Julie Leighton Was Not Sure What to Make of Matthew Thorn, But She Knew He Unsettled Her.

His black evening coat emphasized his broad shoulders. The crisp whiteness of his ruffled shirt accentuated the bronzed tan of his skin.

"I think we have some business to discuss."

Julie frowned in confusion and looked around her casino, Land of Gold, so recently inherited from her father.

Reaching into his jacket, Thorn removed a long envelope and handed it to Julie saying, "This should explain everything."

The shock of her father's letter, written before his murder, forced Julie to sit down. According to these papers, this man was to be her secret partner! There must be some mistake!

Thorn gathered her nervous hands into his larger ones. "I promised your father I would look out for you."

"I release you from any promises you made to my father."

A slow smile spread over his rugged face. "Miss Leighton, I always keep my promises."

Dear Reader,

We, the editors of Tapestry Romances, are committed to bringing you two outstanding original romantic historical novels each and every month.

From Kentucky in the 1850s to the court of Louis XIII, from the deck of a pirate ship within sight of Gibraltar to a mining camp high in the Sierra Nevadas, our heroines experience life and love, romance and adventure.

Our aim is to give you the kind of historical romances that you want to read. We would enjoy hearing your thoughts about this book and all future Tapestry Romances. Please write to us at the address below.

The Editors
Tapestry Romances
POCKET BOOKS
1230 Avenue of the Americas
Box TAP
New York, N.Y. 10020

Land of Gold

Mary Ann Hammond

A TAPESTRY BOOK
PUBLISHED BY POCKET BOOKS NEW YORK

An *Original* publication of TAPESTRY BOOKS

 A Tapestry Book published by
POCKET BOOKS, a division of Simon & Schuster, Inc.
1230 Avenue of the Americas, New York, N.Y. 10020

ISBN: 0-671-50872-5

First Tapestry Books printing May, 1984

10 9 8 7 6 5 4 3 2 1

POCKET and colophon are registered trademarks of Simon & Schuster, Inc.

TAPESTRY is a trademark of Simon & Schuster, Inc.

Printed in the U.S.A.

To David, Drew, Ward and Tanya.
I don't know what I'd do without you.

Prologue

THE CREAKING OF SHIP'S RIGGING ON THE MULTITUDE OF anchored and abandoned vessels nestled cheek to jowl in San Francisco Bay, added an eerie background to the fog-shrouded waterfront. A lone figure made his way cautiously through the night. The dripping of salt-laden moisture from the eaves of buildings lining Commercial Street echoed the footsteps of James Leighton as he made his way carefully across the narrow, muddy gap between the buildings.

He paused and looked quickly over his shoulder as though expecting to see something. But all he saw was the swirling blanket of gray as it isolated him in a world of fear.

Straining to see ahead, he knew it shouldn't be too much farther before he reached his destination. He hurried his pace, hoping he could outdistance his unwanted shadows.

He had realized that he was being followed soon after he'd left his casino. But he had promised Molly he would make this last stop before calling it a night.

A sound behind him made James turn. Outlined against the fog by the muted gaslight on a nearby corner were the figures of two men. Seeing their prey, one of the men raised his arm and a flash of fire and the report of a gunshot signalled the end of James Leighton as he crumpled to the wet ground.

Chapter One

THE FIGURE OF A SLIM YOUNG WOMAN CLOTHED IN black moved slowly through the bustle of Portsmouth Plaza. Her dark brown hair was crowned by a simple black hat of mourning, its dark veil covering her small oval face and hiding the dark shadows of pain that shaded her high cheekbones and determined chin. Her face was set off by a pair of soft lips, and large gray eyes that reflected sorrow as they gazed out on the world. The plain lines of the black bombazine dress could not hide the swell of firm young breasts under its pleated bodice, and its stiff skirt flared out from a narrow waist over the gentle curve of slim hips to reveal trim ankles that peeked out from beneath the hem. Black shoes, which looked too heavy for the tiny feet they encased, completed the picture.

At twenty-two, Julie Leighton felt old. She carried the weight of the world on her slim shoulders. Earlier that morning, she and her sister, Sara, had buried their father. Now they were to meet at his lawyer's office for the reading of his will.

The Plaza had come a long way since its days of grazing land, shanties and tents. It had become the city's main square, evolving and flourishing as had the rest of San Francisco.

Julie passed the many offices, casinos, hostelries and saloons that lined the square and remembered how her father had always said, "If you need a doctor, dentist, a lawyer, an education or to buy or sell anything, you can do it without ever leaving the Plaza."

Many of the merchants and regulars on the Plaza had known her since childhood and they watched Julie pass, exchanging looks of concern between themselves and wondering what might become of their young friend now that her father had died. She held a special place in their hearts, with her quick smile, friendly laugh and warm giving personality. Over the years, Julie and her father had shared in their joys and helped with their sorrows. Now, during Julie's time of need, the people of the Plaza had banded together to watch over her.

They waved and called quiet greetings to the large Oriental who followed in Julie's wake. Lee Tang was a well-known figure. He had been James Leighton's bodyguard for many years. He had been away visiting his family in Chinatown on the night of James's death and he felt a sense of responsibility for his loss. He now guarded Julie perhaps even more closely than he had her father.

Her childhood had been cosmopolitan. In her growing years she had spent many hours playing with the children of many lands in and around the Plaza. The numerous booths set up to display the wares of the world had been her introduction to the diversity of peoples and cultures. To her the Plaza had always been a bazaar that never closed. She had many friends and enjoyed the differences in their languages, food and customs. Life then had been an adventure. But, today she was oblivious to the sounds of hawkers crying out the merits of their wares. The sailors on liberty, with their reckless eyes, and the miners, fresh from the gold fields, greeting each other raucously seemed part of a dream as she threaded her way through the crowds toward a two-storied frame building at the far end of the square.

As she neared her destination a carriage pulled alongside and a man's voice called out, "Julie! Wait a moment."

She turned and waited as her brother-in-law, Adam Raleigh, helped her sister from the carriage. As always, Julie found it hard to believe that Sara was truly her kin. They were as different as night and day.

Their mother had died of cholera when Julie was seven. Sara, being twelve at the time, had been sent back East to boarding school. Over the years, Julie had rarely seen her, except during infrequent vacation trips home from school. The distance being so great between Philadelphia and California, Sara had spent most of her vacations with relatives there. This left Julie alone with her father. Because of his business she had been left on her own for the most part and, as a result, had become self-sufficient and very independent at an early age.

Her sister had become a beauty who attracted notice wherever she went. Sara's honey-brown hair and soft hazel eyes drew people to her. Her soft musical voice captivated listeners when she spoke, but Julie knew her sister's beauty was only superficial. Sara had become vain, self-seeking and above all a snob. She used her beauty to gain the riches and status she craved.

She had been married to Adam for three years, years that had made the two sisters even more distant. Sara had met him at an opera party, given by one of her select friends. He had caught her attention with his raven-black hair, dark eyes and handsome face. She had asked her friend about him and been gratified to learn that he was not only devastatingly handsome, but rich and one of the most eligible men in San Francisco. He owned a great deal of property in the commercial district and rented it out to the shopkeepers and store owners who did business there. His other interests ran from shipping and ranching to racehorses.

By the end of that evening, they had discovered in each other the same need for riches and social acclaim. Their wedding had been one of the most lavish in San Francisco history. Over three hundred guests, two orchestras and catering by the finest restaurant had made it the social event of the year.

Julie remembered reading about it in the newspapers for days. She and her father had not been invited. Sara had said she did not want them to feel uncomfortable amidst all her rich and cultured friends.

Julie knew the real reason. Sara was ashamed of

them, of where they lived and how they made their living. She had confronted Sara with this knowledge and an ugly scene had followed. Julie had thought Sara was going to strike her, but when she pointed out that Sara had never refused the money which had paid for her exclusive schooling and expensive clothes, her sister was reduced to a sputtering mass of fury.

Their father had intervened, defending Sara and saying he understood her concern about them feeling out of place.

He had always had a blind spot where Sara was concerned. She looked so much like his dead wife that he could never believe she was not as sweet and caring. He had even proudly shown the newspaper clippings of her wedding to any and all, not even noticing the looks of pity or the reticent congratulations he received.

He had even gone so far as to suggest that Julie should follow her sister's lead and find a good man, settle down and start a family.

But Julie could not see herself subjugating her own wishes and opinions to those of any man. She had been self-reliant at an early age and found the thought of depending on someone else unthinkable.

Julie watched Adam and her sister move toward her. Sara's dress was black, but the color was the only indication she was in mourning. From its rich fabric and styling, Julie knew it was a copy of a Paris original, designed to flatter and enhance its wearer.

They had left her at the cemetery to return home to their elegant house in South Park where they would receive the polite condolence calls of their friends.

Julie had not been asked to accompany them, which had saved her the trouble of declining. She had re-

5

turned to the casino to thank her father's many true friends who came with gifts of food and flowers to share their own grief with her at his passing.

As the time drew near for the reading of her father's will Julie left this circle of warm support, and Molly had gently admonished her, "Hurry now, I'll take care of things here and join you as soon as I can."

Molly Fitzroy had been her father's partner in the Land of Gold casino; she ran the bordello side of the establishment, while he had overseen the gambling end. When Julie's mother died, she had taken Julie under her wing and helped fill the gap left in her life.

Julie hugged her tightly and prepared to face yet another heavy responsibility. She did not want to sit in some stuffy office and listen to someone enumerate her father's last wishes. If she could have what she really wanted, it would be to wake up and discover the past few days were only an ugly nightmare and her father was still alive. Murdered! She shuddered as the horror of that fact washed over her anew. She looked over to see whether Sara had been affected by this tragedy in their lives.

Feeling Julie's eyes on her, Sara's face changed like a chameleon's and anyone who saw her would have sworn she was grief-stricken. But Julie, who caught the quick assessing gleam in Sara's eyes as she took in the drab simplicity of Julie's gown, had to fight back the urge to say something sharp.

The two sisters silently hugged one another briefly, and Adam pecked Julie on the cheek before they moved together to the walkway leading to the lawyer's office. Lee Tang followed watchfully behind them, his eyes constantly on the alert for possible trouble.

6

The air in the small office was heavy with tension as the waiting drew on. How long would they have to wait? Julie wondered to herself as she looked over at the closed door.

With its five occupants, the room was almost full. Sara and Adam, having chosen to sit apart from Julie and Lee Tang, had taken up a position at the back of the room. But who was the strange man standing next to Adam? Julie had never seen him around the casino or the Plaza. She thought she knew most of her father's business acquaintances and he was not among them. Why was he here? He and Lee Tang apparently knew each other for they were talking softly. Usually Tang was not friendly with strangers, and Julie watched the two men as they talked.

Her gaze moved over the tall, broad-shouldered man standing next to Lee Tang. His sun-gold hair was thick as a lion's mane, and he held himself as casually as one of those great cats; he had an air about him that spoke of agile strength and an awareness of everything that went on around him. The cut of his dark brown coat of superfine emphasized his broad shoulders and sinewy frame. There was leashed power in the long muscular legs that were clothed in tightly fitting tan pants met at the knees by the tops of highly polished black boots. Julie was not quite sure what to make of him or of his presence, but she knew he unsettled her.

A shock went through her as she felt herself pinned by his golden eyes. He scrutinized her as thoroughly as she had him. His gaze traveled from her hair to her feet, and Julie felt as though she had been ranked, sorted and filed. Goose bumps crawled over her skin, even though the room was very close and warm.

She returned his stare coolly. She did not like being judged by any man, especially this one. She sat stiff and still as his tiger eyes moved briefly back to her face before moving away at the sound of the far door being opened.

Molly, a stylishly dressed woman of middle age with red hair and what some might call an overblown figure, entered the room. She was followed by a thin man wearing spectacles and she moved to a chair behind Julie, patting her softly on the shoulder before she sat down.

The thin man took up a position at the heavy wooden desk which faced the waiting group. Adjusting his spectacles and clearing his throat, the lawyer looked around the room checking to see if everyone was present as requested. Noticing the stranger at the back of the room, he frowned slightly and moved to where he waited.

Maybe now, we will find out who he is and why he is here, Julie thought to herself as she watched the lawyer engage him in a softly voiced conversation. But her hopes were dashed when the tawny-haired man nodded twice at something the lawyer had said and, straightening from his relaxed pose, turned and left the room. The lawyer returned to his desk and once again cleared his throat.

Julie decided he must be an associate of Mr. Washburn's who had come to receive instructions of some kind from him. He had nothing to do with her at all. Then why, her mind niggled back, had he stared at her like he had?

Her musings were broken by the solemn voice of the lawyer as he spoke, "Thank you all for coming this afternoon. I realize it is somewhat unusual to have the reading of the last will and testament of the deceased on the same day as the funeral. But it was one of the charges laid upon me by James Leighton when this document was drawn up."

Julie felt her insides grow cold as the finality of the lawyer's words reaffirmed that she was not asleep and dreaming. She was wide awake and living a nightmare.

She could hear Sara's voice, as though through a fog, when she said, "We understand, Mr. Washburn. Please proceed."

The rustling of paper was followed by the lawyer's voice as he read. "I, James Patrick Leighton, being of sound mind and physical condition do this day set forth in writing my last will and testament according to the laws of the state of . . ."

The ponderous tones of the stiff legal phrasing fell on Julie's ears like the breakers of a storm crashing a ship against the rocks. Her mind refused to accept what it was hearing and drifted to more pleasant thoughts and happier times. Times when she and her father had laughed and enjoyed life together.

As a child, she had trailed behind him whenever she could learning as she did all that went into the running of a casino. Her skill and knowledge of the cards and dice had grown over the years and had been a quiet source of pride for her father.

Julie remembered when she'd turned twelve and asked Molly if she and her fifteen-year-old friend, Carlo Ramos, could use one of the rooms on the bordello side of the casino. She and Carlo had grown up side by side and were the closest of friends. Her father had nearly become apoplectic until Molly had shushed him and asked her why they wanted to use one of the rooms. Julie had responded that she knew Molly's girls used them to visit with their friends and talk in private and that she and Carlo needed to do the same thing.

Molly had shot her father a look of warning as he had started to bluster and fuss and, taking Julie by the hand, had sat her down and explained a few things to her she had never known before. She was not shocked at what Molly had told her but disappointed that she and Carlo would not be able to plan his sister's birthday party in private.

From that day on, Julie remembered, she had not been allowed to go on that side of the casino unless Molly was with her. She'd missed visiting with Molly's girls and watching them try on their pretty clothes and fix their hair, but Molly's word was law.

Shortly after that her father had decided she should go back east to boarding school as had Sara. It had taken days of tears and pleading to make him change his mind and allow her to finish her schooling in San Francisco with her friends.

Julie's mind barely registered Adam's pleased exclamation at hearing Sara had inherited all of her father's real-estate holdings or Molly's soft gasp of surprise when she heard James had canceled the notes of loan he'd held against her share of the casino.

Her mind began to drift off once more and she recalled the look of joy on her father's face the day she had finished school at the top of her class.

Her thoughts drifted over the many years and memories, and she was content to ignore the tragic events of the present in favor of these far happier times.

It was Adam's disconcerted explosion of astonishment that finally broke through the shell Julie had erected protectively about herself.

"You can't be serious! Are you certain you are reading that correctly, Mr. Washburn?" Adam demanded as he glared at the poor lawyer.

Molly leaned forward, placed her hand gently on Julie's shoulder and whispered, "Listen Julie. It concerns you, dear."

Julie blinked her eyes a few times as she focused her attention on what was being said.

Mr. Washburn lifted one of the papers from the desk and read aloud, "And to my youngest and more adventuresome daughter Julie, I bequeath my share of ownership in the casino, known as the Land of Gold."

Julie could not believe what she was hearing. She had not thought ahead to what might happen to her now that her father was gone. And the possibility of having to leave the only home she had ever known and loved had never occurred to her until this moment. By leaving her his share of the casino, her father was ensuring she would not have to leave unless it was what she truly wanted to do.

She could not suppress the feeling that she had barely escaped a fate laid out for her by Adam and Sara . . . a fate that conformed to their opinion, or more precisely, Adam's opinion, of what was the proper place and life-style for her.

She turned to look at Sara, and seeing the shock in her sister's eyes, Julie coupled it with Adam's reaction and knew they had made other plans for her future which certainly had not included her remaining at the Land of Gold.

Adam was continuing his tirade, saying, "The man must have been mad. Leaving a gambling hall to an unmarried woman! She could not possibly manage such a place! It would be bankrupt in no time!"

The lawyer raised his voice in order to be heard above Adam's rantings. "There is more."

"More!" Adam gasped, his face turning red. "I think there has been more than enough already!"

Sara placed her hand on her husband's arm and said, "Please, Adam. Let's hear what else Mr. Washburn has to tell us. Maybe it will explain why my father has done what he has in leaving the casino to Julie."

Julie held her breath and took hold of Molly's hand as it rested comfortingly on her shoulder. She dreaded hearing what else her father may have decided. It was more than enough of a shock to find she had inherited her father's share of the Land of Gold. She did not know if she could withstand another such surprise.

The lawyer referred to the papers he held before he continued. "In the event this provision is contested in a court of law by any of my heirs or their spouses, they shall by doing so nullify their own bequests and everything I own shall be left to my daughter Julie."

Julie laughed shakily as she thought to herself, Adam and Sara will think twice about trying to force me to live the way they think I should, now. They both had had their eyes on her father's real-estate investments for years, hoping someday these would belong to them.

Adam's voice cut through the stunned assemblage saying, "Julie, surely you realize your father has left you in a very delicate position."

She lifted her head and stared at him coldly. "How so, Adam? It would appear to me that you and Sara are the ones left in a delicate position. If either of you try to break my father's will, you will be the ones to lose a great deal, not I."

Sara placed her hand on Adam's arm, concern on her face. "She's right, Adam."

He brushed his wife's hand away and returned his gaze to Julie, saying, "That is for the courts to decide."

"I'm afraid not, Mr. Raleigh," the lawyer informed him. "If you should contest any part of this will in a court of law, you will automatically disinherit your wife, regardless of the court's ruling on the contested provision."

"Adam." Sara pleaded for her husband to calm down. His outbursts could cost them dearly, if what Mr. Washburn said was true.

Shaking his head, Adam sat down muttering, "The revenue from that casino is more than my shipping line generates. How can anyone think Julie is competent to handle such large sums of money on a daily basis? It would be hard for a man to manage!"

There was an uncomfortable silence in the room as Sara once again motioned for her husband to watch what he said. She was not any happier with the way things were going than he was, but she was smart enough to keep her feelings to herself.

Molly spoke up. "Julie helped James manage the casino from the time she left school until his death, Mr. Raleigh. She is more than able to handle the task on her own." And she pointed out to him frankly, "If I were you, I would be more concerned with the apparently poor management of my shipping line than worrying about someone else's competency. Why a person might think you felt you should have inherited James's share of the Land of Gold instead of Julie!" She frowned at him quizzically.

"I never said anything of the kind, Mrs. Fitzroy!" Adam vehemently denied her thinly veiled accusation. "I was only thinking about Julie's future well-being." He gazed earnestly about the room as he added, "I feel more than certain that her father intended for her to sell his share of the casino and place the moneys in a protected trust until such time as she marries and her husband can oversee them for her, thus guarding her future. Believe me, I want only what is best for Julie."

In a pig's eye you do, Molly thought to herself. You practically started foaming at the mouth when you heard Mr. Washburn announce that Julie and not your wife had inherited his share of the Land of Gold.

Keeping her observations to herself, Molly said aloud, "I find I must disagree with you, Mr. Raleigh. James was well aware that Julie had no intention of marrying for quite some time, if ever. I cannot believe he would expect her to be without visible means of support. By selling off her inheritance and placing the moneys in trust, she would be homeless as well as penniless."

"Rot!" Adam exclaimed. "She would come and live with Sara and I. As her only remaining relatives, we are in effect her guardians."

And as her guardians, you would have access to any money she had in trust, Molly thought to herself.

Julie had heard more than she cared to hear and stirred herself from her state of self-pity, saying, "As I am of age and have been for years, this guardianship you have alluded to, Adam, is neither legal nor wanted. I have no desire to sell anything. I shall continue to run

14

and operate my share of the Land of Gold as Molly's new partner. So, you and Sara need have no concern for my well-being, or my ability to carry on where my father left off."

Turning to the lawyer, Julie continued, "Mr. Washburn, if you have completed the reading of my father's will, I wish to express my gratitude for the capable manner in which you have handled my father's affairs. And I will bid you all a good day."

Having said this, she rose and, nodding for Lee Tang to follow, turned and departed the suddenly oppressive office to begin the short journey back to the Land of Gold: her home.

Chapter Two

JULIE STOOD AT THE SOLID REDWOOD RAILING ON THE landing atop the wide curving staircase and gazed down at the scene below.

It was the middle of the evening and life on Portsmouth Plaza was its usual milling mix of rough-clad laborers, white-collared clericals, swaggering sailors and silk-hatted dandies out to try Lady Luck or find a pretty and willing companion for a few hours or a night of pleasure.

A great many of these revelers had decided to indulge themselves in the touch of class offered at reasonable prices by the Land of Gold.

In her role as part-owner, with its attendant duty to mingle with her customers, Julie had exchanged her

16

mourning garb for an evening gown of rich emerald green velvet. It had an off-the-shoulder neckline and a creamy French lace bodice that revealed the gentle swell of her breasts above its ruffled edge. The bodice was gathered beneath her breasts by a narrow satin ribbon, the trailing ends of which cascaded down the front of her softly flared skirt.

Her dark hair, styled in the Grecian manner and set high atop her head, except for a waterfall of curls that flowed down her back, gleamed with rich highlights of gold and red as she moved from the railing and down the staircase to where the many lamps and mirrors illuminated the crowded floor below.

Julie strolled through the room greeting customers and answering questions as she kept a watchful eye on the gaming around her. She glanced over to the long mahogany bar that required three bartenders and she watched the busy exchange of gold dust for liquor. Pausing she spoke with Bettina, one of Molly's girls, who tended the large coffee urn at the heavily laden refreshment table slightly beyond the crowded bar.

"Everything going all right here, Bet?" she asked as she took a quick inventory of the provender set out.

"Nothing I can't handle, Miss Julie." Bettina smiled. "We've run out of oysters twice and this is close to being empty." She patted the side of the large urn.

Julie heard the sounds of movement on the high platform behind Bettina and smiled at the musicians as they prepared to add their talented offerings to the clinking of glasses and the babble of tongues that filled the smoky air.

Satisfied that everything was running smoothly, Julie made her way past the many tables in the center of the room. Each had its own contingent of agitated and gleaming-eyed players, and on each were piles of gold and silver of varying shapes and sizes.

Exhaustion was beating a familiar tattoo behind her burning eyes and Julie knew she would be glad when the night was over and she could crawl into her bed to welcome the oblivion of sleep.

She had started up the staircase when a male voice halted her on the fourth step. "Miss Leighton?"

The timbre of the voice was like warm silk. Julie turned to reply and a frisson of shock shot through her as she saw twin orbs of gold calmly staring at her. It was the stranger from earlier that afternoon. He was watching her like a cat watches a mouse and his gaze was almost mesmerizing in its effect.

With effort, she shook herself free from his gaze and said, "Yes? May I help you?" She could not help thinking all the while that if there ever was a man who looked in less need of aid, it was this man.

He had exchanged his earlier attire for evening dress of black. The crisp whiteness of his ruffled shirt accentuated the bronzed tan of his skin and the expert styling of his coat and trousers practically shouted money.

He moved next to her on the stairs, his eyes never leaving hers. His height as he towered over her put Julie at a clear disadvantage. She had to move up a step to be able to look at him without craning her neck.

A slow smile spread over his rugged face as he said, "I think we have some business to discuss."

"Business?" Julie frowned in confusion. What was he talking about? She knew for certain she had no business with him. An idea came to her, easing some-

18

what the turmoil of her thoughts. "I'm sorry, if it is a job you seek, we haven't any openings at this time."

His golden gaze swept over the room before returning to her. "I can see we have all the dealers we need," he commented indulgently as one would to a small child.

"We?" Julie choked as the blood drained from her face. What did he mean by that?

Seeing her reaction, a slight frown creased his brow as he reached out and clasped her elbow in his hand, saying, "I think any more discussion should be in private."

Saying no more, he began to escort her up the staircase to her office at the far side of the landing. Reaching the door, he opened it and stood aside, allowing her to precede him into the elegantly appointed room.

All Julie could think was who is he and how does he know this is my office?

Moving past the understated richness of a velvet sofa and two chairs and over to the far side of the room, Julie took up a position behind a heavy oak desk. She wanted as much space and furniture between her and this man as possible. He unnerved her.

She waited while he took his time in joining her. He moved with casual self-assurance as he took in the floor-to-ceiling bookcases that lined the one wall of the office filled with books and account ledgers. And he smiled as he noted the businesslike arrangement of the safe near the wall by the desk.

His almost proprietary air annoyed Julie no end and she spoke more sharply than she meant to, saying, "I fail to see what we could possibly have to say to one another. I do not even know who you are."

Reaching into the inside pocket of his jacket, he removed a long envelope and handed it to Julie saying, "This should explain everything."

She was almost afraid to take it from him for fear of what it might contain. All her senses were warning her that this man was dangerous and could be trouble. Gathering all the courage she could muster, she accepted the envelope from his hand, her fingers briefly touching his. At the contact, she pulled her hand back as though burned, and her eyes rose swiftly to see if he'd noticed.

He was moving to one of the velvet chairs by the sofa and seemed perfectly content to sit and wait until she had perused the contents of the envelope.

Taking the ivory letter opener from the desk top, she carefully slit open the envelope and removed four sheets of folded paper. Unfolding them, she gasped as she saw that the first sheet was addressed to her and in her father's handwriting. The shock of seeing this forced her to sit down as she read:

My dearest Julie,
    As you are reading this, I know I am no longer there to help you. Please believe me when I say, I know what a shock all this will be for you. But, it was the only way things could be done. The man who brought you this letter is Matthew Thorn. He is a man you can trust and my partner.

Julie's eyes flashed to where Matthew Thorn sat, quietly waiting for her to finish reading what her father had to say. His partner! Her mind was a mass of questions and denials. There must be some mistake!

She looked down again at her father's script and continued reading.

I have known Matt a number of years and have counted him a trusted friend. Realizing the danger of my situation, I sought to protect you and the continuation of the Land of Gold by selling half of my share to him.

Both Matt and I feel it is of the utmost importance that his quarter-interest in the Land of Gold be kept secret until such time as justice is served.

I leave it to the two of you to decide how you wish to go about this. I must tell you that the danger has not ended with my death. Your own life, my dear daughter, may be in jeopardy. None of this will be mentioned in my will, and as far as the world at large will know, you are the sole heir to my half-ownership.

Please do not think I did this because I lacked faith in your ability to run the Land of Gold on your own. I did it out of a necessity to protect you and try to bring my killers to justice. Enclosed you will find a copy of the sale agreement between Matt and myself. Another copy is on file with my lawyer, Mr. Washburn, who of equal necessity had to be informed of my actions in this matter.

Your loving father,
James

Julie folded the letter and scanned the sale agreement that was enclosed. What her father had said was true. He had sold half of his share to Matthew Thorn. It was all written down and witnessed by Mr. Washburn, her father's lawyer.

Folding the sheets of paper carefully and returning them to their envelope, Julie was shaken to her very core. She had no idea what to say to the man who waited so patiently for her to speak.

Rising from behind the desk, she moved across the room and extended the envelope to Matthew, saying, "It would appear we do have business to discuss, Mr. Thorn."

He rose and accepted the envelope as he softly replied, "Please call me Matt. And I will call you, Julie."

"Matt," Julie stammered.

"Please sit down, Julie," he escorted her to the sofa. "Would you care for a drink? I know all of this has been a shock."

Julie allowed him to seat her, but she shook her head at his offer of something to drink. It was as if this were his office and she had come to call on him and not the other way around. She found this very disconcerting and said, "I'm afraid, my father has placed us both in an awkward position. It would be best for all concerned if you would let me buy back your quarter interest and then you would be free to attend to whatever it is you do for a living."

Matt took a seat opposite her and smiled, "I have no desire to sell my interest in the Land of Gold. And as for what I do for a living, let us say, I have many business interests in the community and the Land of Gold is but one of them."

His attitude piqued Julie and she snapped back.

"You seem to find this all very amusing, Mr. Thorn. I see nothing amusing in any of this. Forgive me if I sound sharp, but the past few days have not been easy ones."

"Don't you ever relax?" he asked her curiously. "Your father led me to believe you were a calm sensible woman who would see the necessity of all this. But here you are wound tighter than a bow string and not even willing to try things his way. I always thought your father was a fair judge of a person's character, until now."

Julie could feel her cheeks redden under his keen gaze. He was impossible! Sitting there so relaxed and at home and passing judgment on her character as though he had every right to do so!

"I find it hard to understand his apparent regard for you, sir," she replied.

"The lady has sharp claws beneath her cloak of ice," he commented with a grin. "Don't tire yourself out sharpening them on me, Julie. You will only dull them, I'm afraid."

"Oh!" Julie gasped. She wished she could think of something truly cutting to retort, but a small voice inside her whispered it would be a waste of time even if she could.

Matt watched the play of emotions on her face aware she had no idea how it reflected everything she thought. "We could spend the rest of the night trading insults, Julie. But, come morning we would be no farther along than we are now. I think it would be wiser to settle how we are going to explain my sudden appearance on the scene, don't you?" He raised an eyebrow slightly, a teasing grin on his face.

He did have a valid point in what he said, and though Julie did not want to admit it, her innate honesty forced her to nod in agreement. But her stubborn pride had her saying, "Is there a chance you could disappear as suddenly? It would make things so much easier, if you could."

His sudden laugh made her eyes fly open in surprise. Did nothing penetrate that thick skin of his?

"You do speak your mind, don't you? At least you are honest about not wanting me around," Matt informed her as he leaned forward resting his arms on his knees. He stared at her, a twinkle in his eyes. "It has been a long while since a woman has not been desirous of my company. I find myself curious as to why?" he teased her.

Julie clenched her fists in her lap, fighting an urge to slap the smile from his face. The arrogance of the man was overwhelming!

Leaning back in his chair once more, Matt continued in a more serious vein, "How do you suggest we explain my presence?"

"I have no idea on the matter at all!" Julie exclaimed, wishing he would just go away and never return. The throb in her head had grown into a pounding headache and all she wanted to do was lie down and rest until it went away.

"I doubt if anyone would accept the idea that I was your fiancée from back East, come here to be with you in your time of trouble," Matt mused aloud as he watched Julie's face to see her reaction to what he said.

"I should certainly hope not!" she gasped without thinking. "Even if some would be willing to accept such a preposterous tale, it would not work. I could hardly produce a fiancée from somewhere I'd never been!"

Matt held his arms wide and shrugged his shoulders, saying, "I said it was doubtful. Where do we go from here?"

"Must we go anywhere?" Julie asked him. She smoothed the material of her dress across her lap nervously as she continued. "Why is it so important for us to do anything at all?"

Reaching across the short distance that separated them, Matt gathered her nervous hands into his much larger ones and said, "Because I promised your father I would look out for you. And I always keep my promises."

Steeling herself for the shock she knew would come, Julie raised her eyes to Matt's and, staring at him, said as earnestly as she could, "I release you from any promises you made to my father."

Matt shook his head slowly, saying, "It is not in your power to do such a thing. Even if it were, I would not be able to leave you unprotected from the danger your father felt threatened you."

Julie tried to pull her hands free, but he tightened his hold and she tried to fight the need to cry out and break free. His touch sent a burning sensation up her arms and into her very soul. This is ridiculous, she thought. There is no logical reason for this to be happening. I must be even more exhausted than I thought.

As though sensing her discomfiture, Matt slowly released her hands and sat back in his seat. "You are in danger, Julie," he spoke softly. "Your father was not a man to cry wolf, when there was none there."

Julie's head came up and she paid closer attention to what Matt was saying. For he was right, her father had never been an alarmist.

"When last we spoke, he told me he had a fair idea he was ruffling feathers with his efforts to clean up some of the dives and shanghai parlors in this part of town, especially the ones north of the El Dorado Saloon. He said if something wasn't done about them soon, the entire area would continue to degenerate and would finally reach a point where even the broad-minded people of San Francisco would rise up in disgust." Matt's voice echoed words Julie had heard her father say on more than one occasion.

She knew when she was beaten and her tired shoulders slumped even more at this added knowledge. She was in danger and her father had sent Matt to help her. She sighed softly as she said, "What are we going to do?"

Matt could read the effort it took for her to accept him and replied, "We are not going to do anything. You are going to introduce me to the world as a business acquaintance of your father's, here to advise you. While I am going to try and find out who is responsible for his death."

Chapter Three

THE DAY HAD BEEN TOO MUCH ALREADY AND NOW SHE HAD to deal with this. Julie numbly rose from the sofa and started toward the door, saying, "The sooner we start, the sooner it will end."

Matt saw her shoulders start to shake. Rising from the chair, he stopped her before she could reach the door. Pulling her to him, he held her close and murmured incoherent soothing words as she began to cry.

Her small form shook with the force of her sobs as all the pent-up sorrow and agony of the past few days spilled forth onto his ruffled shirt.

Julie did not question Matt's offer of comfort. She needed a shoulder to lean on and his was there. She cried until she could cry no more, her breath coming in tiny hiccups.

Matt pulled a large white handkerchief from his pocket and silently handed it to her. Julie had to pull back slightly to dry her eyes and the movement made her realize how closely he had been holding her. Rather than embarrassment, she felt a comforting glow of security which she was curiously loathe to give up.

The minutes passed and Matt made no move to release her, as though he too were content to allow things to remain as they were. This startling thought made Julie look up quickly to see if she could read the expression on his face. But his gaze seemed fixed on a point over her head and she could not begin to guess what he was thinking.

"I think you have done enough for today. What you need is sleep," his warm voice told her.

Julie could not agree with him more, but her feeling of responsibility told her she could not as yet give herself up to the arms of Morpheus.

"No, I have work to do."

"Where is your bedroom?" Matt asked her as though she had never spoken.

"What?" Julie stammered, not believing she had heard him correctly.

Before she could say another word, Julie felt herself lifted into his arms and her own arms went around his neck in self-protection.

Turning, Matt looked about the room until he faced a closed door on the far side of the room. "Ah! That must be the bedroom," he commented as he started in that direction.

He had taken but a step when the door to the office opened and Molly walked in, calling, "Julie?"

Hearing her voice, Julie instinctively buried her face against the damp ruffles of Matt's shirt, her heart in her throat. How in the world was she going to explain Matt Thorn to Molly? Molly's next words answered her question more fully than Julie ever expected.

"Matt Thorn! What are you doing on this side of the casino!" Molly exclaimed in surprise.

"Putting a friend to bed, Molly," he replied calmly as he started toward the closed door a second time.

He was halted as Julie began struggling to break free of his hold, practically spitting in anger, "This side of the casino! Put me down!"

"Bed!" Molly choked in dismay.

Matt's lips thinned as he muttered in exasperation, "Women!"

Molly moved across the office and took up a position in front of the closed door, saying, "You are not going anywhere with her, Matthew Thorn."

"Molly . . ." He started to explain as he tried to control the sputtering mass of velvet and lace in his arms.

"Don't you Molly me, you rat! You put her down right now or rue the day you ever met me," Molly threatened him.

"Damn!" Matt bit out between clenched teeth.

The next thing Julie knew she was falling. Before she could cry out in alarm, she landed on the velvet plushness of the sofa, her dress bunched around her knees and the pins from her hair raining about her as heavy tresses fell down across her face and shoulders.

Not waiting to see if she had hit the sofa, Matt moved toward Molly and enfolded her in a bear hug that trapped her arms against her sides.

Julie watched in horror as he lifted Molly bodily and deposited her on one of the velvet chairs.

When Molly opened her mouth to protest, he practically yelled, "Enough!"

The authority in his tone left both women speechless.

"Why I should bother to explain anything to either of you is beyond me!" Matt paced the floor in controlled anger as he glared at them. "But, as the three of us will be working closely together, I would prefer not having to keep looking over my shoulder to see if one of you is about to bash my head in."

Julie opened her mouth to tell him she thought he was the most unreasonable man she had ever had the misfortune to meet. Not only had he let her make a complete fool of herself crying as she had, but he had tossed her aside like a sack of potatoes.

However, Matt's eyes pinned her to the sofa, and the pulsating muscle in his cheek warned Julie that she had better remain silent or incur his full wrath upon her head.

Molly started to rise from the chair, only to subside when Matt barked at her. "I wouldn't if I were you. And stop acting like a she-bear defending her cub."

Molly looked from Matt to the closed bedroom door and glared back at him. "You said you were taking her to bed. What am I supposed to do? Stand aside and give you my blessings!"

"You've been running a bordello too long Molly," he coldly informed her. "I said I was putting her to bed.

30

Your precious lamb was not about to be sacrificed on the altar of lust. You should know me well enough to know I don't make it a habit of bedding females about to collapse from exhaustion."

"That's not even my bedroom!" Julie blurted, immediately sorry she had brought his attention back to her.

"And you! So what if Molly is used to seeing me on her side of the casino. That does not necessarily mean I am a regular customer. And even if I am, what business is it of yours?" he demanded roughly.

"None!" Julie choked.

"You're damn right!"

"But . . . but . . ." Julie stammered.

Matt paused and shook his head. "You'd better say what you're dying to say before it chokes you."

"Am I the only person in San Francisco who didn't already know you? First my father, then Lee Tang and now Molly!" she stated in a breathless rush of words.

"What?" Matt was stupefied.

Seeing the look of shock on his face, Julie gathered her wits, anger helping her to continue. "Personally, I don't care if you live on Molly's side of the casino! But, as part-owner of this establishment I don't like being the last person in San Francisco to know about it!"

"Is that what has you so all fired mad at me?" Matt asked her with a look of surprise.

"And what if it is?" Julie responded defensively as she straightened her dress and tried to push her hair from her face.

Matt's booming laugh filled the room, causing Julie to put her hands over her ears in surprise.

Bending down, Matt pulled her hands away and

smiled at her. "And all this time, I thought you were defending your virtue."

"Don't be absurd!" Julie snapped at him. "I knew perfectly well nothing was going to happen."

Matt raised an eyebrow, inquiringly. "And how may I ask did you know that?"

Julie stared up at him defiantly and replied, "Because I had no intention of letting it."

Matt rose, moved to the one empty chair and sat down laughing. "If I had wanted something to happen, Julie, you would not have been able to stop me."

"Enough of this." Molly spoke up. "I want to know what you are doing here, Matt?"

Julie chewed on her bottom lip wondering how he would answer. Her father's letter had made it very clear that no one else was to know about Matt's partial ownership in the casino. Did that mean Molly was to be kept in the dark along with everyone else?

Her question was soon answered as Matt began to tell Molly everything. Everything, except the way she had lost all control and cried her eyes out on his shoulder.

Julie was thankful to him for leaving her a small bit of pride, even where Molly was concerned. She did not want her fussing about like a mother-hen and if she knew her, Molly would have done that.

"So you were serious when you said you were only putting Julie to bed?" Molly asked after hearing everything, Matt had to say.

"Molly!" both Matt and Julie exclaimed at the same time.

"Okay! Okay! I won't say another word about it."

Molly raised her hands in defeat. "Am I allowed to ask what happens next?"

Julie scooted off the sofa and straightened her dress as she replied, "I don't think anything more is going to happen tonight. We can start worrying tomorrow morning."

"Sorry to disappoint you, Julie." Molly's voice stopped her cold. "The reason I came up here in the first place was to tell you that George Baldwin and some of the other casino owners are downstairs, asking to see you."

"Casino owners? Why are they here?" Julie frowned.

Rising from his chair, Matt moved next to her saying, "Shall we go down and ask them?"

"What!"

Matt shrugged. "We have to start sometime. It might as well be now."

"I can't go downstairs looking like this," Julie protested. "At least give me a few minutes to fix my hair."

"A few minutes and no longer," Matt told her. "I don't want to keep our visitors waiting any longer than they have been already."

True to her word, it was but a few minutes before Julie returned, her hair sleeked back into a shining French pleat. Joining Matt, she said, "Shall we go?"

He extended his arm to her with a smile, "Lead the way, partner."

Julie threaded her arm through his, hissing, "Don't call me that! If you start doing that, you might slip once we're downstairs and we'd be sunk."

Matt patted her hand and laughed softly as they

moved across the landing toward the staircase, "Would you rather I called you, darling?"

Julie stumbled slightly and looked up at him aghast, "Don't you dare! They will all think I'm your mistress!"

"From such a simple word as darling?" Matt teased her as they descended the wide staircase and saw the group of men awaiting them below.

"Matt, please!" Julie pleaded under her breath, forcing a smile of welcome on her face as they reached the foot of the stairs.

Any reply he might have made was lost to Julie when one of the men reached out, took her free hand in his fat one and said, "Miss Leighton, please allow me to offer our condolences to you on the death of your father. He was a credit to the community and will be sorely missed."

Julie tried not to cringe as George Baldwin held on to her hand while his baggy eyes slyly moved over her appraisingly from under heavy lids.

"Thank you, gentlemen. I can't begin to tell you how touched I am by your taking time from your own casinos to come here tonight." She addressed her remarks to them all, but she saw Baldwin's eyes widen as they noticed Matt attentively at her side.

She was saved from having to introduce Matt because one of the men spoke up saying, "Thorn! What are you doing here? I had no idea you knew Miss Leighton."

"Hastings." Matt acknowledged him with a nod.

Seeing the expressions, ranging from surprise to suspicion, on the faces of her guests as they eyed Matt,

Julie took matters into her own hands, saying, "Shall we move to my private table, gentlemen? I do believe you would be more comfortable there."

Not waiting to see if they followed, Julie moved down the last step, her arm still threaded with Matt's, forcing him to accompany her as she crossed the crowded room to a small alcove.

Standing by a chair, she waited for Matt to pull it out for her before taking her seat and waving for the gentlemen to do the same.

After everyone had found a seat, she motioned to one of the bartenders to come over. "Champagne, Lukes. We are going to drink to my father's memory."

The champagne was quick in coming, and Julie waited until each man held a glass before rising. "To my father," she said holding her glass up and taking a drink.

The company followed suit, even though it was more than apparent that many of them almost choked on her words.

Matt watched all this in careful silence, content for the moment to allow her to run the show. It gave him a chance to observe the other men at the table.

Baldwin was next to Julie on her left, with Hastings next to him. Then came Potter, Sherman and Watkins on his left. Not one of them had reason to mourn James's passing. Their operations were some of the very ones he had been trying to clean up.

Baldwin's voice, as he spoke to Julie, drew Matt's attention. He glanced over at his dissipated face, the jowled cheeks and bulbous nose, and he frowned as he heard.

"We came here tonight, Miss Leighton, not only to offer our most sincere condolences, but to also offer any assistance or advice you might need in continuing this grand establishment."

Matt almost cut him off, but a sudden grip on the top of his thigh by Julie's hand, hidden beneath the snowy tablecloth, silenced him.

Looking around the table, Julie smiled what she hoped was a smile of gratitude for their concern, even as she thought to herself, I know more about running an honest operation than the lot of you combined.

Turning back to George Baldwin, she said, "I thank you for your more than kind offer of assistance. But, I'm afraid, I've already accepted Mr. Thorn's offer to advise me. He was a very close business associate of my father's and I am sure I shall manage quite well with his knowledgeable assistance."

Matt thought he could hear Baldwin's teeth grind together in frustration as he looked at him. Leaning over, he whispered in Julie's ear, "Don't lay it on any thicker or I won't last the night."

Beaming up at him with a twinkle in her eye, Julie said, "Thank you for reminding me, Matthew."

Matthew! He frowned. What was she trying to do? She was the one worried about people getting the wrong idea earlier.

Ignoring his frown, Julie faced the table and said, "Mr. Thorn has reminded me I mustn't detain you gentlemen any longer. For, as he so wisely put it, we all have businesses to run."

Having been dismissed, even as politely as Julie had

dismissed them, the men had no other recourse but to bid her a good evening and depart.

Julie remained seated at the table until the last of them had gone, her hand still gripping Matt's thigh. When the last of their callers had departed through the ornate double doors, she felt the hard muscle of his leg beneath her hand and, releasing her hold on him, flushed. "Thank you, Matt. I could not have faced them alone."

"I don't think you need me to help you face anyone," he told her as he massaged his sore leg.

"I'm afraid, I must ask another favor of you, Matt," Julie said as she slowly rose from her seat. "Could you escort me back up to my room? I honestly don't think I can make it on my own."

Matt took a look at her white face and rose from his seat with a muttered oath. "You little fool! Why didn't you let me handle them? You are almost dead on your feet."

She smiled up at him weakly. "You said we had to start sometime."

Taking her arm, Matt told her to lean on him as they made their way across the room and slowly back up the stairs. Reaching the landing, Matt saw Molly hovering near a door next to the office and called to her, "Molly, come and give me a hand."

Molly rushed forward, "What do you want me to do?"

"You show me which room is her bedroom and come help me put her to bed. She's too damn stubborn to know when to quit," Matt replied in a voice laced with anger.

"I am not!" Julie protested as Molly raced across the landing and threw open a door. "I asked you to help me up here, didn't I?"

"You're asking for trouble if you say another word," Matt warned her as he lifted her into his arms and followed Molly into the bedroom.

Chapter Four

JULIE WOKE TO THE RUMBLE OF VOICES AS THEY PASSED HER closed door. Rising, she picked up the blue silk robe that lay across the foot of her bed and slipped into it. By the light that filtered into the room from behind closed curtains, she was disconcerted to discover she had slept much later than was usual for her.

A muffled curse and the sound of laughter made her move toward the door to investigate. Opening her door, she saw two of her bartenders trying to muscle an oversize bedframe through the open office doorway.

Molly was directing their efforts from the hallway, as Mae, one of her girls, waited by her side, her arms filled with bedding. Mae laughed anew as the two men pushed and shoved fruitlessly trying to force the frame past the doorjamb.

"Why couldn't the two of you have waited until the door was removed?" Molly remonstrated with the two men. "Now we'll be lucky if you don't ruin both the door and the bedframe."

One of the men stood upright and, wiping the sweat from his brow, said, "All you told us was to move this frame from the cat house to the office bedroom. You didn't say nothin' 'bout no doors."

Molly looked to the ceiling for strength as she muttered, "Forgive me. I made the mistake of thinking you could figure that out for yourselves."

Drawing her robe about her, Julie tightened its sash saying, "What is going on?"

"Hello, Miss Julie." Mae beamed.

"Good morning, Mae," Julie replied, adding, "you're up early."

Mae shook her head and smiled. "Not really, Miss Julie. You just slept later than you think."

"Oh," Julie murmured self-consciously. She did not like the idea that apparently some things had obviously been decided while she slept. Glancing at the two bartenders and Molly hovering over them, Julie bristled. Apparently some major changes were going on here that she knew nothing about.

Molly looked over at her and said, "Sleep well, dear?"

Before Julie could answer her or receive an answer to her question, Molly cried out, "Lukes! Be careful! You almost ripped the door off!"

The two men ignored Molly and with a mighty heave,

concerted groans and a loud scraping noise, the bed-frame was through the door.

Molly and Mae hurriedly followed to ensure they did not destroy the entire office with their clumsiness.

This left Julie standing alone in the hallway, her unanswered curiosity making her feel crosser by the moment. Determined to find out what was going on, she moved into the now-crowded office, a frown on her face.

What she saw made her frown even more. The two bartenders were waiting patiently by the much-abused bedframe as Molly and Mae stood watching Matt Thorn remove the bedroom door from its frame.

Setting the door out of the way, Matt caught sight of Julie's frowning countenance. "I'm afraid the bed's not set up yet. But if you are willing to wait a few minutes, I'm sure I can accommodate you," he commented as he watched the two men carry the bedframe into the bedroom.

"I am still in my night clothes because I was awak-ened by the sounds of major remodeling, not for any other reason." She glared at him heatedly.

Matt eyed Julie and, noticing the way her hair lay in trailing disarray about her shoulders and the traces of sleep still showing on her face, even as her eyes blazed at him in annoyance, he could not help but grin at her. "Pity. Here I was hoping you'd decided to keep me company." He eyed the bed being set up and grinned at her. "That's an awful big bed for only one person. Sure you won't reconsider? I have a feeling I could get pretty lonely by myself."

Drawing herself to her full height, Julie replied, "I

doubt that very much, Mr. Thorn. You have your enormous ego to keep you company."

"Ouch!" He flinched. "You're definitely not friendly when you first wake up, are you?"

Julie did not make it a habit to bite people's heads off the first thing every day, but in his case she was quite willing to make an exception. Who did he think he was? He'd shown up out of nowhere and in less than twenty-four hours had practically taken over. She would certainly set him straight. "What is going on here anyway?" she demanded.

Molly, Mae and the bartenders were all in the bedroom busily setting up the bed, leaving her and Matt alone in the office. Julie's voice echoed coldly in the air, sounding harsher than she had intended it to sound. But she held her ground and looked to Matt for an answer.

Matt's eyes narrowed as he replied, "Obviously, politeness is not one of your strong points either."

He absolutely infuriated her. Now he was passing judgment on her character! "My strong or weak points are not under discussion here. I would like to know the reason for all this." She waved her hand at the unattached door and the bedroom. "After all I do own this place!"

Matt moved to reattach the door. "Only part of it," he reminded her. "Hand me that. Would you please?" he pointed to a tool lying near her.

Julie picked it up and handed it to him as he continued, "As I am going to be closely involved with things around here, I decided it would be easier if I moved in." He tightened the door hinges and turned to face her. "Besides, how would it look for your advisor to maintain rooms on Molly's side of the casino?"

"I fail to see what difference it makes where you live," Julie told him.

"I knew you wouldn't mind my moving in here," Matt replied, pleased. "I told Molly she was being foolish thinking you would object." He dusted his hands off and placed the tools he'd been using back in their box.

Julie watched him in stunned disbelief. What she had meant and how he had taken it could not have been farther apart. She had meant that she could see no reason the location of his rooms would be of any consequence to anyone. So why make a move? He had deliberately twisted her words to make them sound as though she were in complete agreement with his decision to move in here!

"Where do you suggest we start?" Matt asked her as he moved toward the desk.

"Start what?" Julie choked.

Seating himself behind the massive desk, Matt opened one of the drawers and frowned up at her. "Why, going through your father's papers, of course. I realize you have managed to sleep away the better part of the day, but there's still time. Hopefully we will be able to find something here that may give us an idea of your father's comings and goings prior to the time of his murder."

The nerve of him! It was partly his fault she had been so overtired. Now he was insinuating she was a slugabed. Whatever her father may have seen in him, she surely did not.

Julie's eyes were drawn to the open drawer. Knowing her father's habit for painfully recording everything, she foresaw hours of tedious searching in the remote hope that they might uncover some information useful in tracking his killers.

Clasping her arms in front of her, she was sharply reminded that she was clad only in her nightgown and robe. "Would it be too much to ask that I be allowed to dress and at least have a cup of coffee first?" she heard herself ask him sarcastically.

Matt's eyes widened in appreciation of what he saw. "No need to change on my account. But if it will make you feel more comfortable, you go ahead and change. I'll have some coffee brought up. Maybe it will help improve your mood."

"There is nothing wrong with my mood, thank you," Julie informed him.

But he had already turned his attention on the open drawer in front of him and replied, "You're quite welcome. Do you take cream and sugar?"

She had stomped from the room when Matt looked up with a smile on his face and a gleam in his eyes. He'd made a good start. James had warned him about her independent ways and about her temper. What he had failed to mention was how beautiful she looked fresh from sleep. Shame on you, James! he thought.

Julie returned to her room and discarded her robe and nightgown in a pile on the bed; then she moved toward the large wardrobe and opened its door to stare unseeingly at the dresses within. Infuriated by the way Matt made her lose all her composure she grabbed the first dress she saw.

Pulling on the dove gray gown, she was too intent on

44

scolding herself for allowing Matt to unsettle her to notice the way the color brought out the deep gray of her eyes or the soft flare of the material as it molded itself to her slim figure. Moving to her mirrored vanity, she sat down and, taking a brush in hand, forced her hair into a severe pleat at the back of her head, wishing all the while that she could control her reactions to Matt and his high-handedness as easily as she did her hair.

Turning from the vanity, she failed to see the small wisps of curl already breaking free of their confinement to frame her face as she donned her hose and shoes.

She uttered a small oath when she noticed she had buttoned her shoes incorrectly. Looking at the missed buttons on her right shoe and then seeing more on her left, Julie paused saying aloud to herself, "This is ridiculous! I'm allowing myself to overreact. Common sense and a cool head are what is needed here. Matthew Thorn is no different from any other man."

Rebuttoning her shoes correctly gave her the time she needed to steady her nerves and regain her self-confidence.

When she left her room, Julie felt ready to face almost anything, including Matt Thorn. She only hoped he had ordered the coffee as promised; she certainly could use a cup.

Reentering the office, Julie was prepared to meet any of Matt's presumptuous orders with cool aplomb. But, she was not prepared for his off-handed "Coffee's on the table," since he did not even bother to look up from his perusal of a stack of papers.

Pouring herself a cup of the fragrant brew, she didn't notice his golden eyes appraising her from across the room. She took a much-needed swallow before moving to the sofa and placed the cup on the table in front of it.

Matt's voice sounded behind her as he said, "Your father was quite a record keeper. Come grab a stack of papers and start going through them while you finish your coffee."

As she had intended to do that very thing, Julie put a firm control on her impulse to tell him so and contented herself with glaring at Matt's bowed head as she moved to the desk. Taking a large folder full of papers, she returned to the sofa and settled herself for what promised to be a long and nerve-racking day.

The hours wore on and Julie's coffee cooled, unheeded, as she read. Conversation between her and Matt was limited to the exchange of information as they found it. Slowly and painstakingly they began to reconstruct the three weeks prior to her father's death.

They eventually had a list of all his meetings, visitors and appointments.

Setting the last paper in the stack he was reading aside, Matt looked over at Julie curled up on the sofa, her now shoeless feet tucked beneath her, her shining head bent as she studied the papers in her lap. "You have a beautiful daughter, my friend," he told the departed James.

As though sensing he was looking at her, Julie glanced over at Matt, a questioning expression on her oval face. "Is something wrong?" she asked him.

"No," Matt replied with a smile as he stretched some of the tenseness from his shoulders.

Then, what? Julie wondered to herself.

Rising from his seat behind the desk, Matt moved to

where Julie was, saying, "Why don't we call it quits for now and have some lunch?"

"Lunch?" Julie frowned as she looked at the carved clock on the mantle above the fireplace. "You mean dinner, don't you?"

Matt's eyes followed her gaze and he was startled to see they had worked through the entire afternoon and into the early evening. "No wonder I'm starving! We're calling it a day. Why didn't you say something sooner?" Matt asked her.

"I lost all track of time myself," Julie admitted to him, as she drew her feet from under her and placed the papers on the table next to her forgotten coffee cup.

The sight of her gracefully stretching the tiredness from her cramped muscles created an unexpected stirring in Matt's blood as he took in her unconscious grace. Steady, Matthew, he mused, for she was affecting him in a way he had not felt in a long time.

"I think we have more than earned a good meal," Matt told her, and with a smile, he bent down and placed a gentle kiss on her cheek.

She looked up at him in stunned surprise, saying, "Why did you do that?"

Enjoying the astonished look on her face, Matt took her hands in his. "Why not?" He lifted her to her feet and added, "Go and change, I'm hungry."

"What does my changing clothes have to do with your being hungry?" Julie asked, the confusion she felt reflected in her eyes as he released her hands and turned her toward the office doorway.

Why had he kissed her, she wondered? Her mind swirled with confusing reactions to his kiss, her skin tingled from the impression of his lips.

"We are going out to dinner. Now hurry up," he replied as he gave her a little push toward the door.

"I can't go out with you," Julie exclaimed. "I have work to do downstairs."

Matt shook his head. "Your father told me you were headstrong." He held his hand to his midsection adding, "But, I become grouchy when hungry. So, you had better stop wasting time and go change."

Julie's eyes widened in disbelief. First, he had moved into the bedroom next to hers without even asking. Then he expected her to spend her entire day searching through files with him, ignoring all her other duties. And after all this, he had the nerve to kiss her! Now he was not even listening to her when she gave him her reason for not going with him! And he said she was headstrong! Well! He was about to discover she would no longer endure his heavy-handed takeover of things! He could not make her do what he had arbitrarily decided.

Placing her hands on her hips as she faced him, she spoke in a slow, clear voice, "If you are waiting for me, you will starve. After I change, I will be downstairs where I am expected to be. Not out on the town with you!"

Matt took no notice of her refusal to dine out with him, saying, "I don't remember saying anything about going out on the town. But, if you'd like? Only, after we've eaten mind you."

Julie stared at him in wonder. He couldn't possibly be that obtuse. He was deliberately trying to bait her into losing her temper!

Matt's next remark disturbed her composure even more. "Don't you get hungry?"

"Of course, I do!" Julie returned crossly, "I'll eat something here later. Right now, I'm trying to make you understand that I can't go with you!"

Moving across the room, he took her hands in his as he led her out into the hallway and started toward her room, adding, "You may need a jacket. It might be damp out tonight."

Julie stiffened and tried to dig her heels into the carpet, saying, "Matthew Thorn! Will you listen to me!"

Glancing down at her as they neared the door to her bedroom, he replied, "No."

"No? I said I have work to do!" Julie exclaimed in frustration. "Are you always this bossy?" she asked in annoyance as they halted at her door and Matt reached for the knob.

Matt paused with his hand on the doorknob and replied, "Only when I'm hungry and someone is making me wait to eat."

Looking behind him, Julie saw Molly heading in their direction and called, "Molly! Will you please tell him"—she glared up at Matt—"that I can't have dinner with him! He is being totally unreasonable."

"Why can't you?" Molly smiled.

"What! Not you too!" Julie exclaimed. "You know as well as I do I am needed here."

Molly shook her head. "Lee Tang and I can manage fine while you have dinner. You've been closeted in that office all day. Some time away from here will do you good. Now go along with Matt and enjoy your dinner, I'll keep an eye on things here."

"Traitor!" Julie accused her.

Laughing as she continued toward the office, Molly replied, "Have fun you two."

The whole world was suddenly against her! Julie felt trapped. She threw a disgusted look at Molly's back as it disappeared through the office door.

"Give up?" Matt's voice sounded in her ear.

"After I finish downstairs, I have to finish setting up the work schedules for next week! And then, there are the thank-you notes to the people who came to the wake!" Julie tried desperately to talk her way out of going with him.

A slow grin appeared on Matt's face as he listened to her. Her thin excuses sounded more as if she were trying to convince herself than him. "If I'm not fed soon, I'll be in no condition to take you out on the town," he warned her.

The sound of her stomach growling in protest made Julie's cheeks turn pink with embarrassment as Matt stood there grinning at her. Her excuses were beginning to sound lame even to her, and it was obvious they were having no affect on him. And she was hungry. "All right! You win!" she exclaimed in defeat.

Opening the door to her bedroom, Matt waved her into the room with a laugh, saying, "I'm glad to see you have come to your senses."

"It would seem I have no other alternative," Julie grudgingly admitted. "Even though I think I may have lost any sense I had left," Julie retorted as she entered her room and closed the door in his face.

Matt's laughter sounded through the door as he called, "Don't take too long."

Chapter Five

WHAT WAS WRONG WITH HER? WHY HAD SHE ALLOWED herself to be bullied into dining with Matt, she asked herself with a frown as she moved toward the wardrobe? She seemed to be making a habit of doing what he wanted. Why?

The memory of his unexpected kiss made her shake her head in denial. And why had he done that, she wondered? Telling herself he was only being polite to a new partner and nothing more, she opened the wardrobe door. Choosing a simply cut, dark blue evening gown of silk, she laid it on the bed and then undressed.

Having changed, she sat before her mirrored vanity and redid her hair. Brushing the last strands into place, she made a face at herself, saying aloud, "Matt was only being friendly. So he kissed you. It's not as though you've never been kissed before. He was only thanking you for helping him go through all those papers."

A small voice inside her replied, "Then why are you making all this fuss?"

She was acting strangely where Matt was concerned and a disquieting feeling came over her. Could it be she wished he had kissed her for another reason altogether? Definitely not!

The sound of knocking on her door was followed by Matt's voice calling, "I'm starving out here."

Grabbing an evening purse, Julie tried to regain a tight rein on her wayward thoughts as she took a deep breath and called out in reply, "I'll be with you in a minute."

She paused before opening her door and took another calming breath. Opening the door, she smiled up at him, saying, "Shall we go?"

She was surprised to see he had also changed into evening wear. Somehow she had thought he had been waiting outside her door the entire time.

Matt threaded her arm through his as they started downstairs. Smiling down at her, he asked, "Where shall we go? There's Clayton's or Martin's. Or do you feel like something from the sea? Captain Cropper's has excellent terrapin and oysters."

Julie found she could not help but smile at him as they made their way through the crowded casino to the street. Accepting his hand into the carriage, she replied, "You're the one who's starving. You decide."

Looking up at their driver, Matt said, "Clayton's on Commercial Street and don't dawdle. My lady is quite famished."

"What!" Julie choked as Matt took his seat next to her and the carriage moved off at a brisk pace.

Matt took her hand in his and grinned. "I didn't think it would matter if I told him I was the one who was starving. This way, we reach the restaurant sooner and he feels as though he has aided a lady in distress."

"You made me sound like a glutton!" Julie protested as they took a sharp turn off onto Kearny and continued toward Commercial.

Matt braced her with his body as their speed increased and they dodged the other carriages about them. Matt laughed, "I think he doesn't want you to die of starvation while he's driving."

Julie tried not to lean all her weight on Matt as the carriage rocked. She did not think she could handle another shock. When he had called her his lady, a strange warmth had coursed through her, and she was unsettled by it. What was wrong with her? Maybe she was more hungry than she thought to be feeling so strangely. The little voice inside her mocked, "Coward!"

"Ohh!" she gasped as she was almost thrown into his arms when the carriage tilted dangerously as they came round onto Commercial Street.

Both of them were thrown forward as their zealous driver hauled in on the reins and applied the foot brake at the same time. The carriage came to a shuddering stop and its door was thrown open as the driver announced in a pleased voice, "Clayton's, sir."

Alighting from the carriage, Julie, who expected to see the poor carriage horse a wreck from their wild journey, was surprised to see him tossing his head and snorting as though he had enjoyed the entire episode!

53

Seeing the look of disbelief on her face, their driver said, "Thank you, ma'am. We both owe you a debt. General there used to be a racehorse and he dearly loves it when I have a fast fare."

"You're welcome," Julie managed to get out as she tried to control an overwhelming urge to start laughing.

Matt, his own lips twitching suspiciously, paid the driver, grasped Julie by the arm, and lost no time in escorting her away from the carriage before they both lost all control.

Entering the restaurant, they gave vent to the laughter that overcame them. The maître d' greeted him by name and asked if he would prefer his usual table.

Julie raised an eyebrow in surprise. His usual table?

"Yes, thank you, Stephen," Matt replied.

Taking two menus in hand, the maître d' escorted them through the crowded restaurant to a secluded table off to the side.

After they were seated, Matt chuckled, "I do think you've made some friends for life. Promise me you won't captivate the waiter until after I've been served."

"Only if you promise not to tell him tales about me, while he's serving you!" Julie replied with a laugh. The memory of her reaction to him in the carriage made her say, "That ride was enough to make me wonder if we would arrive in any condition to eat at all!"

Opening the large embossed menu, Matt teased, "Ah! So you admit you are hungry after all."

"How unfair of you! Shall I send for our carriage driver and tell him you lied to him? Why it might break his poor horse's heart," Julie informed him with a straight face.

Eyeing her over the top of his menu, Matt replied, "I

honestly don't think it would matter to either of them. They enjoyed the run, no matter the reason."

Julie folded her hands in her lap and chuckled. "I don't think the two of them really need a reason. Do you?"

"No," Matt agreed. Closing the menu, he asked, "Now that you have admitted you are hungry, would you allow me to order for you. Or do you have a preference?"

"That depends," was her reply. "What do you have in mind for me?"

Matt quirked an eye at her and teased, "As a gentleman, I cannot answer that question. But, I don't suppose you would care for the six-course dinner?"

Remembering his avowed hunger, she added, "Heavens, no! I have never been that hungry!"

"I thought not." Matt grinned. "But, I am. So, if you don't mind?"

"I doubt if it would matter if I did," Julie told him. "I'll watch in awe to see if anyone can truly consume that much at one meal. But, please only a light meal for me."

Matt's reply was cut off as the waiter came for their order. Smiling mischievously at her, Matt said, "The lady will have . . ." He paused.

Julie stared at him warningly.

". . . hot oysters, toast and tomatoes, followed by coffee." Matt finished with a lifted eyebrow in her direction. Seeing her slight nod of agreement, he looked to the waiter and asked, "Is the salmon fresh?"

"River-caught today, sir," was the quiet reply.

Nodding in satisfaction, Matt said, "Then Philip, make it my usual, please."

"Yes, sir!" Philip smiled in agreement.

"Your usual?" Julie asked him curiously.

"You'll see," Matt answered mysteriously.

Julie was beginning to believe there was nothing usual about Matthew Thorn. As the meal began and progressed, Julie could hardly believe her eyes as the courses were set before him. He started out with a steaming oyster soup that was quickly followed by the fresh salmon, fried to a golden turn. Then she watched in growing amazement as he consumed roast beef, boiled ham, and, finally, fried oysters with potatoes and onions.

She found herself sighing with relief when Matt decided against the mince pie and pudding, telling her, "I never have learned to like them when they're made without milk or eggs."

Having finished her light meal ages ago, Julie sipped at her coffee. Replete after his own meal, Matt offered to share his dessert of nuts, raisins and Madeira.

"No, thank you." Julie shook her head. "After watching you, I may never eat again. You said you were hungry, but I never dreamed you were in such dire straits."

Matt cracked a few nuts and separated the meat from the shells, saying, "I seem to recall saying I was starving."

Placing her cup on the saucer, Julie smiled. "Next time I'll believe you."

Changing the subject, Matt said, "I think we found more than I had expected when we started going through your father's papers."

"What makes you say that?" Julie questioned him.

"My father was meticulous about keeping records of practically everything."

"So I discovered," Matt replied. "Although"—he frowned—"I still haven't been able to find out why he was in that part of town at that time of night."

"He was on his way to visit Ah Toy," Julie informed him.

Matt's eyes widened curiously. Why would James be going to visit one of the toughest madams in town at that time of night? "Why haven't you told me this before?" Matt demanded.

Julie shrugged, "Since you never asked, I thought you already knew."

"I didn't," Matt responded grimly. "I sincerely doubt he was spying on the competition for Molly. So, if it is not too much to ask, why would he be visiting Ah Toy?"

"As a favor," Julie replied, adding with a curve of her lips, "a favor for Molly."

Leaning forward in his seat Matt asked, "I say again, why?"

"Have you ever heard of the Barracoon?" Julie asked him.

"Yes. Why?" Matt asked her. He hated the very name and all it conjured up. From what he knew it was based somewhere in Chinatown. It was where many of the unscrupulous brothel owners bought girls to work in their houses. The girls were sold on the block like slaves. Many of them had been kidnapped by, or sold to, the same scum that ran this dirty and clandestine operation. He thought he could guess now what James had been on his way to do the night of his death.

"Molly and my father had hoped to be able to close that hideous place once and for all," Julie explained. "Ah Toy is one of its major customers. She has never cared about the girls who work for her. She buys and sells them like slaves through the Barracoon. She also entices the agents for wealthy Chinese men, in the market for mistresses, to shop there."

"Nice lady," Matt commented coldly.

Julie grimaced in agreement as she went on with her explanation. "My father decided to try and persuade her to end her part in the Barracoon altogether," Julie continued. "He knew it was a risky thing for him to do, but he was willing to take that chance. Since the authorities continue to turn a blind eye to what happens there, he felt someone had to do something."

"Your father may have had more heart than he did sense," Matt grumbled. "That little journey in the night is what may have cost him his life," he said as he sipped at his Madeira.

"Do you think that's why he was murdered?" Julie asked him. "Is that what you found in his papers?"

Matt shook his head tiredly. "I did not expect things to be that easy, Julie. But, if I had known about your father's intention to speak with Ah Toy, it would have helped matters considerably."

"What did you expect to find in his papers anyway?"

"I was hoping to find a trail that might lead me to the answer of who killed him."

"And did you?" Julie pushed him, wanting to know what he had found that she had not.

"For the three weeks prior to his death, I know where he went, who he saw and why he saw them," Matt replied.

58

"So? I found some of that information myself. How will that tell us who killed him?" Julie did not understand how he thought this would lead them to her father's killers.

Matt clasped his hands on the table in front of him and tried to explain. "I plan to visit these people and ask them some questions. Hopefully one of them might be able to shed some light on the reasons for your father's murder."

Crossing her arms in front of her Julie nodded. "That makes sense. When do we start?"

Matt's eyes widened. *"We* don't start anything. I will start tomorrow. You have our casino to run."

"What!" Julie's eyes flashed in disagreement. "I know many of those people as well as my father did. What makes you think they will tell you, a complete stranger, things they would not tell me, his daughter!"

"This is not a series of social visits, Julie! It could be dangerous to ask questions," Matt informed her.

"Don't be ridiculous! I still want to know why you think you will be able to find out more than I could? I cannot sit here and accept the idea that people I have known for years would wish me harm." Julie flared.

"Do you honestly believe your father's murder was the work of complete strangers?" Matt asked her in a cold voice.

Julie flushed. "I'm not stupid! So there is some danger involved. But, I will have Lee Tang with me for protection. Why can't I help? Besides, with two of us asking questions, we could split the list and things would go faster."

Matt swirled the Madeira around in his glass and looked up at her saying, "This is not a matter open to discussion. I work alone. *You* will remain at the casino and do what is required of you there."

Julie wanted to tell him she would do no such thing, but his tiger eyes bore into her with a look of warning. It was as though he could read her thoughts and know exactly what she felt like saying to him. She bit her lip and glared back at him. If it was a battle of wills he wanted, then let the battle begin.

Matt watched in admiration as Julie glared at him in defiance. She had more spirit than he'd thought. He hoped she had more sense than her late father. It was not a game they were involved in, it was a hunt. Quite possibly a hunt to the death. He would have to keep a watchful eye on her. Something told him it was not in her character to give in so easily, especially when it was something she did not want to do. She had fought him once already over coming to dinner. She would fight him again. Of that much he was sure. He planned to win.

A slow smile spread across Matt's face as he raised his glass to her in a toast. A shiver went up Julie's spine, but she acknowledged his action with a slight nod. War had been declared.

Matt paid their bill and escorted a still-silent Julie to a waiting carriage in front of the restaurant. Settling next to her on the seat, he commented, "Enough wild rides for tonight. I told the driver to take it slow and easy."

Julie leaned back against the cushions and rested her eyes. What she needed was time. Time to regain her strength and shore up her defenses. She did not trust herself to reply to Matt's words. She was determined not to let him see she was shaken by their wordless duel in the restaurant. It was as though he had spent most of the day knocking her off guard. Not giving her a chance to think straight.

The feel of his hand on her arm made her start as he pulled her closer to him, saying, "You must be tired. It's been a long day. Rest your head on my shoulder, where it will be more comfortable."

Julie sighed. She was tired and he was right; his shoulder was more comfortable than the lumpy cushion. But it was hard for her to think straight with his arm around her. Her last thought was: Damn! He's done it again!

Chapter Six

JULIE LOOKED DOWN AT THE LIST IN HER HAND AND said, "Tang, we'll start at Sam Isaacs', on Folsom Street. Maybe he can give us some help."

Tang nodded and lifting the reins, started the carriage forward down Washington Street.

Julie was pleased with herself. She had managed to give Matt the slip. And Molly had been nowhere in sight when she and Tang had left. She was determined to help her find her father's killers, with or without Matt's permission. She had risen extra early and compiled a list of names on her own. Now she and Tang were about to visit the first name on that list.

They made good time once they had turned right

onto Montgomery and were nearing Market, but the crush of traffic on Market hindered their progress. And Julie began to wonder if they would ever make it across the crowded street.

After waiting nearly five minutes, Tang saw his chance and hurried the team across and onto Second Street. As they continued, Julie was greeted by calls and shouts from many of the pedestrians they passed along their route. She waved back and smiled. She sat forward on the seat as they turned left onto Folsom. She hoped Tang would be able to find an opening for the carriage near Sam Isaacs' tailor shop.

Though young and not in business for long, Sam had a large clientele. His tailoring was perfection. All the best-dressed men in San Francisco patronized his small establishment.

Julie heaved a sigh of relief. They were in luck. As they neared the shop, another carriage was pulling away and Tang was able to follow in its wake and take its vacated spot.

Julie smiled at Tang as he helped her from the carriage. "Maybe our visit will prove as lucky."

As she moved onto the rough walkway that fronted the shop, she glanced around her at the many carriages and coaches, all jockeying for positions to stop and disgorge their passengers. She shook her head. "Maybe someday in the future when this town is more settled, problems like this will be a thing of the past."

Tang's face remained impassive as he stood to the side and allowed Julie to precede him along the crude walkway. His eyes ever vigilant for possible danger, he still could not help but privately think that she had exercised the usual female illogic. In his mind "more settled" meant more people. And more people meant even less room.

He kept his thoughts to himself as always. Soon they arrived at a glass-fronted door with ornate lettering in gold that read: "Sam Isaacs, Tailor."

Entering the shop, they saw Sam in front of a group of mirrors at the rear. As always his measuring tape was draped over his shoulders. He was helping a gentleman don a superbly cut evening jacket of dark green velvet. Seeing them, he said something to his customer and moved to greet them.

"Miss Julie, how nice to see you again." He turned and called over his shoulder, "Annie, come see who's come to see us."

There was a rustle of movement behind a long narrow curtain at the corner of the room. It parted as a pretty young woman came at Sam's call. Looking askance to her husband, Annie Isaacs quickened her pace. "Julie!" she called fondly as she recognized her and clasped Julie in a warm embrace.

"Annie, love," Julie greeted her in return. "How are you? I'm sorry I haven't been able to visit sooner, but . . ."

Annie patted her on the arm, saying, "We understand. We loved him too. Your papa was a kind man."

Julie smiled her thanks for their warm offer of sympathy. She knew her father had held a special place in their hearts. He had loaned Sam the money to open the shop after Sam had been turned down by the bankers in town because he was a Jew. Julie had come to know both Sam and Annie well during the years they had been in San Francisco. They were honest, simple people who were not afraid to work hard. They had become good friends.

Sam excused himself, returning to the customer waiting by the mirrors. Annie drew Julie with her toward the curtain. "And what can we do for you?" she asked, a questioning look in her dark eyes.

Julie smiled, "I hope you can help me, Annie."

She followed Annie into the living quarters of the shop. Though not richly furnished, the small parlor was immaculately clean and cheerful. The modest sofa and three chairs were strewn with brightly colored pillows, and the small tables were polished to a bright shine. Through a small passage Julie could see the tiny dining room, a golden Menorah resting on the sideboard against the wall.

Taking a seat, Julie explained the reason for her visit and asked Annie if her father had seemed preoccupied or upset when last they had seen him.

Annie shook her head. "You know your papa. He was always with the quick laugh and warm smile. He and Sam took care of their business and then he left. He said something about an appointment he had to keep."

This was news to Julie. "Did he happen to mention where or with whom, Annie? It could be important."

"No. But, he did say he would much rather stay here and have some of my knishes and kielbasa." Annie motioned her to a seat, excused herself and headed toward the tiny kitchen.

Julie made herself comfortable and waited for Annie to rejoin her. Lee Tang entered quietly and took up an unobtrusive position at the entry.

Annie returned shortly, bearing a tray laden with

homemade pastries and a coffee service. Setting it down on a nearby table, Annie handed Julie a cup filled with coffee. Taking a cup for herself, Annie looked at her friend, concern on her face as she said, "I want you to know Julie, I do not make it a habit to be a kibitzer. But it wounds me to see the heavyhearted look in your eyes. You tell Annie. Maybe together we can find a solution, no?"

"I'm afraid there's little you can do, Annie. I'm retracing my father's movements as I told you. And it is really like searching for a needle in a haystack."

Annie set her cup down and noticed Lee Tang for the first time. "Does your Oriental friend mind kosher? He is big enough to need feeding all the time."

"Lee Tang?" Julie smiled at him questioningly. She understood Annie's need to feed anyone who came to her home. But the thought of her worrying about Tang wasting away from hunger made laughter dance in her eyes.

Tang regarded Annie's offer as his due as a man. He did not see what Miss Julie found so humorous about it. But his duty came first; he could not eat and keep watch. He shook his head in reply.

"What does that mean?" Annie questioned with a shrug. "Does it mean he doesn't eat kosher? Or he's not hungry?"

Julie laughed. "I think it means neither. He is my bodyguard, Annie. He probably feels his duty comes before anything else."

Rising from her seat, Annie took a linen napkin and began to wrap some of the flaky pastries. "He would never eat when he came with your father either. He will make himself sick that way. I will send some of this with you. He can have it when he feels it is correct."

Julie saw the look of concern on Annie's face as she looked at Tang, and she graciously accepted the wrapped pastries rather than hurt Annie's feelings. "Thank you, Annie. I'm sure Tang will enjoy this when the time is proper."

"Go on with you!" Annie waved her hand in dismissal. "I would not be able to live with myself if you were hurt because your bodyguard was too weak from hunger to protect you."

Julie glanced at Annie lovingly. "Annie? You said, my father had some business with Sam. Maybe he said something to him?"

Annie shrugged. "That I would not know. Sam, he tells me nothing. What goes on between him and his customers is not for gossip, he says. As if Annie Isaacs would tell the world or something! But, you ask him. Maybe he might be able to help you. Your papa was special to him."

As though hearing his name, Sam entered the room. Carefully avoiding Tang, he moved to join Annie and Julie. Taking a seat across from Julie, he reached over and helped himself to some of the pastries on the tray. "Has my Annie worn your ear to a nubbin? Once she starts I often wonder if she will ever stop." He softened his words with a loving look at his wife.

Annie lowered her eyes and said, "Stop it, Sam Isaacs. You embarrass me in front of our friend, Julie."

Julie knew how much they loved one another and enjoyed the way they teased. She hoped someday to find a man she could love and who would love her as much as the Isaacs loved one another.

Mentally shaking herself, Julie put such thoughts from her mind. "Sam? Annie tells me you and my father had some business before he died. Did he happen to say anything that might make you think he was worried or possibly expecting trouble of some kind?"

Sam thoughtfully chewed his lip for a moment before replying, "He was not a man to blab his business around. But, we did talk about the way things were going to the dogs . . . what with certain elements here in town."

"What elements were those, Sam?" Julie asked him, hoping he could shed some light on her father's state of mind at that time.

Sam paused and Annie admonished him, "Tell her, Samuel. She has a right to know. Maybe it will help."

Sam cleared his throat, before saying, "We talked about alot of things, Miss Julie. How prices are going through the roof and how hard it is for an honest man to make a living. He did say he could do without some of the sharks who preyed on his part of town."

Julie wished he would get to the point. But she was afraid to hurry him. "Sam, did he say who any of those sharks were?"

The sound of the bell at the front door of the shop made Sam rise from his seat. Moving toward the doorway, he replied, "No. But he did say he had the ammunition to harpoon one of the biggest."

Pausing by the curtain, he added, "He did say something about a notebook, Miss Julie. But, the shop began to get crowded and we couldn't talk anymore without being heard."

He disappeared into the shop before Julie could ask

him anything else. She desperately wanted to know if her father had said anything else about this mysterious notebook. She had never known it existed, nor to her knowledge did Molly.

From the sound of the constantly ringing bell, she knew Sam would be too busy to answer any more of her questions today. She would have to be satisfied with what he had told her, but—she frowned—he had given her more questions than he had answers. Things were turning out to be more complicated than she ever thought they would.

Finishing her coffee, Julie thanked Annie for her time, and rose to leave.

Annie clasped her in a farewell embrace, saying, "You be careful, Julie. I know that tone in Sam's voice. Things were serious between him and your papa that day. You take care of yourself."

"I will Annie. And thank you again for everything," Julie told her as she and Lee Tang moved from the tiny living room into the shop.

Annie called to her as she and Tang moved through the shop. "Wait, Julie!"

Turning, Julie waited as Annie hurried to her side. "For shame! You forgot your bodyguard's food."

Glancing up at Tang, Julie was surprised to see what could have been a look of reproach in his eyes. Accepting the food bundle from Annie, Julie found herself apologizing.

Turning, she resumed her way toward the front of the shop. Intent on asking herself why she had felt the need to apologize, Julie did not notice the tall form in front of her.

"Visiting old friends? Or shopping for a pair of pants

to go with your independent life-style?" Matt's voice washed over her like a shower of cold rain.

Shocked to see him, Julie blurted, "What business is it of yours?"

Refusing to move to one side to allow her by him, Matt replied, "None at all. If that is why you are really here. I thought we had settled things last night at dinner. I work alone, remember?"

"I'll try to remember that." She smiled sweetly before adding in a low voice, "Partner."

"Julie." Matt said her name with an underlying tone of steel.

"Yes?" She stared at him unflinchingly.

"Don't try my patience too far. You might not like the results," he warned her.

Goaded by his threat, Julie retorted, "As I am not well acquainted with your virtues, I was not aware patience was one of them." She gazed up at him with falsely innocent eyes.

A grin spread across his face and Matt said silkily, "A situation that can be easily remedied, my dear Julie. I have been told I have many virtues appreciated by the ladies."

To cover the growing disquiet he'd created in her, Julie took refuge in a haughty tone of disinterest and replied, "As I have neither the time nor inclination to pursue this conversation any further, please excuse me?"

With a mock bow in her direction, Matt stood aside to let her by. "Pity. It might have been worth pursuing," he whispered in her ear as she passed.

Julie raised her eyes to look at him and felt an icy tingle run up her spine. Her breath caught in her throat as Matt's eyes promised her he would deal with her later.

After she had left, Matt moved to where Sam Isaacs was waiting and greeted him as one would an old friend. Before he left the shop, he had found out as much as Julie and had ordered two new coats and three pairs of pants. He had been one of Sam's regular customers since James Leighton had brought him to the shop on the day it had opened.

Too unsettled by her encounter with Matt, Julie returned home instead of visiting the next name on her list. Molly met her near the front door, a disgusted look on her face. She told her that George Baldwin was upstairs in the office, waiting to speak to her.

Motioning to Lee Tang to follow her, Julie went up to the office and found Baldwin sitting on the sofa as though he hadn't a care in the world.

He rose to his feet as she entered the room and greeted her with an unctuous smile. "Good day, Miss Leighton."

"Mr. Baldwin," she replied as she moved behind her desk and sat down.

Tang had quietly followed her into the room and taken up a position by the door. Seeing him, Baldwin's eyes narrowed slightly before his gaze returned to Julie. "I've come here today to see if things are running smoothly for you," he told Julie, a false note of concern in his voice.

Looking up at him, she replied, "Is there any reason they shouldn't be, Mr. Baldwin?"

"No. Oh, no," he was quick to answer. "It's just that it's a mighty heavy load you've taken upon yourself. And I thought, that is, the other owners and I thought

71

one of us should stop by and reinforce our offer of the other night."

"Offer, Mr. Baldwin?" Julie frowned at him. "I don't seem to recall there having been any offer, other than advice. And it was explained to you then that Matthew Thorn has been kind enough to act as my advisor."

From the narrowing of his small eyes, Julie could see he was not at all pleased with what she said. That was fine with her; she did not care for him or his friends. They were some of the lowest life in the district. Despite their fancy homes and rich clothing and fawning women, they were still crooks as far as she was concerned. And anything that made them unhappy suited her just fine.

"About Matthew Thorn, Miss Leighton. My friends and I feel we should tell you that he is not exactly what we would call a competent advisor. He has never run an operation like a casino. All his apparent expertise has been in areas like logging, shipping and the like. Whereas we who operate casinos of our own are more than capable and willing, I might add, to lend you any advice or assistance you might need," he said as he rolled an unlit cigar through his fat fingers.

Looking him square in the face, Julie said, "I fail to see how my choice of an advisor concerns you or your friends, Mr. Baldwin." The sooner she could end this visit, the better she would feel. Her insides were twisting into knots with each passing minute.

"That's where I think you are making a mistake, Miss Leighton. What happens here can happen anywhere . . . and, have devastating effects on all of us," he warned her grimly. "Which brings us back to the offer I mentioned earlier. My friends and I are prepared to make you and Mrs. Fitzroy a fair offer for the Land of Gold."

"You mean to buy us out, Mr. Baldwin?" Julie questioned him coldly. "For how much, may I ask?"

He named a price so low it would not even cover the casino's liquor bill for six months. Julie saw red.

"How dare you and your friends insult me with such a ridiculous figure. This casino is worth more than all of yours put together and we both know it." Julie raked him with her eyes. "But as it is not for sale at any price, don't bother wasting any more of my time by naming another equally ridiculous figure."

Baldwin shrugged. "If you want to turn down what may be your last chance at getting anything out of this place before it folds around your ears, that's your choice. But I should tell you, rely on your Mr. Matthew Thorn and see how long you stay in business."

Rising from her chair, Julie asked, "Are you threatening me, Mr. Baldwin?"

Putting both his hands up, he replied, "By no means, Miss Leighton. Merely explaining a fact of business that's all."

"It is more than clear we have nothing further to discuss. Tang will escort you out," Julie told him.

Baldwin had no chance to protest as Tang took a firm grip on his arm and ushered him to the door. Glancing back at Julie with a look of outrage, he called, "You will be sorry, Miss Leighton. Stick with Thorn and you'll be out of business within a month."

"Don't waste your breath," Julie shot back at him.

"And, Mr. Baldwin, a bit of advice. It might not prove wise for you to show your face around here again. Lee Tang is not always this polite."

Julie sank to the sofa as Tang escorted Baldwin from the premises. She was so mad she was shaking. How dare they think she was so stupid as to accept their offer?

She was still on the sofa, stiff with anger, when Molly hurried into the room. "What happened? I saw Lee Tang take Baldwin out."

Julie took a slow deep breath, trying to rid herself of the urge to scream. "He and his friends wanted us to sell out to them," she told Molly through clenched teeth.

"They what?" Molly exclaimed.

Rising to her feet, Julie walked her anger off, adding, "I also was informed of their opinion regarding Matt's total incompetence as an advisor!"

"I hope you told him what they could do with their offer and their opinion?" Molly said.

"I certainly did. I also told him not to show his face around here again," Julie informed her.

"What if he does?" Molly asked.

"He knows he will have Tang to deal with," Julie replied in a hard voice.

Later that evening, as Julie moved through the crowded casino, she nodded to her regular customers as a matter of habit more than anything else. Now that she'd had time for her anger to cool, her mind was on other things. She was still trying to decide why Baldwin had appeared out of the blue as he had.

She was so involved with her tortured thoughts, Julie

did not notice Matt watching her. He had spoken with Molly and been informed of Baldwin's earlier visit. And of what Julie had said. He feared she might try something reckless. She had quite a bit of pride as well as intelligence. And both had been insulted.

He followed her progress through the room with his eyes. He found himself noticing the way the lamplight highlighted her hair and the graceful way she carried herself. He felt a now familiar stirring inside him as he moved to join her.

Julie's first awareness of him was his warm voice saying, "Why so serious? Is business that bad?"

"Don't startle me like that!" Julie exclaimed as she jumped in surprise. "Must you always sneak up on me?" she demanded crossly.

"I do apologize. But, you were so lost in thought I could have hired a band and you still wouldn't have heard me," he told her as he fell into step beside her.

"What were you chewing over so thoughtfully?" he asked her.

"Nothing," was her noncommittal reply.

Matt frowned as he looked down at her. "Nothing? Are you sure it's not a case of your not wanting to tell me?"

Julie cast a sidelong look at him as she moved up the staircase. "That possibility does exist. You do not have to know everything I'm thinking. You might not like it, if you did."

"Try me." Matt challenged her with a smile.

Ignoring his dare, she moved across the landing and into the office. Seeing that he had followed her, she said, "You wanted something?"

Matt's grin widened as he closed the gap between them, saying, "You really shouldn't ask leading questions like that. You might be shocked by the answers."

"Shocked?" Julie gave him a doubtful look. "You forget, I grew up here. I am not easily shocked."

Matt leaned closer and drew her into his arms as he whispered, "Then this shouldn't bother you at all."

Julie gasped as his lips took possession of hers, moving with sensual slowness as he kissed her.

Totally unprepared for his sudden action, it took a few seconds for her to react. She put her hands against his chest with the intention of pushing free, but changed her mind, deciding she would show him she was not that easily shocked.

Matt sensed her aim and deepened his kiss. His hands moved down along the curve of her hips and pressed her closer to him as his tongue moved to taste the sweet nectar of her mouth.

Julie tried to fight the way her body was starting to respond. Even as her hands moved up across his chest to encircle his neck and her fingers tangled in his thick hair, a part of her mind was sending out warning signals. Things were not going at all as she'd planned!

Matt was the one to finally end the kiss and break free. He gazed down at the turmoil in her eyes. And he felt the uneven rise and fall of her breasts against his chest. He wondered if it was all anger he saw in her eyes? Or had he affected her as much as she had him?

Shaken by his kiss and unwilling to let him know it, Julie took refuge in annoyance by saying, "Don't do that!"

"Then I would suggest you stop looking at me like that or I might do it again," he warned her softly.

Not trusting him not to kiss her anyway, Julie tried once again to break free from his embrace. "Matt, will you let me go?" she demanded.

He relented enough to pull back, leaving his hands on her waist to prevent her from running. "I thought you said you couldn't be shocked?" he reminded her.

"I'm not. But, I am too busy to stand here and debate the matter with you. Now go away and let me get on with my work," she ordered with a wave of her hand.

"Now who's being bossy?" Matt commented as he watched the play of emotions on her face.

"Bossy!" Julie strained against his muscular hands.

Matt raised an eyebrow and replied, "Hey, you were the one who started all this by asking what I wanted."

"That was a rhetorical question!"

Matt saw he had better leave before he really made her mad. Loosening his hold on her, he grinned, "You're always so tense. Try to relax. Why not quit early tonight and soak in a hot tub for a while. I hear it does wonders for tension."

Staring at him coldly, Julie replied, "I prefer hot cocoa."

"I'm not surprised," Matt commented blandly. Turning toward the door he added, "I see you have work to do. I'll take my leave and let you get at it."

"Ohh!" Julie fumed as he closed the door behind him.

She did not have long to dwell on her exasperation with Matt. There were far too many other things that required her attention. Gathering the receipts she'd come up for, she returned downstairs.

Moving over to her private table, she sat down and

spread the papers in front of her. She was soon joined by two men, the wine and liquor dealer from whom she regularly ordered and her grocer.

"Please have a seat, gentlemen," she instructed them. When they had settled themselves, she lifted one of the papers in front of her and said, "I have a receipt here, Mr. Duncan, for fifteen cases of champagne, twenty-five cases of whiskey, and twelve cases of blended bourbon. My head bartender tells me you were unable to make good on these deliveries. Why?"

The man shrugged his shoulders and replied, "I can only deliver what I have, Miss Leighton. My own supplier has failed to make good on my order from him. I can fill only part of your order without shorting my other customers."

"Why didn't you tell me about this when I placed my order?" Julie questioned him.

"I couldn't. I didn't know this was going to happen," was his pained reply.

"Deliver what you can then. And, Mr. Duncan, I will expect either a full refund for the undelivered merchandise or a notarized credit voucher first thing tomorrow morning," Julie instructed him.

He sat back in his seat and nodded, "Certainly, Miss Leighton."

Turning her attention to the grocer, Julie raised an eyebrow and asked, "Did your supplier short you, Mr. Grundig?"

His eyes widened with shock. "No, Miss Leighton!"

She held up the receipt of her order with him and said, "Then could you please explain why you also are unable to fill my order?"

"There was a fire at my warehouse and a good portion of my inventory was destroyed," he explained. "But I will deliver as much as I am able, Miss Leighton. I just won't be able to fill your complete order."

"A fire, you say?" Julie questioned him. "I thought your warehouse was one of the new brick buildings and fireproof, Mr. Grundig."

The grocer squirmed in his seat. "It is. The building did not suffer that much damage, but the contents were not fireproof."

"Have you any idea what the cause of the fire was, Mr. Grundig?" Julie asked him quietly.

"No, ma'am." It was a strangled reply.

"I suggest you try to find out and make certain it doesn't happen again," Julie suggested. "My terms are the same for you as they were for Mr. Duncan. Delivery first thing tomorrow and repayment or notarized credit voucher."

"Certainly, Miss Leighton. That is only fair." The grocer nodded swiftly. Neither man wished to lose such a valued customer. They were ready to agree to almost anything she wanted as long as she continued to trade with them.

Before she could call it a night, Julie had dealt with the usual drunken fights, sore losers and a small grease fire in the kitchen.

Moving upstairs to her room, she didn't think she had a muscle that didn't ache or a joint that wasn't protesting. A hot bath sounded absolutely wonderful.

When the tub was filled with steaming water and piled high with fragrant bubbles, Julie pinned her hair atop her head and slipped into its welcome warmth.

Resting her head against the back of the tub, she closed her eyes and let the steaming water soothe the aches and pains from her body.

She must have fallen asleep for a moment or two because the next thing she knew, she could smell hot cocoa in the air. She was afraid to open her eyes for fear she would see what she expected to see. Peeking carefully from behind lowered lashes, she scanned the area. She didn't see anything, only a cup and saucer resting on a chair at the side of the tub. It was enough. She hid as much of herself as she could under the dwindling bubbles and waited. She had no doubt as to what was in the cup or as to who was responsible for it being there. She strained her eyes and ears to see if she could pinpoint where the unwanted visitor was lurking. Minutes passed and soon she realized she was alone.

How had he come in and left again without her hearing him, she puzzled? That it was Matt, she had little doubt. It was just the type of thing he would do. Shrugging her shoulders she decided she could either spend the rest of the night in a tub full of rapidly cooling water, or she could dry off and drink her cup of cocoa. Better yet, drink the cocoa then dry off, she thought. She reached across and lifted the cup, draining its lukewarm contents. Setting it back on its saucer, she rinsed off one last time before getting out.

Chapter Seven

HAVING MADE HER DECISION SHE STOOD AND REACHED FOR the towel she had left nearby. It was gone! Before she could sink down again under the protective cover of the water, the missing towel was wrapped around her and two arms lifted her bodily from the tub and began to briskly dry her. She began to struggle the minute she noticed that her towel was gone, but she was at a definite disadvantage. It was impossible to break free and retain the towel and her modesty at the same time.

"Matthew Thorn! Leave me alone and get out of here!" she ordered as she pushed against him. "You have no business being here in the first place! Now go away!"

"I can't," came his warm response in her ear.

She stiffened in his arms and kicked herself for saying, "And why not?"

"That's my towel you're using."

Julie's eyes flashed to where she had left her towel and saw it had fallen to the floor. He had brought this one with him! "What are you doing here? And why did you bring a towel with you, anyway?" she demanded as she squirmed to free herself.

She felt a rumble of laughter flow through him as he replied, "I know you won't believe this, but I came to take a bath."

"What!" she exclaimed. "I don't make it a practice to share my baths, Matthew Thorn!"

"So I've discovered." His sigh was full of disappointment.

"Ohh!" She thrust her elbow as hard as she could into his midsection and was gratified to hear an "oof" as the arms that held her let go. She lost no time in putting some distance between them. She needed space to be able to think straight and try to figure out how to get out of this.

"You can't deny you have the only bathtub on this side of the building," Matt told her.

"What has that to do with anything?" Julie asked from across the room. She tried to wrap the towel around her, but her fingers were shaking and she fumbled awkwardly.

"Our discussion earlier this evening reminded me that I also enjoy the relaxing qualities of a hot bath before retiring at night," Matt explained calmly. "I thought I could slip in here while you were still downstairs finishing the work you keep reminding me about, and have a nice hot bath. I'd planned on being gone long before you came upstairs."

Julie listened to his story, surprised that she was inclined to believe him. What he said did make some sense. But, what about the hot cocoa? The little voice inside her asked.

"If what you say is true, what about that?" she pointed at the incriminating cup and saucer.

"It's mine. I like cocoa too." Matt smiled. "Imagine my surprise when I came back here with it and found you asleep in the tub. I set it down and started to leave, when I heard you start to waken. I didn't want you bringing the roof down on my head when you caught me leaving. So I tried to stay off to the side and out of the way."

"You could have coughed or something to let me know you were still here," Julie told him reproachfully.

"And have you screaming for Lee Tang? No, thank you," Matt answered. "If you had some idea I was here, why didn't you say something?" he asked her.

Julie couldn't answer him. She probably should have called out to make sure she was alone, but she hadn't.

"Julie? I'm getting awfully tired of fighting with you all the time. And you must be getting cold with only that towel. Let's call it a draw for tonight? Okay?" Matt took a step toward her his hand outstretched.

Julie could not stop herself from taking a step backward as Matt advanced. "No! I mean, don't come any closer. I'm not sure I can trust you."

"Julie? Who are you trying so hard to convince? Me or yourself?" Matt shook his head. "You know as well as I do you can trust me."

"I'm not trying to convince anyone. I am stating a fact," Julie retorted in desperation. "Right now I'm beginning to wonder if I can trust anyone."

Matt moved to the side of the tub, saying in a soothing voice, "There really isn't any reason for you to be so upset."

"No reason! What in the world are you talking about? I have every reason to be upset!" Julie wished he would go away. She was finding it harder and harder to stay calm. He was thoroughly disturbing her, in a way she had never felt before. And it frightened her.

"Why Julie?" Matt said softly as he stared into her eyes.

"Why you ask?" Julie stammered. "You show up from out of nowhere and . . . and whisk me out of the tub and you still have to ask why?"

"Did I scare you?" Matt queried.

Julie took a deep breath and answered shakily, "Yes you did. Why are you acting like this? You've got me all confused."

Matt smiled at her reassuringly. "I never meant to do either."

"Well, you did," Julie told him accusingly.

"I can't say I'm sorry. Because I'm not," Matt continued. "I rather enjoy having you in my arms. But I never wanted to scare or confuse you."

To her surprise she said, "We've only known each other a short time. And not under the best of circumstances. I can't understand why you are acting like this."

"Is it so hard for you to believe I might find you attractive and even desirable?" Matt questioned her slowly.

"Yes," she whispered in reply grabbing the towel as it threatened to slip from her grasp.

Matt held his hand out to her, saying, "Come here, Julie."

She hesitated slightly before accepting his outstretched hand and allowing him to draw her into his arms. You fool, she told herself as Matt cradled her against him.

"I would never do anything to hurt you. You know that don't you?" Matt asked her.

Julie found herself nodding her head, her cheek rubbing against the smoothness of his silk shirt. Deep inside she knew what Matt told her was true. He would never deliberately hurt her. But, if she allowed her new feelings for him to overrule her good sense, she might be courting disaster.

"Julie?" Matt whispered her name.

"Hmm?" she murmured as she rested in his arms.

"Look at me, Julie," Matt told her.

She reluctantly raised her head and gazed at his rugged features as he asked, "Do you trust me?"

"Why?" She frowned.

"I want you to promise me you won't go off on your own again. Let me finish the questioning of the others," he told her.

"Ohh!" She raged as she beat her hands against his chest. "You tricked me! All this sincerity was just to get me in a mood to agree to step aside and let you be the boss."

Matt pulled her head back down on his shoulder and stroked the tense muscles in her neck, saying, "You know better than that, Julie. Stop fighting me. You will only wear yourself out."

"I don't like fighting with you." Julie sighed in exasperation. "You make me do it."

"I do!" Matt exclaimed. "I haven't been able to make you do anything you didn't want to do. You have fought me every step of the way. And now you say I make you fight with me. It doesn't make sense, Julie."

"I know," she admitted. She could not even begin to explain to him how he made her feel. And even if she could she was not certain she should. He had too much power over her already.

"Julie? Do I have your promise?" Matt persisted. He wanted to hear from her that she would no longer interfere and make it harder for him to concentrate on what he had to do. He had spent too much time already worrying about her when he should be searching for her father's killers.

Relaxed by the soothing caress of his strong hands, she protested sleepily, "I'm too tired to fight anymore, Matt."

"Then don't," Matt advised as he lifted her into his arms. Rising from the sofa he started toward her bedroom.

Julie put her arms around his neck not caring where they were going. She had done all the fighting she could for one day.

She felt so warm and safe in Matt's arms. She could not remember ever feeling as secure as she did now.

Julie dozed, her head on his shoulder, while he carried her with ease. A frown wrinkled her brow as he laid her down on the bed and her arms slid from around his neck when she sank into the fluffy softness of the mattress. She opened her eyes and watched as Matt removed his jacket and boots before lying down beside her.

When he gathered her into his arms, it felt perfectly natural to her and Julie sighed softly. The feel of his lips as they caressed her forehead and cheek sent tiny waves of pleasure through her. More than content to be in his arms, she tried to snuggle closer.

Matt welcomed her apparent acceptance of him. His lips trailed gentle kisses down her cheek to her throat, while his hand traced the curve of her waist as it flowed into her hip. The feel of the rough towel molding itself against her soft skin made his breath quicken.

Julie relaxed even more as a languor filled her, and Matt took possession of her lips with a kiss that sent tongues of fire through her. She gave no conscious thought to what might happen should things continue the course they were on. She was too caught up in the wonder of how Matt was making her feel.

She threaded her fingers through his thick golden hair and marveled at the way its strands wrapped around her fingers. Almost as though they had a life of their own.

Time became meaningless; she was lost in a cloud of sensation. Matt's hands drew circles of pleasure across her shoulders and back. His fingertips left a path of gentle awakening along her collar bone and down across the tops of her breasts, where they swelled above the towel.

Julie felt herself begin to tremble and Matt sensed her growing response. He smiled softly as he lowered his head and his lips retraced the path of his fingers.

She was adrift on a sea of feeling and did not protest

when he undid the fold of her towel. Slipping it from her, Matt slowly began to draw it away.

Julie felt cool air across her breasts as Matt moved away to discard his shirt. Then he gathered her close to him and she gasped at the feel of his warm hand cupping her breast. His skin against hers felt like a branding iron. She sensed her breast swelling in his hand as though it welcomed his touch.

When he lowered his lips to tease its rosy peak, Julie was shocked to hear herself moan with delight. She stroked the corded muscles of his back, exploring each and every sinew and curve. His skin felt smooth and supple as it rippled beneath her hands.

A hollow ache that she had never felt before began to build inside her and she arched herself against him, her breath coming in little gasps.

His lips brushed teasingly against her breasts, and she thought she would die as he ever so slowly traced patterns of fire across her abdomen and hips with his tongue. His lips blazed a trail of kisses from the tops of her thighs to the tips of her toes.

Matt gazed at the sight of Julie's thick hair tumbling in waves over her silken shoulders, down past her narrow waist to her softly curved hips, and he held his breath in wonder. She was exquisite. A feeling close to reverence flowed through him. Never had he seen such beauty.

The need to make her his gathered strength and he rose from her side to strip away his clothes. Bending over her, he saw the gleam of desire in her thickly lashed eyes as she watched him.

He groaned aloud as her slim fingers tentatively traced the muscles of his chest with feather softness.

Had she any idea what she was doing to him? From her innocent openness he suspected this was her first time with a man. A heady feeling of responsibility came over him. It was his place to initiate her into the full joys of what could be one of the sweetest times between a man and a woman.

Placing a tight rein on his own need for her, Matt lay beside her. His hands began to stroke and caress her satin-smooth skin with deliberate slowness. She moved against him and bit her lips to try to hide the tiny moans that escaped her.

Trailing his fingers over the incredible softness of her inner thighs, Matt knew neither of them could wait much longer. Moving onto his knees, he placed his hands beneath her hips and lifted her to meet him.

Their joining ignited such a surge of feeling that neither felt anything but the burning desire to fulfill their union. They moved as one, lost on the spiraling staircase of completion. Their climb was a dizzying coil of shared passion that ended in a starburst of pleasure as they reached the top.

Having scaled the heights and reached the pinnacle they slowly drifted back down, entwined in each others arms.

Awareness of her surroundings slowly returned and Julie felt adrift on a warm sea of contentment. As she relived what they had shared a sudden feeling of panic threatened to overwhelm her. What had she done! She had never acted this way before in her life! How could she have allowed things to go as far as this? Did she have so little control where Matt was concerned that her body betrayed her and her mind refused to admit the danger he posed?

Matt felt her withdrawal from him as she tried to cope with the realization of what had happened between them. He knew this time was as critical as any they had shared. He had to be certain she did not try to hide from the truth. Looking at her he saw the reflected turbulence of her thoughts in her eyes.

"Oh, no," she gasped.

"Julie?" he tried to make her look at him. But, she closed her eyes as tears began to stream silently down her cheeks.

What he must think of me! I may as well ask Molly for a job! She cried to herself. She felt like rolling into a ball and hiding her shame and misery from the world.

Seeing her tears, Matt frowned. "No, Julie. There's no reason for tears."

Julie could barely look at him, but she had to tell him. "I'm sorry."

"Sorry?" Matt cradled her close to him. "I don't understand." He watched her face hoping to find an answer there. "Explain it to me, Julie. Did I do something to frighten you?"

Seconds passed before he heard her whispered reply. "No. I frightened myself."

Matt's arms tightened around her protectively. "How? By being warm and alive and giving?"

How could she tell him she was afraid of how he made her feel? She couldn't. She had lost control of everything. She had to try to save what little pride she had left. She shivered involuntarily.

Matt knew he had to find a way to make her tell him what was wrong. Things between them might never be the same if he didn't. He could see how she was fighting the tears that continued to stream down her cheeks unchecked. "You must tell me, Julie," he told her softly. "Together we can handle whatever it is."

Julie raised her eyes to his and wiped the tears from her cheeks with the back of her hand, saying, "I can't."

Matt took her hand in his and asked, "Can't what, Julie?"

"Tell you," she stammered, her eyes glimmering with unshed tears.

Her response triggered Matt's temper and he tightened the grip he held on her hand, saying, "You're not leaving here, until you do."

Her eyes grew wide at the steel in his voice. And fear crept up her spine. She recognized the uncompromising expression on his face as he stared at her. She would have to come up with a plausible excuse or be forced to tell him the truth. Something she wanted to avoid at all costs. She would not humiliate herself to satisfy his curiosity!

The atmosphere was rich with the lingering threads of awareness. Matt watched her, the memory of shared desire flickering in the depths of his golden eyes. He could see by the erratic pulse at the base of her throat that Julie was beyond her depth, vulnerable, and, frantically trying to find a way to escape.

"Let me go, Matt," Julie said quietly as she tried to pull her hand free.

"Why? So you can run and hide?" Matt asked. "Pretending nothing happened won't make it so, Julie."

Her head snapped up and she retorted, "Don't say that!"

Matt leaned back and shook his head from side to side. "Where is that honesty and fairness you pride yourself on now, Julie? Why won't you face the truth?"

"And what truth is that?" Julie challenged him.

"You tell me," Matt replied calmly.

Trying even harder to break free of his hold, she gasped, "The truth? You want the truth? The truth is you are gloating over the fact that you can add me to your list of conquests."

Matt released her hand and smiled as she scrambled from the bed and bent to grab the towel. "Is that what you believe? It's quite a nice excuse to keep you free of any of the responsibility for what happened between us."

"An excuse!" Julie exclaimed as she tried to wrap the towel around her. "There is no excuse for what happened here tonight."

Matt rose from the bed, and she took a step backward not fully trusting what he might do. He laughed softly. "I think you are afraid to face the fact that you are a fraud."

"Fraud!" Julie stopped and stared at him.

"You have fooled yourself and others for years with your pose of self-sufficiency. That cool regard of those who might threaten your control of your life is only a front. Tonight, you discovered you can lose that precious control and be a warm and passionate woman." He paused before adding, "And the discovery scares you to death."

Julie wrapped her arms about herself as his words stabbed at her. No! You're wrong! She denied them in her heart. You're the one who makes me feel that way.

92

No power on earth could make her say the words aloud. Doing so would give him a power over her that she was not ready to give.

"No!" she murmured, unaware how she was exposing the torment she was going through.

Having dressed, Matt moved toward the door. Turning he told her softly, "Yes, Julie. Nothing can be settled until you are willing to admit the truth to yourself. When you do, we will settle what is between us."

She watched him leave the room. She felt totally drained. Moving to the bed, she sank down on the edge, her legs no longer able to support her. Why was all this happening? She couldn't possibly tell him what her heart even now was telling her. She was in love with him.

The persistent tingling of her skin reminded her of what they had shared. She had responded to him in a way she had to no other man.

He had taken her to heights she had never dreamed existed. But when she had drifted back to earth and the reality of what had happened began to set in, he'd wanted even more. He'd wanted her to bare her very soul to him.

She felt so vulnerable. Too much had happened too soon. It frightened her to discover she could respond to a man as she had to him. Her burning eyes moved to the closed door. He had been so angry when he left. But, how could she explain things she didn't understand herself?

Why had he made love to her? Did he think she was like one of Molly's girls? The possibility made her blood run cold. That had to be the reason. He was used to taking his pleasure at any time he desired. She was only a convenient female and nothing more.

Too hurt to think about it any longer, she rose from the bed. Moving to the dresser, she automatically reached for her night clothes even as she tried to quell the pain that burned inside her.

Chapter Eight

THE NEXT FEW DAYS WERE PURE TORTURE FOR JULIE. Try as she might, she could not forget what she and Matt had shared, nor his angry departure from her room. She tried to lose herself in work. When that didn't help, she began searching for the notebook Sam Isaacs had told her about. But even as she searched, the persistent memory of Matt's lips against her skin and of the way she had responded to him made it almost impossible to concentrate.

She had not seen Matt since that night in her room. He had risen early and left before she awakened. She had dreaded having to face him, for fear he would be able to see the love in her eyes. She soon discovered that his absence was far worse. She found she was always looking over her shoulder, expecting him to be there, or listening for his voice as she moved through the casino at night.

By the end of the day, she would sink exhaustedly into her bed and pray the next day would be better.

She had come close to tearing the desk and the office apart in her search for her father's notebook. But with no success. Hunt as she might, she could find no trace of it. She thought it strange that her father had never mentioned its existence to her.

After searching everywhere she could think to look, she asked Molly, "By any chance have you seen one of my father's notebooks lying around anywhere?"

Molly replied, "Your father kept all his papers and notebooks in the desk. If it's not there, I don't know where it might be. Why? Is it important?"

That had been a ticklish question. She knew she couldn't tell Molly the truth. If she knew, she would forbid Julie to do anything but turn the notebook over to the authorities, or worse, to Matt. "Not really," she answered. "I just thought he might have another one around here somewhere."

Added to the problem of the missing notebook, they were suddenly plagued by a rash of accidents. First, Lukes almost lost a hand when the mirror behind the bar came crashing down while he was restocking. Then Bet was burned as she tried to stop the coffee urn from toppling from its table. Neither of them had been badly injured, but Julie wondered how and why both accidents had happened.

The bar mirror had been replaced only a month

before, and the new one had been securely fitted into place. The coffee urn was too heavy to have fallen by itself. What had caused them to fall?

Everyone was becoming jumpy. The previous evening two of Molly's girls, Pearl and Mary, had been attacked in their rooms and viciously beaten. Their attackers had escaped before either girl had been found.

What had begun as merely a spate of unfortunate incidents was fast turning into something very ugly.

Two of her Faro dealers were accused of cheating. Julie had had to fire one on the spot. Lee Tang had thrown him out onto the street as a warning that cheating was not tolerated at the Land of Gold. The second dealer had been falsely accused by a poor loser, widely known to be a loud-mouthed troublemaker. He'd bellowed even louder as he followed the crooked dealer out onto the street.

The most recent incidents had happened simultaneously, wiping out any thought that they were not deliberate. A large rock had come crashing through one of the front windows of the casino, and then a gun shot through the broken window had narrowly missed Julie.

That morning, the musicians had given notice, saying they could no longer work there. When pressed for a reason why, they had answered that they didn't feel safe on the high platform with all the accidents that had been happening.

Julie had the music platform thoroughly checked for safety. Still, the musicians refused to stay if they were expected to use it. She finally had resorted to moving some of the gaming tables and setting up an area on the main floor for them to use. This was the only way she could keep them from leaving, but it meant she would be losing revenue from the lost tables.

In the midst of all this chaos, Adam and Sara paid her a visit. It was the first time she'd seen them since the reading of her father's will, and the gleam of curiosity in Sara's eyes as she viewed the room, made Julie wonder what she was up to. Sara was the one Julie didn't trust. Adam was more than obvious in his disapproval of what he saw. "Julie! I heard word at one of my clubs of all the problems you've been having," he informed her smugly. "Maybe now you will agree that running such an establishment is not a job for a woman?"

Julie smiled up at him and said, "But, Adam, didn't you also hear at one of your clubs that I have a man helping me?"

"What!" Adam and her sister had exclaimed.

It was the only good thing that had happened all day. Julie thoroughly enjoyed seeing them caught by surprise.

"Who?" Adam demanded curtly.

"A close business acquaintance of father's. A Mr. Matthew Thorn," Julie replied with quiet dignity.

Sara began looking around the room. Not seeing anyone she didn't know, she said, "Where is he? We would like to meet him."

Good question, Julie thought to herself, but replied, "I'm sorry. He's not here at the moment. I know he'll be sorry to hear he missed meeting both of you." She paused for a moment before adding, "But, you have seen him."

"We have?" Adam frowned. "When was this? I do not remember any such meeting."

"He was at the reading of father's will. The tall man in the back of the room," Julie explained.

"Him!" Sara came close to hissing through her teeth. She had not liked the looks of him. He was not someone to tangle with. And now he was working with Julie.

"Yes," Julie answered. Glancing across the room, Julie looked back at her visitors, saying, "I'm sorry I haven't time to chat. As Adam has pointed out, there is quite a bit of work involved in running a casino."

Adam had put up his hand to forestall her, but she ignored it, saying, "If you let me know the next time you will be calling I'll try and have more free time. Now if you will both please excuse me."

She had not waited to hear their answer, but had hurried to the kitchen and away from them. The last thing she wanted now, was for either of them to begin asking pointed questions she could not answer.

Matt's continued absence started to raise eyebrows. The whispers as to why began to grow louder. Julie tried to cope with the nervous casino staff, while Molly did her best to reassure her frightened girls.

At night, things were no better. Julie would lie awake unable to sleep. Her body felt lost in the big bed. She may have shared it only once, but the emptiness she felt inside told her it was enough. Rarely was she able to fall asleep for more than two or three hours.

The tension of holding the casino together combined with the lack of sleep began to take their toll. Dark circles formed under her eyes and she lost her appetite.

By the third day, Molly started wondering about

Matt's continued absence. She had been having thoughts of her own regarding the cause. She decided to find out if what she suspected was true.

"Did you and Matt have a fight?" she asked Julie in the office one afternoon.

"What makes you ask a question like that?" Julie hedged cautiously, as she closed the account book, in which she had been marking the day's entries.

Molly made herself comfortable on the small sofa, saying, "He didn't look very pleased with things the other night. I know the two of you had been together and thought maybe you'd had another one of your arguments."

Rising from her seat, Julie carried the account book to the shelves and replaced it. "You make it sound as though all we ever do is argue!" she laughed self-consciously.

Molly raised an eyebrow at her. "I would hope you both are too smart for that." She smoothed the skirt of her dress as she added with a teasing tone, "There are other more rewarding pastimes."

Julie froze in her tracks. What was Molly hinting at? Had she guessed?

"From the way your face is turning red, I would hazard to say you've already discovered some of them."

Julie turned her back to Molly and returned to straighten the books lined in front of her. This conversation was becoming dangerous. Molly was entirely too sharp not to pull the truth from her if she allowed her to go on.

"Molly! Stop teasing me!" Julie ordered. "You know as well as I do that Matt is a business partner."

"So?" Molly said. "For a business partner he's not around much. Besides, that doesn't mean he can't be anything else."

Returning to her seat at the desk, Julie picked up a sheet of paper and pretended to be engrossed with it. "If you say so," she commented with what she hoped was disinterest.

"I know so." Molly frowned. "And what is so all fired interesting in that laundry bill?"

"What?" Julie stammered.

"You've been staring at it for the past five minutes," Molly informed her.

"I was only going over these figures," Julie lied.

"Right," Molly disagreed. "And someday they'll elect a madam mayor." She turned to face her, saying, "Come on, Julie. What's going on between you and Matt?"

"Why should anything be going on between us?" Julie stalled as she moved to the rack ladder which leaned against the book shelves. Pretending to need one of the books from the top shelf, she began to climb. Frantically, she tried to think of something to say that would keep Molly from pestering her. She had enough on her hands without Molly prying into things.

"You tell me?" Molly persisted.

"Tell you what?" Matt asked as he unexpectedly entered the room.

His reappearance after nearly a week's absence took them completely by surprise. There had been no word from him during the entire time. Now he reappeared on the scene as though he had only stepped out for a few minutes.

He stood in the doorway and looked up at Julie as

she stared down at him from her precarious perch atop the ladder.

The impact of his golden eyes staring into hers sent a thrill of apprehension up her spine. His look told her he had not forgotten a thing that had happened between them.

She started down the ladder thinking she would feel safer on the floor. She had made it only part way down when, without a word to her, Matt moved to the ladder and reaching up clasped her about the waist. Lifting her from the ladder, he set her on the floor before continuing to one of the chairs. Sitting down, he smiled at Molly. "Please don't let me interrupt. You were saying?"

Shifting herself on the sofa, Molly replied, "Never mind what I was saying. Where have you been all this time?"

"Around," was his laconic answer.

"What!" Molly snapped. "Is that the best you can do! You disappear without a word then suddenly reappear and all you can say for yourself is 'around'!"

"That's right." Matt nodded agreeably.

Looking over at Julie, he said grimly, "I've already heard about the 'accidents.' Are you okay, Julie?"

Julie could only nod numbly. Seeing him again had brought all the defenses she had so carefully erected around herself over the past week crumbling down. He still had the power to make her pulse leap and her heart pound. Damn him! Why did he have to come back? Julie railed to herself.

Hiding his surprise at the dark circles under her eyes and the way her clothes could not hide the weight she'd lost, Matt said, "I'll want to go over them with you later."

Returning his full attention to Molly, he added, "Now, why don't you fill me in on the rest?"

"The rest?" Molly frowned at him.

"For instance, what were you badgering Julie about when I came in?" Matt asked her.

"I was not badgering her! I was simply asking her what was going on between you two," Molly answered him. Leaning forward and eyeing him coolly, she said, "Maybe you could tell me?"

Julie could still feel the imprint of his strong hands on her waist. She tried to ignore what it was doing to her senses, as she heard Molly's words. Oh, no! How could Molly ask him something like that? "Molly!" she exclaimed.

"What business is it of yours?" Matt asked carefully.

"Anything that affects Julie is my business," Molly informed him. "I don't like what I've been seeing around here and I want some answers."

Julie's strangled cry of response went unheard.

Crossing his legs and resting his booted ankle on his knee, Matt's expression was closed and unreadable. "We had a disagreement."

Julie gripped the edges of the desk to keep from fainting. Disagreement? What was he talking about? Everyone knew they'd rarely agreed on anything from the day they'd met. What was he talking about?

Glancing over at Julie's white face and back to Matt, Molly said, "I knew it! What was it about?"

"I refused to let her go off on her own and question some of the people her father met before he died,"

Matt replied with a steady voice. "She tried taking off on her own and managed to visit the Isaacs. But, fortunately, I arrived on the scene and prevented any further visitations."

Eyeing him dubiously, Molly said, "Is what he says true, Julie?"

"Yes," was all she could say in reply. Her heart was thudding against her ribs so loudly, she was surprised no one else could hear it.

"Then, that's where you've been all this time? Visiting these people?" Molly asked him.

"That's right," Matt returned. "And Julie has had to remain here. Something that, as you may have noticed, does not agree with her."

Molly frowned and digested his explanation, not sure whether she should believe it. She had been so certain that something else was going on between them she found it hard to accept. "If what you say is true, then why has she been tearing this place apart hunting for something?" Molly figured she'd trapped him.

Reaching into the inside pocket of his jacket, Matt pulled out a small brown notebook, saying, "She was looking for this."

Julie gasped aloud, causing Molly to look at her and ask, "Is that what I think it is, Julie?"

"Yes, my father's notebook," was all she could reply. He's had it all along! Her mind screamed at her.

"The one you asked me about?" Molly probed.

Julie nodded mutely, too shaken to trust her voice. How did he find it? How long had he had it? Why had he kept it from her? The questions boiled inside her, but she had no answers to make her feel any better.

"What are you doing with it?" Molly asked him as Julie waited with bated breath to hear his reply.

Tucking it back into his pocket, Matt replied, "Using it."

"For what?" Molly demanded. "If it belonged to James, then it now belongs to Julie. What gives you the right to use it?"

Rising from his seat, Matt shook his head saying, "You are correct in saying it once belonged to James, but incorrect in saying it now belongs to Julie. It's mine."

"Hold it a minute!" Julie protested. "Just because you have it doesn't mean it belongs to you!"

"I'd say it does." Matt dismissed her challenge as he patted his coat pocket. "But, in any case, it's mine. Your father gave it to me before he died."

"He what!" Both women looked at him in disbelief.

Recovering slightly, Julie went on, "Then why did we spend all the time we did going through his papers? If you already had the notebook, there was no need to look any further."

A frown of consternation appeared on Matt's brow. "I had my reasons."

"Reasons! You had your reasons!" Julie fumed. "What kind of an answer is that?"

Looking into her eyes, Matt replied, "The only one you're going to get."

"Why didn't you tell anyone you'd be gone?" Molly asked him.

"I work alone and answer to no one," he informed

them. "Why not ask Julie why she insisted on taking off on her own, Molly?"

"Stop trying to change the subject!" Molly warned him.

"I'm not. I'm closing it," Matt told her as he turned to leave the room.

Hurrying to intercept him, Julie grabbed him by the arm and said, "Oh, no, you're not!"

Looking down at her hand on his arm and back to her face, Matt slowly smiled. "I think I already have."

Pulling her hand away as though burned, Julie exclaimed, "I want to know why my father gave you his notebook. I don't have the patience to play any of your games!"

Matt turned so that Molly couldn't see his face as he said, "If you don't like games, could I suggest something else?"

Julie glared up at him and hissed between her teeth, "No!"

"No?" Matt shrugged. "My, what a short memory you have."

"My memory is fine. Maybe you're not that memorable," Julie snapped at him.

His eyes darkened slightly. "Do you have that many to remember?"

Julie could not help flinching as though she'd been slapped in the face. Could he have said it any plainer? He considered her no differently than he did the prostitutes who worked for Molly.

Matt saw the pain that clouded her eyes. What was this? Surely, his words hadn't hurt her, or had they, he frowned? Something strange was going on inside that pretty head of hers and he was going to find out what it was.

"What are the two of you fighting about now?" Molly asked from across the room.

"Should I tell her?" Matt tested Julie, a glint in his eyes.

Julie's face whitened with anger and she snapped back, "She wouldn't believe you if you did. She knows I have better taste."

"Julie?" His eyebrows went up as he questioned her softly. The sooner the two of them talked alone the better. For some reason or another she was entirely too defensive.

Fed up at being ignored, Molly rose from the sofa. Moving beside them, she demanded, "What is going on?"

Julie knew she had no control over what he said. Looking over at Molly, who frowned at her in puzzlement, Julie's shoulders slumped as she said, "Do whatever you like, Matt. You will anyway."

"Would one of you answer me!" Molly's voice rose in consternation.

"It's nothing, Molly. Julie was only reading me the riot act for being gone so long. That's all," Matt explained quietly as he stared at Julie, trying to puzzle out what was wrong with her.

"And well she should!" Molly agreed. "Things around here have been hectic as hell this past week. You should have been here to help out, not gallivanting around visiting people you don't even know."

Tired of Molly's nosy nagging, Matt placed a gentle

hand on Julie's arm, saying, "I would like to see where these accidents happened. Would you show me?"

"Downstairs," Julie replied dully as she led the way from the office.

Knowing when she was not wanted, Molly let them go without her.

Chapter Nine

THE CROWDED ROOM PULSATED WITH THE SMELL OF cheap whiskey, stale smoke and unwashed bodies as the less than savory clientele of the Jackpot Saloon pushed tightly around the gaming tables.

All were intent on trying to beat the odds of chance and the rigged wheels of the house. That the games were rigged was common knowledge, but few of the gamblers complained. Not too picky about their own standards of honesty or behavior, their kind was not readily accepted at the more honest houses, and they knew if they did complain they could end up out on the street with a busted head.

And the Jackpot was no different than any of the

other gambling dens they could afford to patronize. Here at least the whiskey was cheap and so were the women.

On the far side of the room, away from the rabble was a large table set in the corner. At this table, engrossed in conversation sat the same five men who'd visited Julie on the night of her father's funeral.

George Baldwin struck a match on the underside of the table and carried it to the end of his black cigar. Lighting the cigar, he waved the match out and tossed it onto the table, saying, "Things are progressing, gentlemen. Granted they are not moving as swiftly as some of us might like, but I'm confident that Miss Leighton is finding it harder than she anticipated to run a casino."

Sly chuckles and evil grins were the response to his words. "But, accidents can happen to anyone, can't they?" one of the men remarked.

"Yes. Isn't it a shame that poor Miss Leighton seems to be having more than her share lately?" another laughed cruelly.

"Do you think we should try buying her out again, George?" Potter asked with an avid smirk.

Shaking his head, Baldwin replied, "No. She's too stubborn to lie down and quit this soon, but given time, she might see the futility of things and come around to our way of thinking."

Raising his glass in a toast, Watkins said, "Here's to the fortuitous circumstances that have made life even harder for our lady owner."

Sherman shook his head wonderingly. "You're right there. Her suppliers not being able to fill her orders couldn't have worked more in our favor if we'd planned it. I'm kinda surprised we didn't think of it ourselves, but it makes no difference, it's happened anyhow."

"I still say things are taking too long," Hastings announced. "Matt Thorn is no fool. And I for one don't want to end up facing him. Isn't there some way we can remove him from the picture? I'd certainly like the odds better if he weren't around."

"If we took any direct action against him, we'd tip our hands!" Baldwin hissed in reply. "We have to be careful and patient. Things are going according to plan. By this time next week, our Miss Leighton should be more than ready to accept our offer. Until that time, I don't want any of you trying anything on your own and fouling things up." He glared at his companions warningly. "Do you hear me? I don't want any more bullets through smashed windows!"

He stared at them until he received their sullen replies of agreement. "We all have too much at stake here to go off half-cocked and ruin everything. We rush things and the results could be our necks," he informed them. "So, you keep to our agreement and let me handle things. No more ideas of your own!"

"Isn't there anything we can do? Set up a few more 'accidents' or something?" Hastings pushed, still not happy with the idea of playing a waiting game.

Baldwin frowned, "Maybe, but you leave the details to me. I'll set something up to ensure Miss Leighton gets the message."

"It had better be good!" Hastings muttered. "Thorn's no fool. He'll track right back to us if we're not careful."

Baldwin scowled and slapped the palm of his hand on

the table, saying, "That's why I don't want any problems from any of you! I told you we can't take any direct action against him. He has to be handled differently! And, I'll attend to that."

"What about Molly Fitzroy? Are we going to forget about her?" Potter asked nervously.

Glancing over at Watkins, Baldwin said, "Watkins has his orders where she's concerned." Pausing to place his fingertips together, he sneered, "In a few days, she will have other things to worry about and no longer be a problem."

The men all looked at one another with nods and smiles. Watkins was known to have his methods of handling "problems."

Julie had spent the remaining part of the afternoon showing Matt the "accident" locations and taking him to see Pearl and Mary who were recovering slowly from their beatings.

During all that time, Matt had been businesslike in asking questions and listening to her answers. He had questioned Lukes and Bet and listened carefully to their replies. Not once during the entire afternoon did he say a word about where he had been or whom he had seen. Nor did he mention anything about what had happened between him and Julie before he had left.

Julie's nerves were feeling strained to their limit. She wished he would say something and get it over with. Instead all he did was look at her with an expression in his eyes that told her the subject was not forgotten.

Now, it was the middle of the evening and activity at the Land of Gold was in full motion. The tables were full and the bar busy as she made her way through the room toward her private table.

Taking her seat, she gazed around her keeping a watchful eye on things. A movement from the far side of the bar made the hair on the back of her neck stand up. Matt was heading in her direction and he looked none too pleased.

From the stern expression on his face to the purposeful way he strided toward her, he reminded her of a stalking mountain cat.

"What is this foolishness I've heard about you agreeing to be dealer for a high stakes game?" he demanded as he reached her side.

Looking up at him, Julie calmly replied, "There is nothing foolish about it. It's part of my duties."

Pulling a chair out, he sat down next to her, saying, "Duty? That's no reason to expose yourself as an open target. With all the problems around here, we don't need you adding to them."

"Are you ordering me or advising me, Mr. Thorn?" Julie asked in icy tones.

Sucking in his breath with exasperation, Matt leaned over and looked at her commandingly as he replied, "I'm telling you. The entire idea is dangerous. Everyone knows when there's a high stakes game going on and they come to watch. With a crowd like that surrounding the table, anything can happen."

Julie stubbornly shook her head. "I disagree. It is probably one of the safest places I could be. No one is going to try anything with that many witnesses."

113

Matt's jaw clenched and his hand grabbed her arm. "This is not something I'm willing to discuss," he informed her coldly.

"I'm glad to hear you say that. Neither am I." Julie glared steadily back at him. Looking down at his hand on her arm, she added, "Now unless you are planning on causing a scene, I would suggest you let go of me."

Matt withdrew his hand as though he had been burned. "You will not be dealing," he stated flatly.

Julie's eyes widened and she snapped, "I think I will. There isn't anyone else who can do it."

"Molly can do it," Matt told her.

Julie laughed, "Molly's ability with cards is limited to a game of Patience. There isn't any way she could deal a high stakes game."

"Then one of the other dealers," Matt insisted.

Looking about the room with its crowded tables, Julie commented, "You'd have me alienate an entire table of customers by pulling their dealer? That doesn't sound like good business to me. I'm the only one they requested and I'm the only one available." She waited for him to challenge her last statement.

Matt knew what she said was true, but that didn't make it any easier to accept. The possibility of something happening was still great. "If you insist on going through with this, I want Lee Tang positioned near you," he told her.

"He always is when I'm dealing," Julie replied with a smile as she rose from her seat. "Now if you'll excuse me? My players are waiting for me."

Matt sat, stern-lipped, as he watched her move to a center table with five waiting men. It was meager satisfaction to see Lee Tang take up a position behind and to her left as Julie sat down.

Julie opened the sealed pack of cards in front of her and skillfully shuffled them as she greeted each of the players. "Shall I introduce everyone? On my left is Mr. John Simpson of Sacramento, next to him, Mr. Douglas Adams of San Francisco. On Mr. Adams's left we have Mr. Paul Carter of Los Angeles. On his left, Monsieur René Dubonne, late of Paris, France, now San Francisco. And on my right, Mr. August Linquist of Chicago."

The men all acknowledged one another quickly, anxious to get on with the game. Having ordered a round of drinks on the house, Julie lifted the shuffled pack of cards from the table in front of her and said, "Gentlemen. The buy-in is one thousand dollars with a one hundred dollar ante. Betting will be in increments of fifty dollars and the game is five-card stud. The house will take ten percent as its cut." She smiled at each of them in turn. "Are there any questions? If not, shall we begin?"

Each of the men placed his money in front of him and Lukes gathered it in, replacing it with chips. Having done so, he carried the small cashbox to Julie and placed it next to her on the table.

"Let's get those cards dealt, Miss Julie. I feel lucky tonight," the dark-haired rancher across the table from her said.

"We all start out feeling lucky, Carter," the older man next to him quipped. "It's the one with the biggest pile of chips at the end of the game, who is."

"That's the God's truth! Your pardon, Miss Julie," said the well-dressed gentleman on her left.

"There's no need to ask pardon for the truth, Mr. Simpson," Julie replied as she placed the deck in front of him to cut.

He cut the cards and tossed his ante into the middle of the table as did the other players. Julie held the cards carefully saying, "Pot's right. Good luck to you all." She expertly dealt one card down around the table and then said, "Your bet, Mr. Simpson."

The same scene was repeated over and over again for the next three hours. The piles of chips grew and waned with each hand. During the entire game, Julie tried to keep things on a friendly footing, so as to avoid any buildup of tension among the players. She knew that they all were regulars at most of the big-stake games in town, but she did not want any trouble to erupt at this one.

René Dubonne eased his tension by flirting with her outrageously. The rancher, Carter, chewed thoughtfully on a toothpick and the others each had their own way of relieving any stress they might be under.

Julie was used to René's flirting and knew he meant nothing by it. She teased him back as she dealt, knowing it was harmless, but Matt, who had moved to the side of the table to watch the play, had a different idea altogether. He didn't like what he was seeing one bit. As far as he was concerned there was no need for the Frenchman to be so forward nor for Julie to act as though she were enjoying his fulsome and flowery words.

It was close to dawn before the game finally broke up. Everyone was drained, but August Linquist was very pleased. He came away from the table the big winner, having accumulated close to fifteen thousand dollars for one night's work.

With the house's cut, Julie knew they might break even for the tables she'd had to eliminate to reposition the musicians. She handed the cashbox to Tang and rose bidding the gentlemen farewell. She was exhausted but pleased that everything had gone without a hitch.

She started toward the staircase, with Tang close behind. She had reached the foot of the stairs when Matt joined her. Looking up at him, she could not resist saying, "Nothing happened. I told you I thought it was highly unlikely anything would."

"What do you mean nothing happened!" Matt almost snarled at her.

Shocked to see him like this, Julie gasped, "That's what I said."

"Then what do you call your behavior in encouraging that Frenchman? Flirting with him like that! It isn't surprising he practically asked you to sleep with him!" Matt informed her.

"René?" Julie laughed. "It was nothing! He always flirts to ease the tension." Placing her hands on her hips, she added, "And there was nothing wrong with my behavior! You are hunting for something to complain about!"

"Nothing! From where I stood it sounded like he had other ideas in mind for relieving tension," Matt's voice was accusing.

Julie could hardly believe any of this was happening. If she didn't know better she would be tempted to think Matt was actually jealous of René! But since that was as absurd as thinking René meant anything by saying what he had, she dismissed the possibility. She couldn't help but feel disappointed in Matt though. She'd thought he had more strength of character than to hold a grudge because she had been proven right about the high stakes game and he had been proven wrong.

"From now on, you keep your distance from the customers," Matt ordered her. "I don't have time to pull any overamorous swains off you."

Incensed by his attitude, Julie was more than ready to tell him what he could do wih his insulting accusations and autocratic ways when she saw a tall, dark-haired man coming toward them from the front of the casino.

Matt stood waiting impatiently for Julie to agree and provide a better explanation of what had gone on with the Frenchman. The one she had given him was worthless. Why, anyone with eyes in his head could see by looking at the Frenchman that he was serious.

Instead, Julie's face lit up and she brushed past him, her arms opened wide, a joyous cry on her lips.

"What the hell!" Matt muttered as he turned to see her being clasped tightly in the arms of a man he'd never seen before!

The product of an Italian mother and a Mexican father, Carlo had matured into a devastatingly handsome man with jet black hair growing in thick waves and framing an aristocratic face. He had piercing black eyes and a build that reminded one of his ancestors who'd fought in the coliseum of ancient Rome.

Matt watched dumbfounded as the stranger kissed her and Julie did not resist. A mist of anger began to well up inside him. What kind of game was she playing? How many others did she kiss so readily?

Clasping a happy Julie to his side, the stranger spoke to Matt, saying, "Isn't she unbelievable?"

Matt glared at him in silence not trusting himself to speak. Unbelievable was not the word he was thinking of at the moment.

Not receiving a reply, the dark-haired man shrugged and said smilingly to Julie, "Do you think Molly would let us use one of her rooms?"

Matt waited for Julie's hand to flash out and strike the newcomer on the face. Instead, he was not pleased to see that, rather than being offended, she was laughing!

"You'll have to ask her this time," she said.

Having seen and heard more than enough, Matt interrupted, asking, "This time?"

His words penetrated Julie's fog of happiness, and she realized with a start that Matt had no idea what they had been talking about. He had made up his own mind again, just as he had about René!

"Matt, it isn't what you're thinking," Julie started to say. "This is—"

She was cut off by Molly's cry of, "Carlo!" as she joined them and the two hugged.

Even that came as no surprise to Matt. It stood to reason that Molly would know him if he and Julie were so close.

"Molly?" Matt called to her.

"Yes?" she replied.

"This gentleman was inquiring of Julie if she thought you would allow them the use of one of your rooms," Matt informed her.

That should take care of the both of them, Matt thought to himself. He waited for Molly's swift refusal. He knew how adamant she was about Julie and the bordello side of the building. Consequently he was totally unprepared for the wave of laughter that washed over him.

"Lord Almighty, that brings back memories!" Molly exclaimed as she laughed fondly at Julie and the man she'd called Carlo.

"Molly, Matt's serious," Julie informed her. "He really believes that Carlo and I want to use one of your rooms."

"What!" Molly turned and looked at Matt. "I think you are barking up the wrong tree, Matt."

Crossing his arms in front of him, Matt replied, "I'm only repeating what has already been said, Molly."

"I don't believe it! He is serious!" Molly shook her head in disbelief.

"It would seem that Matt has taken up a new hobby, Molly," Julie observed.

"What?" Molly frowned, not sure what was going on here.

"Jumping to conclusions," Julie explained as she eyed him. "Not only does he think Carlo and I truly want one of your rooms, but a few minutes ago he accused me of practically seducing René Dubonne."

"René!" Molly exclaimed in surprise. "I think his wife, Julienne, might have something to say about that!"

Eyeing Matt closely, Carlo saw something neither woman could see. And, with a satisfied grin to himself, he decided it was time he stepped in. Moving away from Julie, he extended a hand to Matt, saying, "I think you and I should have a talk, *amigo.*"

More than curious to hear what Carlo might have to say, Matt nodded his head briefly and followed Carlo over to the bar, leaving Julie and Molly to watch them both with consternation.

"Well, how do you like that?" Molly remarked.

"I don't," Julie replied. What in the world did the two of them have to talk about? They didn't even know one another!

Julie felt as though she had been betrayed as she saw Matt suddenly throw his head back and laugh aloud at something Carlo said.

She was doubly angered to see Carlo clap Matt on the back at hearing his reply. What were they talking about?

As though hearing her thoughts, both men turned and raised their glasses in a toast to her before continuing their conversation.

"They appear to be getting along fine, Julie," Molly observed cheerfully.

"Too fine for my taste," Julie replied as she moved up the staircase.

Chapter Ten

JULIE FELT AS THOUGH HER HEAD HAD JUST TOUCHED the pillow when the sound of knocking at her bedroom door awakened her. She tried burrowing under the covers, but the sound refused to go away.

"Go away!" she groused at the door.

Silence followed her words and she sighed as she snuggled her cheek more comfortably into the pillow. Maybe now she could get some sleep, she thought to herself fuzzily.

The unexpected feeling of the bed sagging under added weight made her eyes fly open. She moved her head and saw Matt's face as he sat looking at her with a smile.

"I said, go away!" she repeated.

Closing her eyes again, she tried to ignore him, hoping he would take the hint and leave. The last thing she wanted on awakening was a confrontation with him. That it was to be a confrontation she did not doubt. After the night before, it could be little else.

"I heard something being mumbled. But, I couldn't make out what it was," he replied.

"Now you know. Go away!" Julie dismissed him, her eyes still closed as she tried to get back to sleep.

Matt's hand on her shoulder, shaking her, made her snap angrily, "Unless the building is on fire or it is a matter of life and death, I don't wish to be disturbed." She flounced away from him, snuggling once again into the pillow.

"Well, the building is not on fire," Matt mused aloud. "But, I think my reason for being here might be classified as a matter of life and death."

"Whose?" came her muffled voice.

"Does it matter?" Matt asked carefully.

Turning over and sitting up in the bed, Julie crossed her arms in front of her and replied with barely controlled tones, "Yes. If it's mine, I would like to be informed. If it's anyone else's, it would depend on whom it is."

"I think we may have a slight problem then," Matt told her. "You see, it's mine." He held his hands up to forestall any resonse from her, adding, "I realize that I am anything but popular with you after last night. But, I am even less popular with Molly and just about everyone else in this damned place."

"So?" Julie frowned. "That's your problem. You

123

should have thought of the consequences last night. Is that why you barged in here? Are you expecting *me* to do something about it?"

"No. Not exactly," Matt hedged.

"Then exactly why did you barge in here uninvited?" Julie demanded impatiently.

"Hey! Don't get all riled at me!" Matt defended himself.

"You enter my room uninvited and wake me up unnecessarily to tell me everyone is mad at you," Julie returned. "And now, you sit there with that injured look on your face and tell me I have no reason to be angry!"

"If there had been any other way to go about this, believe me, I would have taken it," Matt tried to explain. "But, after having cold coffee poured in my lap and burned eggs served for my breakfast, I could not see any other alternative if I hoped to survive until you were up for the day." Matt went on with his explanation hoping to appease her. "I even tried leaving to eat somewhere else, but Tang blocked the door and wouldn't let me out!"

"If you don't get to the point, cold coffee and burned eggs will seem pleasant after what I am going to do to you," Julie warned him. "Keep it up, and you will find Tang's displeasure a happy memory!" Julie folded the sheet down neatly in front of her and rested her arms across her middle, adding with emphasis, "I become violent if I haven't had enough sleep!"

Determined to have his say before Julie completely lost her temper, Matt quickly said, "Doesn't it mean anything that I came to apologize."

"Go on," Julie informed him, "I'm listening. There's a chance I may yet spare your life."

Matt ran his fingers through his hair and looked toward the closed door, muttering, "Damn!"

"Language like that certainly won't help you any," Julie scolded him. "Now, you were saying something about an apology?" she reminded him. "I have yet to hear one."

"God, woman! What do you expect? Blood?" Matt demanded of her.

Glaring at him, she replied, "I may draw some shortly!"

Matt took a deep breath and began, "After talking with your friend, Carlo, last night, I realized I may have misjudged you."

"What do you mean *may* have misjudged me!" Julie interjected. "And as far as Carlo is concerned he is a rat! Deserting me like that to spend all his time with a complete stranger!"

"As I was saying, I *may* have misjudged you." Matt situated himself more firmly on the bed. "As Carlo pointed out to me, I should have seen there was nothing between the two of you."

"And why is that?" Julie asked suspiciously.

Matt smiled sheepishly. "If there had been, he wouldn't have asked you about a room but would have whisked you away right then and there. And the hell with Molly!"

"He said that!" Julie exclaimed.

Matt nodded and shrugged adding, "It's what I would have done."

"I can't believe I'm hearing this!" She shook her head. 'I must be dreaming with my eyes open!" Julie balled her fists and hit the bed. "Did it ever occur to either of you that I might have something to say about all this? I certainly would not allow myself to be whisked away!" She paused to stare at him heatedly. "You are admitting you *may* have misjudged me and my relationship with Carlo. But what about René Dubonne? Are you willing to admit you were wrong about him also?"

Matt frowned slightly before replying, "I guess I could have been mistaken there, but I still think you should keep your distance from the customers!"

"How generous of you to guess you could have been mistaken!" Julie said scathingly. "Somehow I can't help but feel all these confessions of yours might sound more sincere if they were honest admissions that you were wrong in not trusting me! But instead, they are the result of you and Carlo discussing me behind my back! And only after the two of you spent the remainder of the night together in the bar, laughing and drinking!"

"I'm admitting I may be wrong! What else do you want?" Matt demanded.

"I suppose it never occurred to you to believe me?" Julie accused him. "Is it too much to expect you to trust me? Obviously it is!" She answered her own question. "But, let Carlo buy you a few drinks and you'd believe him if he told you I danced naked for the customers on the first Saturday of every month!" Julie practically shouted at him.

"You don't?" Matt said with a teasing light in his eyes. Even as mad as Julie was at him, he found he was beginning to enjoy himself. He was finding her more and more desirable with each passing minute. She had no idea how she looked, her cheeks flushed with anger and her hair cascading about her across the pillow as her eyes flashed sparks. Sparks that were feeding a fire inside him.

Julie was in no mood to be teased. She leaned forward putting her hands out to push him off her bed, but Matt's hands stopped her. He smiled at her as he pulled her closer to him. Bending down, he teased her lips with his own before taking full possession of them with a kiss that made struggle impossible. Julie had all she could do to keep from collapsing against him from lack of air.

Why does he make me so mad, she raged to herself? No one else has ever been able to make me lose my control like he does. And when I do lose my temper he laughs at me! Her thoughts tumbled about, confused by the feel of his hard chest against her breasts and his strong arms about her. She felt as though she were caught in a whirlpool.

Slowly and inexorably she felt her anger evaporate to be replaced by a flickering flame of need that burst to life at the core of her being. Julie fought both it and Matt by pushing away from his lips and gasping, "Don't do that!"

"What? Apologize? Or this?" Matt asked as he drew her back and kissed her again. "Or this?" His lips moved to the side of her neck and up to nibble on her ear. "And I guess I can't do this either?" He lifted her in his arms and laid her across his lap to bend down and reclaim her lips with his own.

Matt was awakening her senses as he had the last time, but now she didn't have the convenient excuse that she was too tired to fight him to explain her actions away. She shuddered in his arms as his lips traced patterns around her ear.

The rush of sensation that flowed through her made Julie's senses reel. I shouldn't be letting this happen again, she thought frantically to herself. I should push him away and make him stop! Her mind tried to cope with the conflicting feelings he was arousing in her. Part of her insisted she make him stop, while yet another part of her was saying, let it go on.

She found herself losing a war on two fronts: one being the knowledge that Matt thought of her only as an outlet for his desire and nothing more; the other being that what was happening went against every rule she had ever held dear. All she knew was her heart telling her it was right and good.

Julie knew what would be the final outcome if she did not protest now, but she couldn't. All that mattered to her at the moment was the fact that she was in the arms of the man she loved. Everything else could wait. That she would more than likely regret her decision, she refused to even consider. It was a decision her heart demanded she make.

Matt reveled in the scent of her hair as it draped about them like a curtain. He trailed kisses from her ear to the hollow of her neck. His hands stroked and caressed her sides through the thin material of her nightgown. He felt her quivering response as she lay in his arms and it inflamed his desire even more.

The realization that he loved her came not with a blinding flash, but from a quiet peace within him. She was the woman he had been destined to make his from the dawning of time.

He knew that she cared for him; her giving of herself

told him so. But he wanted her love. The thought of losing her was one he feared above all else. He would have to make her his before the world. Hopefully with time and patience she would come to love him, but until that time, she would still be his.

Succumbing to the rising tide of desire that was welling within her, Julie felt an even deeper need to be closer to Matt. She lifted her arms and with her hands on the back of his head, she pulled his lips back to her own.

For the first time, she became the aggressor. She teased and nipped at his lips, tracing the outline of his mouth with her dainty tongue before tentatively feeling the hardness of his teeth. The confidence his acceptance of her actions instilled gave her the needed courage to venture into even bolder territory. She gave as well as received and explored the inner recesses of his mouth with her tongue which dueled with his.

"Don't!" Julie cried out as Matt leaned away from her and pulled her hands free of his neck.

Slipping her from his lap and onto the bed, Matt rose and, gazing down at her with passion-filled eyes, said, "Don't what, Julie?"

"Leave me," she answered him. She knew he was giving her this last chance to say no. But, it was impossible.

Matt smiled, "I won't."

Julie watched in fascination as Matt discarded his shirt and undid the belt at his waist. The rippling play of muscles across his chest and shoulders as he moved stirred her. Her hands remembered the power and strength of those muscles and her breath came a little quicker.

Seeing her watching him, Matt asked, "Is anything wrong?"

"No." Julie shook her head. "Everything's fine. I have decided this is better during the daytime."

Matt's eyebrows went up. "And why is that?"

"The light's better and there's more to see." Julie chuckled warmly.

"Oh really?" Matt bantered. "Are you enjoying the view?"

Unused to dissimulation, she answered him truthfully. "Yes I am. Has anyone ever told you, you've a beautiful body?"

"Not lately," Matt told her with a shake of his head as he removed the last of his clothing. He liked the unknowing openness of her. She had never learned to be coy or play games as other women did.

Julie discovered she liked looking at him and did not feel in the least embarrassed at doing so. He could pose for a statue, she thought as her eyes took in his broad shoulders, narrow waist and the ridged flatness of his abdomen. His lean hips tapered down into heavily corded thighs and calves, all perfectly proportioned. She was fascinated with the way his manhood seemed to have a life of its own. Even from across the space that separated them she could feel its radiating power.

Moving back to the bed, Matt knelt at the foot and lifted the hem of her nightgown. Raising it, he pulled it up and over her head to toss it away. Lying down next to her, he cradled her against him and nibbled at her neck saying, "Does this mean you've forgiven me?"

"Not quite," she murmured. "You haven't finished apologizing yet."

Matt could not help but laugh. "I've heard it called many things by many people, but never by that name."

Taking time to fully explore and know each other, they made love slowly and lingeringly. Julie thought she would go wild with the pressure that kept building within her. Matt carried her time and time again to the peak but would prolong the exquisite torture even more by slowing his caresses and teasing her breasts with his lips.

Julie found that each time she let her hands and lips wander wherever they willed, Matt's response added to her own mounting exhilaration. It made her happy to be able to give him pleasure.

When they coupled, their joining sent wave after wave of nerve-tingling excitement through them. Julie heard a voice cry out in ecstasy and vaguely wondered if it were her own.

As they moved closer and closer to total completion, a bud of unbelievable sweetness began to take root and grow, unfurling its petals until it stretched itself upward in full bloom. They both clung to one another as they were tossed on a sea of incredible release.

Drained of all craving but that for the contentment of resting in each other's arms, they nestled together and quietly marveled at the richness they had shared.

Matt pulled Julie closer against him and chuckled, "Now isn't this much nicer than fighting?"

Julie nuzzled her cheek against his shoulder and asked, "Do you make it a habit to always apologize like that?"

A smile creased his rugged face as he looked down at her and replied, "Only in special cases."

Moving her arm across his middle, she poked him in the ribs saying, "And how many 'special' cases are there?"

He could not help but jump; her fingers had found the sensitive point just above his hip bone and she was almost driving him crazy with her tickling. He gritted his teeth to keep from grabbing her hand and giving her the advantage of knowing she had found one of his weak points. If she knew what she was doing to him she would be merciless until she had the answers to her questions. Taking a deep breath, he rolled, pinning her beneath him on the bed and saying, "You want to fight?"

Laughter bubbled from her and she stared up at him wide-eyed and said, "Would it mean another apology?"

Matt placed a kiss on the tip of her nose and replied, "That would depend on whether or not you agreed to fight fair."

"I always fight fair!" Julie insisted stubbornly.

Rolling back on his side and drawing her with him, Matt laughed, "No wonder you lose."

"Oh!" Julie reached over to tickle him again. She was going to show him.

"I wouldn't suggest that," Matt warned her as his hand grabbed hers and held it prisoner.

Julie tried to pull her hand free, but it was impossible. Matt could hold her as easily as a feather. He wasn't even exerting himself and she was helpless. "Matt!" She tried to cajole him.

Placing another kiss on the tip of her nose, he murmured, "I'm busy. Don't bother me."

Julie began to squirm, trying to break free of his hold. Bringing her other hand forward she tried to tickle him under the covers. A wrestling match ensued with both of them laughing and battling to become the victor. The bedding twisted around them as they struggled and their breathless laughter filled the room.

They were so intent on besting one another that neither of them heard the bedroom door open. The first awareness they had of no longer being alone was Carlo's voice saying, "See I told you they were getting along fine, Molly."

Molly's gasp sliced through the air like a knife through butter.

The two playful combatants on the bed froze. Julie snuggled as close to Matt as she could to hide what the twisted sheets did not. Matt turned and looked at the visitors, a broad grin on his face. "Congratulate me, *amigo*. I'm about to be married."

Julie's gasp was an echo of Molly's as she reached her hand under the edge of the twisted sheet and grabbed at his leg, her nails digging in. "I never agreed to that!" she hissed so only he could hear.

On the pretense of rearranging himself to better converse with Carlo and Molly, Matt rolled onto his back and pulled Julie with him whispering, "I think you'd better or face Molly alone."

While Matt pulled the sheet up covering her as she rested against him, Julie peeked over at Molly and saw the outrage and anger on her face. The thought of facing her alone and of the hell Molly could make of her life made Julie groan, "Oh dear!"

"Married?" Molly exclaimed suspiciously, as she took in the scene before her. "I should hope so! I may not be a prude, but some things I will not tolerate! Carrying on like this under my very roof! You should

133

both be heartily ashamed of yourselves!" Molly scowled. This was certainly something she had not expected to see or hear and she did not like to think it might be repeated. Julie was not like the girls who worked for her and she wanted to make certain that Matt knew it.

But, this was surely not anything like what she had envisioned when Matt had stomped upstairs and passed the office over an hour ago, muttering to himself about "Damn females!"

Seeing him, she had become worried and had tried to get Lee Tang to follow him. His usual stoic expression replaced by a wide smile of approval for Matt's actions, the normally obedient bodyguard had astonished her by shaking his head in refusal. Then he'd had the temerity to block her exit from the office! She had tried to physically push her way past him, but he had gently brushed her aside like a fly.

Enraged at his uncharacteristic behavior, she had begun to yell at him and argue that he was failing in his duty to protect Julie by acting the way he was. He had listened to her ranting and raving in silence and had repeated the shaking of his head as she once again tried to leave the office.

Consequently, she had been forced into pacing the office for the past hour. Worried and feeling ready to scream the roof down, she had heard other footsteps on the landing outside the office and had called to whomever it was for help.

She had breathed a heartfelt sigh of relief as she saw Carlo Ramos.

Concern on his face, he'd joined her. She had quickly explained her fear for Julie's safety and been astounded to hear Carlo laugh aloud. He had spent the next ten minutes trying to convince her there was nothing for her to be so worried about, that Julie was perfectly safe and that, as they both knew, she was more than capable of protecting herself should that unlikely need arise.

Refusing to believe him, she'd insisted on seeing for herself. If it had been any other man but Matt, she might have believed Carlo, but for some reason, Julie did not act like herself around Matt and that worried Molly.

After speaking quietly with Lee Tang, who smilingly stood aside to let them pass, Carlo had escorted her to Julie's room. Reassuring her all the way, Carlo had opened the bedroom door and they had entered.

The sight that had greeted her eyes and ears was anything but what she had expected. The room had been filled with relaxed easy laughter and two figures were busily wrestling amidst the tangled covers of the bed.

Now Matt's welcoming greeting to Carlo, informing him that he and Julie were to be married, was almost more than she could take.

"Julie?" Molly called.

"Yes, Molly?" Julie answered trying to hide her feeling of being trapped in a situation over which she had no control.

"Is what Matt says true? Are the two of you getting married?" Molly demanded in the tones of an outraged mother.

Glancing over at the formidable expression on Molly's face, Julie dug her nails even deeper into Matt's leg and hissed under her breath, "You'll be sorry for this."

Snaking his own hand under the covers to try to pull hers free, Matt grimaced slightly. "I'm beginning to see what you mean already."

"Julie!" Molly demanded an answer.

Releasing her hold on Matt's leg and drawing the sheet with her, Julie sat up and looked over at the woman who had been more of a mother to her than anyone else in her life and realized she could not disappoint and hurt her by denying Matt's claim. "Yes, Molly. Matt and I are to be married," she told her.

Molly's next question took both Matt and Julie by surprise. "When?"

Not receiving an immediate answer, Molly continued, "The sooner the better as far as I'm concerned. It is more than apparent you've already jumped the gun once. I don't want it happening again. You will be married this afternoon."

Molly's words fell like thunderclaps of doom on Julie's ears, while Matt welcomed them. He had seized the opportunity Carlo and Molly's unexpected entry had given him and it had paid off even more than he'd hoped that it would. He had been satisfied to have Julie's agreement to an engagement. But Molly's insistence on their marriage that day was music to his ears.

"Molly! I can't marry him today!" Julie protested in desperation.

"And why not?" Molly pinned her with her eyes. "You've already bedded him. The least you can do is allow yourself to be made an honest woman. Your poor father is probably turning over in his grave!"

Carlo put his hand on Molly's arm, saying, "Molly, not so rough."

Julie buried the tears that burned within her and

replied to the truth of Molly's words. "I'm sorry, Molly. I never intended for anyone to be hurt by any of this."

"I don't appreciate your setting yourself up as judge and jury regarding the behavior of my future wife," Matt told Molly in tones of steel. "There is nothing wrong when two people choose to express their love for one another behind the privacy of a closed door. You have no right to blame her for what happened here. I think you owe her an apology for even being here."

Placing her hands on her hips, Molly advanced toward the bed with fire in her eyes. "You speak of rights! What gives you the right to speak to me like that Matthew Thorn! After what you've done here, you're lucky I don't have you arrested! Or have Lee Tang give you what you really deserve! The only thing stopping me is the fact that it would make Julie a widow before she's a bride! Taking advantage of her like you have is called rape by decent people!"

Hearing Molly's voice rise shrilly in anger as she lashed out at Matt, Julie felt panic inside. My God, Molly thinks this was all Matt's doing, she realized! I can't let him take the entire blame. I was as much a part of things as he was. "Molly! Stop it!" Julie exclaimed, cutting her off.

Molly looked at Julie, shocked to hear her speak like that. All she had been doing was trying to force Matt to accept the responsibility for what he had done.

"Molly," Julie said softly, "it wasn't like you think at all! Matt didn't force himself on me. It was as much my idea as it was his."

"Do you realize what you're saying?" Molly asked her, a sad feeling in her heart as she realized her little girl had grown into a woman. A woman with a mind and desires of her own. A woman who was truthfully admitting her own complicity in what had happened here this day.

"Yes, I do," Julie steadfastly replied.

"Why, Julie?" Molly asked her quietly. She thought she knew why, but she wanted to hear it from Julie.

Julie had been afraid Molly would ask her that question; she knew she could never answer her with the truth. Not with Matt there to hear every word. The last thing she wanted was for him to know she loved him. Everything was becoming complicated enough without him having that knowledge to use against her.

"Julie?" Molly asked anew.

"Molly!" Carlo interrupted. "Why waste all this time asking questions? If there is to be a wedding this afternoon, don't you think we should start making the arrangements?"

Molly was caught. She could not demand that Julie answer her and ignore Carlo's reminder of the work to be done if the wedding she had insisted upon was to take place that afternoon.

Turning to face Carlo, she said, "You're right there's a lot of work ahead. I can ask my questions later."

"*Amigo?*" Matt called from the bed. He had been waiting, as curious as Molly to hear Julie's reply, but he now decided to be more patient. He was to be married that afternoon and other details had to be considered first.

Carlo paused as he started to follow Molly from the room. "Yes, my friend?"

"You will stand up with me, won't you? I can't think

138

of anyone else I would like to have for a best man," Matt said to him.

A smile creased Carlo's brown face and he replied, "But, of course, I will, *amigo!* I feel I have a vested interest in this marriage." Laughing he departed from the room leaving Matt and Julie alone.

Waiting until she was certain they would not be disturbed again, Julie attacked Matt saying, "Why did you say we were getting married! You know as well as I do, we never discussed anything like that. Now you have us both trapped!"

Matt rose from the bed and began to dress as he answered her. "You make it sound like a fate worse than death! You didn't see the look on Molly's face when she first saw us and I did! I didn't fancy the idea of being drawn and quartered! I saw a way to avoid bloodshed, in this case mine, and took it!"

"You did this to save your lousy skin!" Julie accused him, joining him by the side of the bed and confronting him.

Pausing as he rebuttoned his shirt, Matt shook his head and smiled. "Not just mine, my dear. Your skin was as much in danger as mine." He reached over and traced a line across her collarbone and down between her breasts. "And I think you had better cover some of that luscious skin of yours before we are invaded again. When word spreads of this wedding, we will be swamped with the curious along with the well-wishers."

Julie could already hear the sounds of footsteps out on the landing. They echoed the truth of Matt's words and she hurried to dress.

The next few hours she was to remember his words

even more vividly. She had no idea how, but it seemed as though the entire Plaza suddenly knew she was to be married that afternoon and had come to offer help and congratulations. What she had hoped to keep a secret was now turning into an excuse for a massive party!

She was taken over by Molly and her girls and not given a chance to do anything but follow their instructions. Each of Molly's girls was as excited as if this were their own wedding that was going to take place.

Matt had been hustled away by Carlo and Julie knew he was experiencing close to the same thing she was. Even Sam Isaacs had shown up from out of the blue with a brand new dark suit for Matt to wear!

Seeing Sam, Julie found herself hunting the now-crowded casino for a sign of Annie. She knew she would not miss this if she could avoid doing so.

Annie Isaacs did arrive and it was not long before Molly and her girls found themselves taking orders for a change. Annie took over, saying, "I've more experience than any of you. I married off five sisters back in the old country and three of Samuel's here."

She wasted no time in issuing orders right and left. The other women soon found it was far easier to follow them than to protest. In any case, Annie ended up with things the way she thought they should be.

Annie even ordered Lee Tang to go to the flower vendors and buy everything they had!

Having given orders to everyone within the radius of her voice, Annie took Julie by the arm and escorted her back up to her bedroom saying, "Now we decide what you will wear."

Julie followed the path of least resistance and allowed herself to be sat on the edge of her bed as Annie

140

threw open the doors on the wardrobe and stepped back to gaze thoughtfully at the contents.

"So okay, white is out. We go with a nice pastel to flatter your pretty hair and skin," Annie commented as she began to sort through the dresses.

"Annie!" Julie exclaimed in shock. How did Annie know she was no longer entitled to wear the white of a virgin bride?

Annie turned and looked over at her as she draped a pale daffodil yellow dress over her arm. "What is wrong? You don't like the color?"

"No," Julie answered in a pained voice. "Does everyone know?"

"Know what?" Annie frowned as she pulled out another dress of rose-colored silk. She laid the two dresses on the bed and, looking up, saw Julie's white face.

"Oh!" she said as she rushed to Julie's side and put her arm around her. "You mean about you and Matt forgetting the preacher usually comes first? No, my sweet! I don't think it has even occurred to anyone else. Me? I know the signs too well not to be able to tell."

"Signs?" Julie gulped, wondering if they were written all over her face for the world to see.

"Calm yourself. They're not that obvious to the world," Annie informed her with a hug. "To tell you the honest truth, I am surprised this didn't happen sooner."

"What!" Julie was aghast.

Annie patted her shoulder and laughed. "You forget. I saw the two of you in our shop. Sparks like that fly only if love or hate is involved and it was not hate I saw in your eyes."

"Oh Annie! What am I going to do?" Julie was so relieved to be able to talk to someone who understood.

"What is this! Do I see tears?" Annie looked at Julie's face with concern. "Tell me. We will take care of whatever it is that upsets you this way."

"Matt doesn't know. He thinks I'm like one of Molly's girls." The words spilled forth almost faster than Julie could control them.

"What is this? You must tell him! He has the right to know you love him!" Annie insisted. "This is no way to begin a marriage! Marriage is hard enough when two people know they love and are loved. But, this is tragic. I will go tell him how wrong he is!" She started to move from the bed.

"No Annie!" Julie stopped her. "I don't want him to know."

"You don't want him to know!" Annie sank back on the bed. "You want your husband to think you are no better than a woman who gives herself for money? I can't believe this of you. Why do you want to create this misery for yourself?"

"He doesn't love me, Annie," Julie confessed. "He told me himself the only reason he suggested we be married was to avoid Molly's anger."

Annie listened to the pain in her friend's voice and felt there had to be some way to ease it and make things right. Julie was too dear and sweet to be allowed to make herself suffer like this.

"Come now! You think about what you are saying. Do you really believe Matthew Thorn is afraid of Molly? Afraid enough to marry someone he doesn't love? I refuse to believe such a thing and you should too!"

LAND OF GOLD

When she listened to Annie, Julie saw how ridiculous Matt's reasons sounded. When had she ever seen him afraid of anything? Never. He must have other reasons he was not telling her for going through with this marriage.

"The casino!" Julie exclaimed, placing a hand over her mouth as the truth dawned on her.

"What about the casino?" Annie questioned, wondering if Julie had become unstrung by all the tension she was under.

Julie's mind was working as fast as it could. Everything was becoming clearer and clearer to her. Matt was marrying her for her share of the Land of Gold!

"Nothing, Annie. I was only thinking out loud." Julie reassured her worried friend. Seeing the still-doubtful look on Annie's face, Julie tried to throw her off the track by saying, "You're right, Annie. I will talk to Matt tonight after all the confusion has died down."

Annie hugged her and beamed with approval. "See I told you we would take care of things! Now we pick out the dress you shall wear, no?"

"Yes. Now we can pick out my dress, Annie." Julie forced a smile.

Her mind was only half on what Annie was saying as she held out dress after dress. To Julie it didn't really matter. She had every intention of taking care of Matthew Thorn before any wedding could take place. She would take away any necessity for him to marry her at all.

143

Chapter Eleven

AFTER LEAVING JULIE TO TAKE A BATH PRIOR TO DRESSING for the wedding, Annie scurried off to check on the other preparations.

Julie waited until Annie was gone and then climbed out of the tub. Wrapping a towel about her, she peeked out her door. Seeing Mae, she called to her, "Go and find Molly and tell her I would like to speak with her."

Mae giggled her best wishes before agreeing to find Molly and tell her she was needed.

Hurrying, Julie finished her bath and quickly dried off. Shrugging her shoulders, she lifted the daffodil-colored dress from the bed and donned it. She was in the process of buttoning the final few buttons when

Molly came bustling into the room with a harried look about her.

"Thank goodness, Father O'Brien agreed to give you a dispensation from the reading of the banns. He happened to be with the bishop when my message arrived and the bishop, dear soul that he is, granted a dispensation and the ceremony can take place here at the casino instead of at the church," Molly rattled off. For one of the few times in her life, Molly was unsure of how to act now that she was alone with Julie.

"Mae said, you wanted to see me?" Her voice cracked slightly with tension. "Is it important? There is still much to be done."

"Molly! Don't be like this! Please," Julie said. "I need your help."

"You should have thought of that before this," Molly said without thinking. Then realizing what she had started she decided to get it all out into the open before it festered and ruined their relationship forever. "I can't say I'm not disappointed in you, because I am. But . . ."—Her voice trembled—"you have been like the daughter I never had. I tried to do the best I could by you after your mother died. I even dreamed of the day you would be married at the cathedral in the long white gown your mother wore. Now . . ." The words trailed off as she looked at Julie sadly. "I forgot you are only human like the rest of us."

Taking a deep breath, Julie took Molly's hands in hers and said, "Oh, Molly. I love you and I'm so sorry all this has happened. But, please listen and try to understand. I'm asking you to trust me one last time. I haven't the time to explain now, but I want to see Mr. Washburn and Matt in the office before the ceremony."

"What do you need a lawyer for now?" Molly frowned. "You plan on making out your will at a time like this?"

"Please, Molly, trust me! Everything will be fine." Julie tried to convince Molly of the importance of her request. Already she could hear the rumble of gathering voices downstairs telling her that the many self-invited guests were arriving. Time was running short, if she hoped to pull off her plan.

"Oh, all right. If it's that important, I'll have them there in five minutes." Molly started to leave the room and paused to add, "But whatever it is, it had better not take too long. There're over two hundred people downstairs expecting to see a wedding. And see one they will."

Julie hurried to the office and, closing the door behind her, ran to the desk and scrambled around in the drawer for a piece of paper. Finding one, she laid it on the desk in front of her. Opening the ink well, she dipped her pen and began to write. She had nearly finished, when the door opened and Molly entered with the lawyer and Matt close behind.

"Mrs. Fitzroy said you wished to see me, Miss Leighton?" the lawyer said, puzzled at the summons.

"Yes, Mr. Washburn," she said handing him the paper. "I would like you to go over this to make certain that it is legal and binding. Then I would like you and Molly to witness it after Mr. Thorn signs it."

The lawyer scanned the paper in his hand and his eyes widened as he read. "But, this is a prenuptial agreement stating that Mr. Thorn relinquishes all rights to your share of the Land of Gold upon your marriage, that even though married you shall retain full possession and control of all that belonged to you prior to the marriage!" He turned a shocked face to Matt. "While prenuptial agreements are not that rare, the contents of this one make it very unusual, Mr. Thorn. I must advise you that you are in no way obligated to sign such a document."

"Is it legal and binding, Mr. Washburn?" Julie pressed him for an answer as she stared unblinkingly at Matt daring him to make an objection.

"Well, yes it is, Miss Leighton. But, it is highly unorthodox," he stammered.

"Thank you, Mr. Washburn. That's all I needed to know," Julie informed the flustered lawyer. Placing the paper flat on the desk, she looked over at Matt and said, "Sign it."

"Julie!" Molly gasped, not believing she would actually go through with such a thing and endanger the approaching ceremony.

Matt moved to the desk and accepted the pen from Julie's hand. He did not even bother to read what the paper said, but quickly signed his name at the bottom of the sheet and handed the pen to Molly for her to witness.

Julie sat in stunned surprise. She had been certain he would refuse to sign it! So certain that she had never given a thought to what might happen otherwise. She watched silently as Molly scrawled her signature and handed the pen to the lawyer for his.

Matt, watching the growing dismay and confusion on Julie's face, said to her, "That's not the reason I'm marrying you."

"Then what is?" she choked out.

Matt merely smiled and said in reply, "See you at the altar, my dear."

Julie was numb with surprise. Nothing was going as she had planned! Matt had almost laughed in her face as he'd signed the agreement. She had fully expected him to refuse to sign it. She had also never expected to have to go through with this farce of a wedding!

Handing the paper to the lawyer, Molly briskly instructed him, "You take care of this. It's your job. I will take care of mine. Come on, Julie. Everyone is waiting for us."

Julie allowed herself to be led from the office. She numbly accepted the bouquet that was thrust into her hands as she reached the top of the staircase.

Her eyes widened curiously when Carlo held out his arm for her to take. "I am doing double duty. I give the bride away and I stand up for the groom," he informed her as the musicians began to play.

Julie's face paled as she realized there was no way the wedding would be stopped now. Carlo patted her hand as it lay still on his arm, and he teased her, "I did say I had a vested interest in this marriage."

Annie Isaacs, smiled up at her from her position on the step in front of her. "Poor Father O'Brien nearly fainted when he found out I was to be your matron of honor. He mumbled something about wondering if your bishop's okay to do whatever was necessary included a Jewess in the wedding party. But, he said it's okay because my heart is in the right place even if my Sabbath isn't."

Hearing the opening notes of the processional,

Annie started down the staircase. Julie and Carlo followed two steps behind her.

The staircase had never seemed longer to Julie. Looking out ahead of her she saw a sea of smiling faces, all watching and waiting for her to join Matt in front of the makeshift altar, at the far side of the room.

She made a beautiful bride in her dress of pale daffodil yellow silk. Her hair was pinned up with tiny curls escaping to peep out from beneath the crown of daisies and wild flowers Molly's girls had made in place of a veil.

Moving down the aisleway left open through the rows of hastily moved chairs, Julie had her first glimpse of Matt. He was standing by the makeshift altar near Father O'Brien. He looked magnificent in the dark suit Sam had brought with him. His thick hair glistened with signs of having been newly washed and his rugged face showed every evidence that this was indeed one of the happiest days of his life. Julie felt confusion at seeing his expression. Why was he marrying her, she thought desperately?

His eyes locked with hers and she felt as though they were pulling her toward him with their golden power.

Reaching Matt's side, Carlo handed her arm to him and then took his place by Matt's. Seeing this, Father O'Brien winced slightly and looked to the heavens for understanding, before saying, "We are gathered here today before God and in the presence of this company to join this man and woman in the holy sacrament of matrimony."

Julie went through the entire ceremony as though caught in a dream. She answered when and where she was supposed to, but could not remember the words as soon as she'd spoken them.

The first realization that she was now actually Mrs. Matthew Thorn came when she heard the priest announce to the gathered throng that they were man and wife.

She felt Matt's lips claim her own at the same moment she heard her sister Sara scream, "Oh my God, no!"

Sara and Adam had arrived at the moment the priest had completed the marriage rite. It was too late. There was nothing either of them could do now about halting this catastrophe. When they had received word of the ceremony they had rushed to put a stop to things if they possibly could.

The last person on earth either of them wanted as a brother-in-law was Matthew Thorn! So overcome by the shock of seeing that things were beyond their control, Sara had cried out and collapsed in a faint in her husband's arms.

Adam carried her to a nearby chair, saying to the concerned onlookers, "She will be all right in a moment. She's only upset because she missed being here for the entire ceremony. Julie is very dear to the both of us."

No one said a word, but many unconvinced glances were exchanged. They knew the true feelings between their Miss Julie and her uppity sister and did not believe a word Adam had said.

The happy people of the Plaza crowded around Julie and Matt voicing their congratulations and joy. Matt kept his arms around Julie and tried to shield her from the unknowing crush of the crowd.

Julie could not see beyond the few smiling faces in front of her as Matt and Carlo joined together to push a way through the guests toward the reception area. She caught only a glimpse of Adam's face as they moved by him. His expression was anything but pleased.

Reaching the reception area, Carlo turned and faced the assembly with raised hands requesting silence. The noisy guests shushed each other and listened to what he had to say.

"My friends, let the celebrating begin!"

A loud cheer went up at his words and the rafters rang with the sounds of happy laughter. It did not take long for the festivities to spill out onto the Plaza. From there word spread and soon most of the Plaza resembled a gigantic fiesta as the crowd increased.

Having recovered from her faint, Sara insisted that she and Adam push their way to the bridal table. Reaching there, she hid the hatred she felt for her sister beneath a sweet smile as she said, "We were sorry to miss the beginning of the ceremony, Julie dear. But when the message came telling us of this surprising event, we were entertaining. It would have been the height of bad manners for us to rush off and leave our guests without a host or a hostess." Leaning across the table, she placed a kiss on Matt's cheek saying, "Welcome to the family, brother dear." It almost choked her to say the words, but she knew she had to make amends for her earlier outburst.

"Thank you, Sara." Matt stared her straight in the eye. "I hope to be an active member in family affairs. It's nice to know I am such a welcome addition."

Sara paled slightly and would have swayed on her

feet but for Adam's steadying hand. "An active member?" she whispered nervously.

Placing his arm about Julie's chair, Matt smiled at his new wife before answering Sara's question. "Julie and I believe that a husband and wife should share everything equally."

Julie reached under the table to dig her nails into his leg, but he had anticipated her action and moved his leg out of her reach. "Patience, my dear," he said teasingly. "She is anxious about the night to come," he told Adam and Sara with a wink and a grin.

Sara gasped audibly and Adam spoke quickly to cover her outcry. "We must take our leave now. We have an engagement tonight at the opera with the mayor and his lovely wife. Congratulations to you both and may you find as much happiness in your marriage as Sara and I have in ours."

Not trusting herself to speak, Julie smiled and waved as Sara and Adam departed. "They must be afraid they'll miss the opening curtain," Matt whispered in her ear. "After all they have only three hours in which to prepare themselves to meet with our illustrious mayor and his wife."

Julie could not stifle the giggle that spilled forth at his semiserious tone of concern. "Why did you say what you did to Adam?" she whispered back.

"You mean about our agreeing to share everything equally?"

"You know perfectly well that's what I mean," Julie told him.

"Let's say, I felt like rattling their pompous composure. It took all of Sara's control to prevent her from gagging when she kissed me," Matt replied. "I'm sorry to tell you this so soon after our wedding, my dear, but I can't say I care overly much for your relatives."

"It pains me as much to have to admit this, but unfortunately, it would seem we have found something we can agree upon," Julie answered back.

As the afternoon progressed Molly rushed to and fro trying to keep everything from crashing about their heads in total confusion. Most of the guests had brought food and drink. The bar and the tables next to it were groaning under the weight of dishes and delicacies from many lands.

It was early in the evening and the majority of the revelers had moved out onto the Plaza. Hearing a loud crash from the kitchen area, Molly went to investigate. She never saw the fist that hit her and sent her ricocheting across the room. Before she could react to protect herself or call out, another blow connected with her jaw and it was quickly followed by a rain of blows that sent pain lancing through her.

She collapsed to the floor and tried to curl into a ball to avoid the boot that began kicking her in the back and ribs. As she faded into unconsciousness she heard voices raised in angry yells and the sound of the back door of the kitchen slamming as her assailant fled.

Julie looked up curiously as Lee Tang bent down and whispered something in Matt's ear. Matt's face became stiff with anger and he rose from his seat, saying, "Molly's been attacked."

"Oh my God!" Julie cried as she quickly rose to follow Matt and Lee Tang.

Entering the kitchen, she saw Molly battered and bruised as she lay with her head cradled lovingly in Bet's lap. Bet looked up, tears streaming down her face and asked, "Who would want to hurt Molly? She never hurt anyone."

Julie knelt beside her and put her hand out to gently stroke Molly's forehead. There was a gash at the side of Molly's mouth and her cheek was badly bruised and swelling. Her hands were clasped in front of her chest protectively. It was clear she had been kicked several times. Her dress showed the imprints of a booted foot. And from the way she was beginning to moan, she had injuries they could not readily see.

"Has the doctor been sent for?" Matt asked in a hard voice.

As if in answer to his question, a young man carrying a fat black bag came into the kitchen and knelt down beside him.

Matt moved out of his way and lifted a stricken Julie into his arms. "She'll be all right. The doctor's here now."

Turning her to face him, he gazed into her eyes and asked, "Will you be all right? Carlo and I are going to see if we can find out who was responsible for this."

Julie nodded unable to take her eyes off the injured Molly lying so helplessly on the floor.

"Lee Tang, stay with my wife," Matt ordered before hugging Julie and moving out the back door to where Carlo waited for him on the porch.

The carefree gaiety of the crowded casino succumbed to a somber cloud of shock and disbelief as word of Molly's beating spread through the crowd.

There were rumbles of dismay, outrage and anger as Lukes and one of the other bartenders made their way through the room bearing Molly's unconscious body.

Julie and the doctor followed closely behind them, grave expressions on their faces, as they accompanied the stretcher party up the wide staircase and across the corridor.

Once the group had disappeared from view a reaction began to swell in the previously subdued audience. Molly was one of them, and many felt as though they had been personally assaulted by this senseless and violent calamity.

The crowd milled about whispering and talking among themselves. Stern and frightened faces replaced the carefree and happy expressions of a few minutes before.

Tough, hardened men used to the harsh ways of life in the West became blank-faced and steely-eyed as they silently scanned the room. Women were scarce enough in the West, but women like Molly, who understood them and accepted them for what they were with no questions, were rare.

The wives and girl friends of these men, as well as the women of the Plaza, felt threatened. They knew it might have been one of them lying so still on that stretcher. Molly had not been the first to be beaten. They remembered two of her girls had also suffered the same fate.

Why? The conjecture grew as word spread and flowed out onto the still festive Plaza. The discordant sounds of musical instruments halting in midnote echoed through the open doorway. The voice of someone announcing what had happened was soon drowned out by the cries of shock and outrage that followed the dreadful news.

The overriding question in the minds of all who listened was why? Why would anyone want to attack Molly? Was there a madman loose among them?

These questions were repeated over and over as the unsettled crowd began to break up into groups. A number of the men left to join Matt and Carlo in hunting for her attacker. While a group of the women banded together to see if there was anything they could do to help.

The remainder either wandered home, stunned by what had happened, or slunk away into the side streets and alleys of the Plaza. The uncaring freeloaders knew there was no reason for them to hang around any longer, now that the chance for free food and drink was gone.

Annie Isaacs felt a sharp stab of painful memory as she watched the scene before her. She had seen this same reaction more times than she cared to remember. Her people had never had an easy life, but toward the end this scene had been repeated over and over in their small village in Poland. Young girls raped and beaten because they were Jews. Old men and women run down in the street by horsemen and carriages. She and Sam had lived through the terrible times of persecution and, having decided their children would not, had come to America. Here they also found persecution and bigotry because of who and what they were, but they endured it all because they were in the one country in the world that promised them a better life for their children.

Now, seeing those who wanted to help and knowing what needed to be done, she took responsibility upon her shoulders and stepped in on behalf of Julie and the injured Molly. She accepted the press of offers from the ladies to help. She lost no time in organizing them into work parties.

Under her direction the vast cleanup and removal of the scattered tables, chairs and half-devoured food was soon under way. Realizing the necessity for the volunteers to be able to do something to keep themselves from feeling terribly helpless in the face of this traumatic attack on one of their own, Annie let no hands remain idle. She put anyone with two hands to work; even the children were given tasks to keep them occupied and out of their mothers' hair.

Annie kept a watchful eye on the volunteers as she fielded the many questions of the curious as well as tactfully dealt with those who wanted to speak personally with Julie.

Those who wished to offer their sympathy were told they should return in a day or so when things had settled down enough for visitors. But those who were gawkers or just plain nosy came face to face with the implacability of Annie Isaacs.

Try as they might, they were deterred time and again by the watchful and determined Annie. She chased them all away, heaping invective upon their heads and telling them that they should be ashamed of themselves for wanting to pry and be titillated by someone else's misfortune.

Those who persisted and attempted to sneak upstairs and spy for themselves were halted by the intimidating Lee Tang. He had taken up a position near the top of the staircase to bar the further progress of any who managed to find their way past Annie.

The casino was slowly beginning to resume its normal appearance when the sound of a rushing carriage halting abruptly out front filtered through the air, and Sara and Adam Raleigh appeared through the doorway, clothed in rich evening wear.

They ignored everyone around them and made their way straight to where Annie stood guard. Sara sniffed and looked down her pert, but haughty nose at Annie as Adam rudely insisted they wanted to see Julie. Neither of them saw any reason to put themselves out by being polite to anyone as unimportant and noninfluential as the wife of a Jewish tailor, but Annie crossed her arms in front of her and stared both of them straight in the eye as she stubbornly refused to let them pass.

"Julie can't see you now. She is extremely busy upstairs with the doctor," she informed them coldly.

Sara's face took on an unbecoming flush and she started to shoulder her way past Annie and try to ascend the staircase. "Out of my way, you insolent bitch!" she ordered the unmoving Annie.

"Coming from you, I accept the compliment," Annie replied calmly. She was not in the least impressed by their rudely superior airs. She had become accustomed to dealing with their type of social bigotry at an early age. Steadfast in her resolve not to let them bother Julie, she moved onto the staircase and placed herself in front of the advancing couple.

Sara looked up and put out a hand to push Annie out of her way but halted with a quick intake of breath when she saw Lee Tang take up a position next to Annie.

"I insist upon seeing my sister!" she nearly shrieked in outrage.

Annie smiled unsympathetically at her and replied, "As I have already told you, your sister is too busy to see anyone. If you feel it is so vital that you see her, you may wait downstairs until she is free."

Adam puffed out his chest and moved in front of his wife saying, "How dare you speak to us like that! Do you realize to whom you are speaking?"

"Perfectly well. And I am not impressed," Annie replied unmoved by his pompous show of aggression. "I repeat, you may wait downstairs until Julie is free."

She glanced up toward the corridor leading to Molly's room before adding, "Julie might be able to see you in three or four hours. There are a few people ahead of you, waiting, so it may be even longer."

Sara placed her hand on Adam's arm and said, "Are you going to let this . . . this person keep us from seeing Julie!"

Adam patted her hand and replied, "Calm yourself, Sara. I will handle her."

"Handle me?" Annie raised her chin. "Aren't you afraid of soiling your hands, Mr. Raleigh?" Her lips quirked in a *moue* of a smile. "And, such a shame it would be to muss up your fine clothes!" Annie shook her head slowly. "From their cut, I would guess you're on your way to the opera, no?"

"What time is it? We can't be late!" Sara gasped white-faced—Annie's mention of the opera reminded her of their original destination.

Adam shot a look of venomous dislike at Annie before turning to his wife and saying, "I am fully aware of that fact, Sara."

Turning to Annie he delivered an ultimatum, "We

can't wait here all night. We have an important engagement with his honor, the mayor. Inform Julie at once that we are here and wish to see her immediately!"

Noticing the look of interest on Annie's face, Sara hastened to say, "We were on our way to the opera, when we heard word of Molly's terrible accident. Knowing how devastated my sister would be, we hurried over here to be with her." If, Sara had hoped to gain Annie's sympathy with this tact, she was soon dissuaded.

"I hope your friends will understand when you are unable to keep your engagement," Annie replied. Shrugging her shoulders as though it were nothing she could do anything about, she added, "What a shame, but if as you insist you must speak with Julie, it will mean missing tonight's performance."

Left with the choice of returning downstairs and waiting who knew how long to see Julie or continuing on their way to meet with the mayor and his wife, Sara glared at Annie and said with tight-lipped dignity, "Inform my sister that we were here! And, that *you* took the responsibility for not allowing us to see her."

"I would be delighted to, Mrs. Raleigh," Annie stated as she began moving down the staircase thereby insuring Sara and Adam's retreat. "As soon as she is free, I will inform her of your presence."

Bending to whisper in his wife's ear, Adam intoned, "We can't stay here all night. We will have to see her some other time."

"But, Adam," Sara whispered back, "what if Molly should die? Then who will Julie have to turn to but that husband of hers! I feel it is imperative we be here to protect our interests."

"No Sara." Adam disagreed. "We will be notified before anything drastic happens. In the meantime, we must protect our interests with the mayor."

Ignoring Sara's disapproving pout, Adam turned to Annie and said, "Our time is too valuable to waste sitting around this place. Please tell my sister-in-law to send a messenger to our residence to set up a time when it would be mutually convenient for us to meet. Inform her that we wish to speak with her at the soonest available time."

"That I will do, Mr. Raleigh." Annie, who now stood on the bottom tread with Lee Tang still at her side, smiled.

"See that you do, Mrs. Isaacs!" Adam reaffirmed his order as he took Sara by the arm and they departed.

Julie was unaware of the battle going on in her behalf as she saw to the settling of Molly. She was too busy with the doctor to have a thought for what was happening downstairs.

Making certain that Molly was well settled in her room, Julie went out to speak with the doctor. She listened very carefully as he explained the type of care Molly would need.

Once Molly had been moved to her room upstairs, he had been able to examine her more carefully and found she had a cracked cheekbone, mild concussion, bruised kidneys and three cracked ribs.

Having wrapped her ribs and sutured her cheek, there was little more that he could do for her but see that she had complete bed rest and constant care. Time would have to heal her other injuries.

The doctor had briefly considered having her transferred to the hospital, but since there was little that could be done there that could not be done here, he decided that if possible he would prefer not to move her again.

Having observed the care and concern evident on the faces of the bartenders who had carried Molly gently up the staircase to her room and the considerate way Bet, Julie and Mae had hovered around Molly's bed, he knew she would not lack for care and attention.

He gave Julie a list of instructions as to what he wished done in the treatment of his patient. He explained that he would spend the remainder of the night with Molly and that if her condition showed any signs of worsening she would have to be immediately transferred to the hospital.

"Worsening?" Julie seized on the word.

Seeing her distress, the doctor took her by the arm and escorted her toward her own room saying, "I said 'if,' Julie. Now you are overwrought and overtired, I want you to go to bed and get some rest. I don't wish to have two patients on my hands." He stood and watched as she opened the door and started into the room.

"But, what if . . . ?" she started to say.

"I'll send someone to get you should she regain consciousness before morning," the doctor reassured her calmly.

"My hus— Matt isn't back yet." Julie tried to delay being left alone in her empty room.

"Julie," the doctor's voice was threatening. "Do you want me to prescribe a sedative for you?"

"No!" Julie had always hated the thought of drugs. She had seen enough of the opium dens that catered to the sicknesses of others.

Having been the Plaza doctor for a number of years

he was well aware of her aversion. He deliberately used her reaction to such a suggestion, turning his offer into a threat of action if she didn't willingly agree to retire for the night.

Seeing through this ploy to force her willing cooperation, Julie sighed heavily, "All right, Doctor. You win. I'll go to bed. But," she amended her coerced agreement, "I want to know the minute Matt returns or . . ."

"Yes." The doctor cut her off. "I promise you will not be forgotten. Now go to bed!"

Julie entered the room and closed the door behind her. Leaning against it, she hugged herself tightly as she struggled to stop the flood of anguish that washed over her.

She gazed over at the turned-down bed, a gossamer nightgown of sheerest film lay draped over its foot. She could guess where it had come from. It was a special gift from the warm-hearted Bet and Mae. Another sign of the love that surrounded her. They had wanted her wedding night to be something to remember always.

She laughed bitterly, "Some wedding night!"

Molly lay in her room beaten unconscious, and her newlywed husband was out somewhere combing the streets of town in search of the one responsible. It was indeed a night she would never forget.

Chapter Twelve

JULIE HAD NO IDEA HOW LATE IT WAS WHEN SHE WAS A-
wakened by the sound of voices. It was still black
outside, and the casino sounded unnaturally still and
quiet. She was used to the continual sound of the
wheels spinning on the roulette tables and to the cries
of winners and losers alike filtering up from the crowded gambling room below. But, all the wheels and tables
were silent tonight. The Land of Gold had remained
closed after what had happened that day.

Thank God, for Annie! She had taken most of the
burden on her shoulders by taking charge as she had.
Julie smiled slightly, sorry she'd missed the confrontation between her stalwart friend and Sara and Adam.

From what she had been told it was a scene enjoyed

by many. She knew she would hear Sara's denunciation of Annie in scathing invective the next time she saw her. But, she could not help wondering, how did Adam and her sister hear about the attack on Molly so quickly? They had left at least two hours before the attack occurred, yet they'd returned within twenty minutes after it happened. Could it be they knew an attack was to take place? Julie shook her head, unwilling to accept the possibility that her own sister could be behind such a vile act. Her mind must still be clouded by sleep and she wasn't thinking clearly. What was it that had awakened her? Voices out in the hallway, she remembered.

She listened carefully for a few seconds to see if she could make out the voices. Her heart went to her throat as she recognized the deep timbre of Matt's voice just outside the bedroom door as Carlo's words echoed in the background. He was back!

She threw off the covers and hurried to the door. She desperately needed to know what they had found. Had they caught the man who'd done it? Did they know who was responsible? Her hand stopped in midmotion on the doorknob as she heard a change in the tone of Matt's voice.

She could not make out the words clearly, but he was saying something to Carlo about "that bastard Baldwin." She froze hardly daring to breathe.

These voices outside her door were not the same voices that had laughed and talked for hours the night before. Now they held an undercurrent of steel, of barely leashed violence and of something she was afraid to even consider . . . death!

Carlo was saying something to Matt and Julie felt

herself propelled back in time to another place where she had heard that same voice come from the lips of her friend.

She shivered as she heard the deadly menace in Carlo's voice. Something she had hoped never to hear again. She had first heard it years ago, when Carlo's favorite, younger sister had been pressured by one of the crib owners to become one of his whores. Marie had refused and tried to run home, but the crib owner had had one of his hired toughs stop her and show her what happened to someone who told him no.

Marie still bore the scars from the knife that had slashed at her face and across her body. She had almost died from the viciousness of her wounds.

When he had seen his sister, Carlo had gone nearly mad with rage. He had tracked the crib owner down and slit his throat before throwing his body into the bay. Julie was one of the very few who knew what had happened and the memory made her sick with dread. He had sounded deadly then, but now he made the hair on the back of her neck rise with fear.

Leaning her ear against the door panel she strained to make out what else they were saying. What could have happened to make her childhood friend sound this way? Even more important, what had happened to make Matt become the stranger she was hearing?

"I will tell you, Matthew. This Baldwin is like pus from a running sore. He spreads his infection and contaminates everything he touches," Carlo was saying with clipped biting words.

"He is only part of the problem, Carlo. There are others. Others, just as dangerous. He is only a part of the sickness that is eating away at the guts of San

Francisco," Matt replied. "The people behind this reign of terror are not dumb and neither is Baldwin. He knew better than to show himself anywhere but in a public place, surrounded by people who could state under oath in a court of law that he had been there all night. In fact, he prefers letting others do his dirty work," Matt explained with terse anger. "Today was only a small sample of what these people will resort to in order to achieve what they want."

"Baldwin and those like him are worse than the shit the rats that infest the waterfront leave in their wake!" Carlo spat out in disgust. "We must clean out this infection before it spreads any further."

"I agree," Matt replied in a tone that made Julie begin to tremble.

"I have little doubt Baldwin is the one who ordered the attack on Molly. But, without proof, we can do little as far as going to the authorities," Matt went on.

"The authorities! He owns most of them already! What good are they against him!" Carlo insisted. "We should drag him out of his filthy casino and deal with him the way he deserves!"

"No, Carlo. We must move carefully," Matt reasoned. "If we lose our heads and charge in after him like stampeding bulls, it will gain us nothing. We have to wait and watch and pick our time carefully." This uncompromising tone of promised retribution frightened Julie more and more as each second passed.

"Then we will deal with him in our own way and on our terms!" Carlo grated harshly as he slapped his hand against his leg.

"He has many eyes and ears. If he gets wind of what we are planning, he'll try his damnedest to stop us. You know he has set a price on my head. And, more than likely yours after tonight," Matt warned him.

"I know, *amigo*," Carlo replied, as he laughed coldly. "I would love to see someone try and collect."

"Before we are through, we shall see many, who will attempt that and more, my friend," Matt replied.

Julie could not stop the gasp that escaped her lips. She froze waiting to see if she had been heard by the men. A hollow feeling invaded her when she no longer heard them talking. They'd heard her!

Her frozen muscles instantly responded to the impetus of fear and she raced back to bed and quickly climbed back under the covers with her back to the door. She frantically tried to steady her breathing as she heard the bedroom door slowly open. She could feel the floor vibrate slightly from the weight of their footsteps as they moved silently across the floor and halted close to the bed.

"She's asleep," Matt said softly.

"Are you certain?" Carlo asked suspiciously. "I heard something from inside this room." He looked around the room as though expecting to find the cause of the noise he was sure he had heard.

Looking back at the bed, he said, "She has a wild streak in her, Matthew. One that has led her into trouble many times over the years. I pray she has slept the night through untroubled."

He moved to look out of the curtained window and to see that it was locked. Returning once again to the side of the bed, he looked down at the sleeping Julie. "If she should find out what we are planning, my friend . . ." Carlo's voice trailed off; then he softly added, "Watch over her."

The two men exchanged glances of understanding. Each knew the other loved this woman who lay on the bed in front of them—one as a sister and dearly beloved friend, and the other as the woman he had made his before the world. Neither was willing to see anything happen to her, if he could prevent it.

Julie fought the desire to open her eyes and see the expressions on their faces. Hearing their voices had made her feel trapped, but why had they stopped talking? Did they know she was not asleep? She tried to keep breathing slowly in and out hoping they would not guess she had heard what she had.

Matt gazed down at his sleeping bride and felt a swell of anger against those who had caused their marriage night to end in this way.

The demons who preyed on defenseless women and old men had matched wits with more than they had bargained for this night. A number of them would no longer prowl and do their masters' bidding.

He felt a stab of intense protectiveness wash over him as he thought of the danger she was in. He had always sworn he would never let a woman get under his skin as she had. How she had done it, he couldn't say. He had no idea as to when it had happened, but it had. She had a hold on him that made him want to kill anyone who tried to hurt her in any way.

She looked so young and helpless as she lay there. It was well that she slept. The horror of tonight's events was not for her eyes or ears. His eyes were drawn to the rise and fall of her shoulders as she breathed and to the way her hair trailed wildly across the pillows, as though even she had been struggling with demons of her own as she slept.

What demons haunted her? he wondered, an aching, bone-heavy desire to make her tell him, so he could slay them for her, came over him. He shook his head slightly as he scolded himself, You aren't in any condition to fight a fly let alone mythical demons!

Looking down at her, he wanted nothing more than to crawl in beside her and hold her in his arms.

After the bloody business in the alleyway tonight, he needed to feel her softness against him to block out the memory of what he, Carlo and the men who had joined them had been forced to do to save their skins.

They had tracked Molly's attacker to a dark alleyway in Chinatown and had gone in after him. The alleyway was long and narrow and was strewn with the garbage of the opium dens and cheap dives that formed its walls. They had rounded one of its many corners and been ambushed by a number of knife-wielding toughs.

Even though skilled in many ways of bringing death to those who gave him no other choice, Matt had never liked killing. And he prayed he never would. But no fiercer man lived when provoked beyond his limit. He had taken on two of their attackers himself and had tossed one against the wall with such force that he had heard the splintering of the man's backbone when his body had connected with the heavy-timbered building. The other had tried to slash at him from a low crouch, but Matt had instinctively kicked out, knocking the knife from his hand and the teeth from his head. He was wrestling with a third man when another came at him from the rear. If Carlo had not seen the man sneaking up behind him, he would not now be able to contemplate holding Julie in his arms.

"There's nothing here, Carlo," Matt replied in a very

subdued voice. "But even if there is, I'm too tired to worry about it," Matt said wearily. "We'll finish making our plans in the morning. There is little that can be done tonight."

Julie could sense them moving away from the bed as Matt walked Carlo to the door. "Sleep well, Carlo. And thank you again for what you did."

"It was nothing!" Carlo replied, offhandedly. "You would have done the same if it had been me."

Julie forced herself to remain still and to seem relaxed as she heard the sounds of Matt's undressing. The feel of cool night air across her as he lifted the covers and crawled in beside her sent gooseflesh racing over her. She bit her lip to keep from gasping as his strong arm moved over the curve of her hip and pulled her tightly against him. She could feel every angle and ridge of his naked form through the thinness of her nightgown as he held her close. Panic began to build in the pit of her stomach. Surely, he was not thinking of claiming his rights as a husband now!

She remained immobile and waited. Time seemed to move as slowly as a glacier. What is he waiting for? her mind screamed. One of his legs moved over hers pinning her to the bed. She felt a tightening of her scalp as he nestled his head in her hair and she could feel his warm breath on her ear. As effectively as though bound with a rope, she was trapped! There was no way she could move.

The added warmth from his pressing body flowed over her, making her feel oddly secure and comforted. A flicker of feeling began to grow inside her and Julie realized with a pang that she wanted him! Even though he'd frightened her, speaking as he had with Carlo, she still wanted him! She wanted to feel his lips on hers, his hands caressing her breasts. A hollow ache began to grow in her loins and she tried not to shake with the surprise and shock of it. She wanted him to make love to her! She wanted him to bring her alive and quench the fire that was even now smoldering inside her.

A deep rumble against her back and the sound that filled the air told her he was asleep. He had fallen asleep!

Bitter resentment and frustration stung her. She had been willing to forget all that had happened between them that day and let him make love to her, but he had fallen asleep! She tried to break away from his hold; the sharp pain in her head and the tightening of his arm as it lay across her were galling proof that even in sleep he could make her his prisoner.

She spent the remaining hours until dawn trapped in his embrace and torn by the knowledge she had acquired that night—knowledge about herself and about this man she had wed and who now held her in his arms.

He would always have the power to make her want him. Even as he lay, exhausted, next to her, he exerted a hold on her more powerful than the arm that held her or the leg that covered hers. Not only was her body a captive, so was her heart.

Whatever had happened tonight, she knew Matt's actions had been filled with danger and death. A new terror joined the unfulfilled desire that raced through her blood. Matt could have been killed! She knew that as well as she knew her own name. It was a realization that came from the most primitive depths of her soul.

Adding to this fear were the words she had overheard: "If he gets wind of what we are planning, he'll try his damnedest to stop us. You know he has set a price on my head. . . ."

The words kept echoing in her head as sleep claimed her.

When Julie woke the sun was high in the sky and she was alone. Only a rumpling of the bedcovers and a lingering presence in the air gave proof that Matt had ever come home.

Sitting up, Julie stared in fascination at the evidence that he had lain beside her. She had not been dreaming after all. Matt had come back the night before! And Carlo had been with him! She had not dreamt the conversation she had overheard between them!

The memory of what she had heard made her pale. She had first been exposed to violence and the harsh realities of life as a young child. And she recognized the sound of unbounded determination and strength in the grim harshness of Matt's voice, as he so coolly advised the hotheaded Carlo, to have patience.

The first time she had seen Matt at Mr. Washburn's office, she had sensed the subtle aura of danger that marked him. He had reminded her then of the cunning and deadly cougar. His very eyes had set her natural defenses to react by cascading gooseflesh over her. She had responded instinctively to him. He had awakened in her a primitive mingling of fear, curiosity and sensual awareness. Now she felt this same fear anew.

Who was this man she'd married? She knew him to be astute and calculating when it came to business. He was well liked by Molly and the girls who worked for her. He had been a trusted and valued friend to her father. But, for all this, he remained a mystery to her.

She knew him as a man who could unsettle her without even trying. He was someone who had taken over her life and channeled its course to his arms. He had been a gentle and sensitive lover. He had taught her things about herself and about passion she had never learned at Molly's knee.

Now he was showing a side of himself that terrified her. She found it close to impossible to reconcile the gentle and sensitive lover with the implacable and dangerous man she had overheard the night before. He is doing it for you. He is defending and protecting his mate, her little voice told her. She did not want to be the cause of bloodshed and violence! She had to put a stop to their plans before more people were hurt!

She felt a twisting inside her as she realized she did not want to lose him. She wanted to grow old with him and bear his children. If he and Carlo were not stopped, she might never have that chance. Somehow, she would have to handle things on her own. The sound of Matt's voice as he spoke, in such deadly earnest, to Carlo echoed in her ears.

Her hand moved of its own volition and traced the outline of his head on the pillow next to her.

A shadow of the desire she had felt the night before nestled, coiled, deeply inside her. It nudged at her nerve endings as a reminder that her love for him was one-sided. Is it, her little voice asked? She tried to ignore the doubt raised in her heart. It was more than she dared allow herself to hope.

A burning ache clutched at her throat. Where had he gone? Had he gone to meet with Carlo to complete their plans? Maybe, they had already left to put their plan into action! The possibility made her leap from the bed and hurry to wash and dress.

Brushing her hair into a quick fold at the back of her head, she pushed pins into it as she hurried to the door and out onto the landing.

Looking to the right and left, she wasn't sure which way to try first. Cursing at herself for being so indecisive, she moved toward Molly's end of the corridor, praying to find Matt and Carlo there.

Opening the door to Molly's room, she entered and scanned the room hopefully. Disappointment flooded through her as she saw Bet look up from giving Molly a drink, for they were the only ones in the room.

"Miss Julie? Is something wrong?" Bet asked with a frown.

Moving closer to the bed, Julie replied, "No, Bet. I was only looking for someone." She turned her eyes to the injured Molly and asked, "How is she?"

"I'll live." The slurred response came from Molly's swollen lips.

"I never doubted that for a minute," Julie lied as she stared down at the battered woman.

"Who?" was all Molly could say as her eyes demanded more.

Julie knew what she meant and replied, "I don't know. Matt and Carlo went after whoever it was. And, I haven't talked with them since they came back." There was no way she could reveal what she had overheard the night before.

Molly closed her eyes briefly due to the effort it was costing her to speak. "Why?"

Julie had her suspicions, but they were not for

Molly's ears. She crossed her arms in front of her and shook her head as she answered tightly, "I don't know."

Molly closed her eyes again and Julie thought she might have fallen asleep, she was so still. But as she was about to turn and leave, Molly's eyes opened and pinned Julie with an intense stare. Her words were harsh and guttural as she gasped them out slowly. "Let Matt . . . handle . . . this."

"He already is," Julie replied carefully. "Now you rest and get well. I'll be back later to see you."

She was at the door, when she heard, "Promise!"

Turning she faced the bed and saw Molly staring at her intently. She was waiting for her to give her word that she wouldn't become involved.

She couldn't promise to let Matt go off and fight her battles for her. She knew in her heart that everything that had happened was aimed at one thing, putting her out of business. Even Molly's beating was meant as a sign to her to accept Baldwin's offer and sell out.

But, God help her, she couldn't tell Molly the truth or allow her to think she was going to try and settle things herself. So, begging forgiveness from the Most High, she lied once again. "Yes."

Molly closed her eyes and a sigh could be heard as she relaxed against the pillows. Bet, who had watched the interchange, now looked at Julie and mouthed the words, "Be careful!"

Julie was not surprised that the wise and caring Bet had seen through her lie.

Bet realized, as clearly as Julie, what was going on and the danger of what had to be done. Bet also loved

Molly dearly. The two young women looked at the resting Molly and then again at one another in agreement. Molly would never know the secret they shared.

Julie inclined her head slightly in acknowledgment of Bet's warning and left the room, closing the door behind her.

Moving toward the stairway she passed the office. Pausing she peeked in, on the off chance that Matt might have returned to his old room, not really expecting to see anyone.

A feeling of relief swept over her as she saw Matt sitting at the desk, while Carlo paced the floor nearby.

Taking a deep breath, she entered the room calling, "Good day, gentlemen."

Matt looked up from the papers set in front of him and Carlo turned pausing in midstride to smile at her warmly. "Good day to you, *cara mía*." Carlo greeted her with a kiss on the cheek.

"Julie." Matt nodded and allowed a small smile to crease the seriousness of his expression.

The room became filled with a tense, uncomfortable silence, as though she had interrupted something they didn't want her to know about. Determined not to give them the chance to complete any plans that she wasn't aware of, she moved to the sofa and sat down, drawing one of her legs beneath her.

"I must have been more tired than I realized. I didn't hear you come in last night," she told them. "When did you return?"

Matt's eyes glinted briefly as he replied, "Late. We had a few things delay us."

A few things! How could he sit there and be so calm

after what she supposed had happened? "Really?" she said, turning her gaze to Carlo and adding, "what about Molly's attacker?"

Carlo exchanged looks with Matt and said, "He will not be troubling anyone else."

Julie was hard pressed to conceal the chill that ran up her spine at his words. Memories of Carlo's methods made her afraid to ask the next question, but she did, "Is he dead?"

Matt rose from the desk and moved to the sofa saying, "He wasn't the last time I saw him."

"What?" Julie was perplexed at the smiles she saw on their faces. She looked from one to the other hoping for an explanation. "I don't understand. Carlo says he won't be causing any more trouble and then you say he isn't dead."

"By now he is resting as comfortably as possible in the hold of Captain Crenshaw's ship." Carlo shrugged. "Whether or not he survives the voyage I'm not in a position to guess."

"He was shanghaied!" Julie exclaimed. "How did that happen?"

Matt laughed and waved a hand at Carlo, saying, "Ask him; he was there. I was ah . . . otherwise occupied at the time."

Julie was torn between asking what had occupied him and demanding an answer from Carlo. Her curiosity about Molly's attacker won. "Carlo!"

Carlo brushed an imaginary piece of lint from his immaculate velvet jacket and replied nonchalantly, "I was escorting him to the authorities." He raised his eyes when Julie could not suppress the sound of disbelief she felt at hearing his words. "As I was trying to say," he continued, "when Captain Crenshaw and a party of sailors happened by. They offered to relieve me of my burden and the long journey to the police station, and I accepted their offer."

"You didn't!" Julie's hand flew to her lips. She was as surprised to hear Carlo had accepted such an offer as she was by the idea that Carlo was truly going to the authorities. She knew how he felt about them, even before overhearing what he had said to Matt the night before. "You let one of the worst captains on the coast take your prisoner!"

"It was late and I was tired." Carlo shrugged. "Boomer's a big man! And it was still a long way to the police station. So . . ."

"Boomer? Not Boomer Wagner!" Julie was shaken to hear the name of the man who'd attacked Molly.

Seeing them nod, Julie shuddered. Boomer Wagner was a big man, standing well over six feet and built like a redwood. He would do anything for the right price and had no conscience. Some even said he enjoyed watching his victims suffer. How Molly had not been killed outright, Julie would never understand. She felt no sympathy for him. He deserved far worse than the hardship of being a member of Captain Crenshaw's crew, willing or not.

"Could he have been responsible for my father's death?" The words spilled forth of their own volition and Julie waited stricken-faced for a reply.

Carlo's face clouded and his brow crinkled in a frown as he said, "We don't know, *cara*."

"We didn't have time to question him," Matt explained further as he took one of her small cold hands in his. "But with his reputation, I wouldn't doubt it, if the price was right."

"Oh," Julie murmured, and her shoulders sagged as she said, "it could have been Boomer or any number of men like him. We won't ever know for certain who did it, will we?"

"That is a possibility you may have to face, Julie," Matt answered her. "But that doesn't mean we will stop looking. There is always a chance someone will become careless and give himself away when he's drunk or bragging. Men like Boomer are known more for their brawn than for their brains."

Julie listened to him, desperately wanting to believe him. Her father's killers had to be found and brought to justice. The thought of them never having to pay for what they did was something she could never accept.

"What about those who hire men like Boomer? Are they as dumb?" Julie asked.

"Maybe not as dumb, but they can be as careless," Matt replied as he stroked the inside of her wrist with his thumb.

The effect on her already sensitive nerve endings was immediate. A sharp tingling began to run up her arm and down into her very core. She pulled her hand away hoping Matt did not guess her reason for doing so.

"How so?" She tried to divert his attention by asking him to explain further.

Matt's eyes glinted briefly with the knowledge that he knew why she had moved her hand before he replied.

"They feel protected because they are invisible. They never have any traceable connection with the beatings, killings or other crimes they order. Their hired muscles get away with a few beatings, or worse, and they begin to think they are invulnerable."

"Aren't they?" Julie prompted. She could not see how they weren't.

"They are not always as careful as they should be. When that happens they leave themselves open to discovery," Carlo explained as he sat on the arm of the sofa next to her.

"You mean you can find out who they are and stop them?" Julie asked hopefully.

"It's not as easy as that, Julie." Matt crushed her rising hopes. "We can follow the trail their carelessness leaves and try to track it back all the way to the one in charge. But, sometimes, we lose the trail before we can do that."

"Then what happens?" Julie asked them.

"We wait for them to become careless again," Carlo answered her.

"But what if they don't?" Julie demanded. "Wouldn't they be even more careful than before if they know you have come so close?"

Carlo smiled at her and said, "You would think that would be the case. But more often than not, they feel even safer because we were close and still did not find them."

She did not see how things could be as simple as they said they were. But she knew, simple or not, she would have to see if she could find this trail they spoke of and trace it back to its source. "Have they been careless this

181

time?" Julie asked them as she looked from Carlo to Matt.

"Why do you want to know?" Matt asked her. "This isn't anything you could handle. Carlo and I will take care of things. You take care of yourself, Molly and the Land of Gold."

Chapter Thirteen

JULIE FROWNED AS SHE MOVED ACROSS THE LANDING toward the staircase. Things were definitely not going as she had planned!

Matt and Carlo had quite effectively shut her out. After telling her about Boomer Wagner, they had been as close-mouthed as clams. She had tried every way she could think of to find out where they were going, but it was as though they had an unspoken agreement where she was concerned. No matter how hard she tried, they kept changing the subject back to either how pretty she always looked first thing in the morning, or, as in Matt's case, to quite unexpected apologies for leaving her alone on their wedding night!

She could see by the way they were gathering themselves to leave that she hadn't much time to find out what it was she needed to know. But she did not want to let it slip that she had overheard their conversation of the night before, and that meant she had to be careful what she said. Keeping that to herself made things difficult and limited what arguments she could use without arousing their suspicions. She found herself becoming very frustrated. And she suspected they both knew it! What she hoped neither of them did suspect was just how much she knew already.

Almost frantic, she had tried to find out where they were going by asking Matt if he would be nearby should she need to reach him. But that had been to no avail. Matt had merely repeated his admonition for her to stay and take care of things, adding that Lee Tang knew where they would be and she could reach him by sending word through him, while Carlo had gone all serious and protective as he told her it was better she didn't know where they were going or why. None of which helped to make her feel any better.

Matt's giving her orders as though she were a recalcitrant child infuriated her no end. Carlo's treating her as though she could not understand what was going on, because she was a woman, irritated her. He should know better than most, that she was fully capable of understanding. When, in his mind, had she changed from an intelligent friend into a mindless female? She was the same person she had always been. He was the one who had changed. But, why?

When Matt and Carlo had each kissed her on the cheek and bid her a good day as they'd left the casino together, Julie was no wiser about their plans than when she'd awakened that morning!

What can I do now, she thought in exasperation? She knew she would not be able to get any information from Lee Tang. And with Molly laid up in bed, the running of the entire Land of Gold was on her shoulders. This, added to her normal duties, was more than enough to keep her occupied a full twenty-four hours a day. It was almost as though the men had planned it that way! Circumstances couldn't have been better for them. Now if she wanted to break free and begin investigating on her own, she would have to delegate as much of the work as possible or be swamped completely!

She moved down the stairs, thinking there had to be some way for her to handle things. She was not about to sit in the background where Matt and Carlo were so confident they had trapped her. But what would she do for a start? She had no concrete idea as to where Matt and Carlo might have gone. She suspected they were going to check up on Baldwin and his cronies. Something she planned on doing herself if she could. She realized it might be impossible to trace Molly's beating or any of the other accidents that been happening back to them. She would have to be extremely careful.

She paused near the bottom of the staircase and reviewed carefully in her mind what her options were. She could try to follow Matt and Carlo. But that was risky. The last thing she wanted was to run into them when she was supposed to be at the casino. If they discovered her, they would probably bring her back and, at the very least, would lock her in her room. That was if she were lucky. She had no doubt in her mind that they could think of far worse things to do in order to keep her safely out of their way. They had both been

185

very insistent that she stay out of things. She knew there was no way she could do that, but she fully intended to do her best to stay out of their sight!

How was she going to manage that and still get to the heart of things? she wondered.

Matt and Carlo were after the same people she was. There had to be another way. What about picking up where her father had left off? Or should she go and try to speak with Ah Toy herself? No. Speaking with Ah Toy wasn't a very good idea. She shook her head. Ah Toy was well known for her dislike of other women. And what could she say to her? She couldn't very well ask Ah Toy outright if she'd had anything to do with her father's death! Julie's thoughts went round and round. This was getting her nowhere! She unconsciously stamped her foot in aggravation. Time was wasting! Maybe some coffee would help her organize her thoughts.

Reaching the main floor, she looked around her at the now-empty gaming tables. For the first time, she found herself glad her father had insisted on not opening for business before dusk. If, like some of the casinos, they opened at noon or, like others, on a twenty-four hour basis, she would never have any time to herself. She moved toward the kitchen thinking that if she needed anything it was the time to think and the space in which to do it.

Returning from the kitchen with a cup of coffee, she sat down at her regular table. While sipping her coffee, she began to slow her whirling thoughts and formulate a plan of action.

She would go through her father's papers one more

time to see if there was anything she had missed earlier, although she would much rather have a look at the notebook he had given to Matt. Something told her that what she needed to know was there. First, she would search his room to see if he'd left it behind; then she'd go over her father's papers one more time.

Having reached these decisions, she quickly finished her coffee. Leaving instructions with Lukes for the restocking and provisioning of the bar and kitchen, she moved back upstairs and through the office to Matt's bedroom.

Standing in the doorway, she surveyed the room to see if she could spot a possible hiding place for the notebook. She was not fool enough to think Matt would leave it out in the open where anyone could find it, but he might have hidden it somewhere in the room.

Starting with the wardrobe, next to the doorway, she began to systematically search every nook and cranny she could find.

After two hours of searching and flinching into a frozen state of terror anytime she heard a noise that might mean Matt and Carlo had returned, she still had not found the notebook. Sitting back on her heels, she stared around the room one last time, refusing to admit what she knew was the truth. The notebook wasn't there. Straightening, she brushed the dust off her hands and skirt while she surveyed the room to be sure she hadn't left any traces of her search. Satisfied that Matt would never know she had been there, she returned to the office.

She sat down at the desk and, with a sigh, began to go over her father's papers. She had nearly gone through the lot, with only the barest of results, when there was a knock at the door. She looked up as it opened and Mae and Pearl came into the room.

"Miss Julie?" Pearl called.

"Yes, Pearl? What is it?" she replied.

Looking nervously at her companion before speaking, Pearl said, "We dunno which rooms we are supposed to have tonight."

"What?" Julie frowned.

Clearing her throat and moving closer to the desk, Mae said, "What with Miss Molly hurt and all, none of us knows what we are supposed to do."

"Why, what you usually do, of course," Julie replied in surprise, wondering what had brought them to her. "We still have a business to run. You girls do whatever it is you usually do for Molly, and I'm sure we will manage fine until she is back on her feet."

"You don't understand, Miss Julie." Pearl tried to explain. "Miss Molly would tell us which rooms we were to use each day. She didn't like us always using the same rooms."

"Why is that?" Julie asked, wishing she knew more about the bordello side of things than she did. "Don't you have regular rooms?"

"No." The two prostitutes shook their heads.

"Some of the rooms are much fancier than the others. Miss Molly says it's better if we all share the rooms. That way nobody gets used to having just one room," Mae told her.

"And that way, there ain't any fighting amongst ourselves to see who gets the fancy rooms. Miss Molly says we all take better care of things if we know we all get to use them," Pearl added.

"Oh." Julie sighed. "And you want me to say who gets which room for tonight?"

The two nodded. "We don't know who else to ask. Bet won't let any of us see Miss Molly. She says Miss Molly needs her rest and don't need to be bothered by us."

"Bet's right," Julie said distractedly, and she thought for a moment before asking, "there are eight rooms aren't there?" She wished she could remember the complete layout. It had been years since she had been through any of the rooms, except for the large dormitory-style room, just below the attic, where the girls all spent their time off and slept.

"Yes'm," Pearl replied. "Four of them are simple. Two of them are decorated with pretty wallpaper and, the other two are the biggest and fanciest, with big brass beds and mirrors."

"I see," Julie said, thinking that Molly not only played mother to her girls, but King Solomon as well. "Who used the fanciest rooms last?"

"Bet and Mary," Mae replied. "Pearl and I had the pretty ones and the other girls switched off using the simple ones."

"Then, Bet and Mary will use two of the simple rooms tonight. You two will use the fancy rooms. The others can decide between themselves which of them stay with the simple ones and which of them move to the pretty rooms tonight," Julie told them.

"Yes, Miss Julie." They smiled.

"Girls, it's more than obvious you know more about how things work in the bordello than I do." Julie sighed. "I think I will need you to help me and each other. So, Mae, you and Pearl will be in charge of assigning the rooms. I want you to be fair and see that everyone gets an equal chance at the fancy rooms. Okay?"

"Sure thing, Miss Julie!" they exclaimed in unison. They visibly puffed up with pride at her show of trust. She was permitting them to handle things for her, and they were not about to let her down.

"Which room will you be using, Miss Julie?" Pearl asked her, already taking her new assignment to heart.

"What!" Julie choked. "I have a bedroom of my own already! When I put you in charge of room assignments, I meant you would assign the bedrooms, where you take your clients, not all the bedrooms in the building!"

"I understand that Miss Julie." Mae nodded and smiled. "I don't think you understand. You see, Miss Molly always had one of the rooms for herself. She would take care of some of the special customers personally," Mae explained. "Now that you are taking her place, we need to know which room you'll be using before we can give out the other rooms."

"Special customers!" Julie looked from Pearl to Mae in shocked surprise. All this was news to her. She was finding out with each passing minute just how sheltered Molly had kept her. "Certainly, no one is going to expect me to take Molly's place! Everyone must know by now why she won't be working for a while." Julie looked at them hopefully. "And, that I am newly married!"

"Sorry, Miss Julie." Pearl shook her head slowly. "It will be expected that whoever takes over for Miss Molly takes over all her duties, not just some of them."

"All?" Julie swallowed quickly. "But I couldn't

possibly . . ." she started to say as the two nodded in answer to her question.

Julie felt a trap beginning to close around her and she wasn't sure what to say, so she asked, "Molly has her own room?"

Seeing them nod once again, she took a deep breath and asked, "Which room does she normally use?"

"The Gold Room," they replied.

"You're certain it's expected?" Julie again tried to avoid having to agree to something she had no intention of doing if she could possibly avoid it.

"I'm afraid so, Miss Julie." Mae smiled understandingly, although she knew there was no way she could force Julie to do what Molly did. Molly took care of the special customers, as she called them, only because she enjoyed it. Mae made a mental note to say something to Pearl about this before they returned to the others.

"Then I guess I will have to use the Gold Room." Like hell I will, she thought to herself. It was an eventuality that she would do her best to avoid at any cost.

"Miss Julie?" Mae asked softly.

"There's something else, Mae?" Julie was afraid of what she might hear next. For all she knew, Molly might have an entire string of private customers! She did not need any more problems! She had more than enough as it was.

"Where do you want us to put our earnings?"

"Earnings?" Julie didn't immediately understand what she was saying. "Oh!" she said when she realized what Mae meant. Here at least was something she could handle. "Did Miss Molly have any special way of managing them?"

"I dunno if it was special." Pearl frowned. "But, we all have cigar boxes we keep our earnings in. And at the end of the night, we take them to Bet. She counts them and gives us our share before turning the rest over to Miss Molly," she went on, explaining to Julie.

"I see," Julie commented, thinking to herself that it was a good thing Bet was in charge of that aspect, for she had no idea what the charges were. Or what share went to the girls!

"Let's keep it that way," Julie suggested. "Tell Bet to bring the remainder to me. I'll put it in the safe, until Miss Molly is well enough to handle things again. Now, is there anything else I should know . . . or, that needs to be taken care of?"

"Only one thing I can think of now, Miss Julie," Pearl answered.

"And what is that?" Julie asked, her heart in her throat. She wasn't sure she really wanted to hear the answer.

"Miss Molly would let any of the girls who wanted to keep their share in the safe," Pearl responded. "Some of us don't feel safe keeping it upstairs in our rooms."

"Fine." Julie sighed in relief. Something else she could cope with. "We will continue with that practice. Just have Bet collect from those who want their earnings in the safe," Julie instructed her. "Tell her I said to count it first and to give each girl a receipt. That way we will be less likely to make any mistakes."

"Miss Julie?" Mae cleared her throat. "I think I should tell you that some of the girls are afraid to work tonight. I've even heard a few of them talking about leaving."

Julie felt no surprise at hearing what Mae was telling

her. But she knew she would have to quiet the girls' fears before they spread and everyone became too afraid to work or left.

"Thank you for telling me, Mae," Julie soothed her. "I can understand why some of the girls are afraid. It's only natural to be frightened when people around you are getting hurt." She paused before continuing, "Tell them that Mr. Thorn and Señor Ramos have caught the man responsible for Miss Molly's beating. They've seen to it that he will not be returning to hurt anyone else. And, Mae, as far as those who want to leave are concerned, it's their choice. They can leave or stay. Neither Miss Molly nor I would try to hold anyone who didn't want to be here."

"I think they're lily-livered cowards!" Pearl spat. "Miss Molly would never run out on any of them if they were in trouble. But they can't wait to make tracks when she's in trouble! I say we are better off without them!"

"Not everyone can be as brave as you, Pearl." Julie tried to explain how the others felt. "It's not that they don't care. But, they have a harder time feeling safe after what has been happening around here. Don't be too hard on them."

Pearl looked down at the floor before looking back up at Julie and saying, "I'll tell them what you said about the man who did it being caught. But I still think they should be ashamed of themselves for being so yellow-bellied."

Julie rose from her seat and moved next to Pearl, putting an arm around her shoulder and saying, "Weren't you afraid after you were hurt?"

"Yes," came the mumbled response.

"Did Miss Molly force you to go back to work before you felt you were ready?"

"No," Pearl answered in a whisper.

"That's right. Well, I think Miss Molly would want you to have patience with the others, Pearl. You have seen many things the other girls have never seen. Being one of the oldest, you should try to remember that many of the younger girls have only worked here for Miss Molly and nowhere else. All this trouble is new to them and it frightens them," Julie told her.

"Maybe you're right, Miss Julie," Pearl said as she tried to understand. "I'll try and be more patient."

After her parents had died, Pearl had gone to live with an uncle she had never known. He had been a drunken gambler who beat her. Thanks to him, she had been plying her trade since the age of fourteen when he began selling her to anyone who had two bits of silver to rub together.

She had run away when she was sixteen. She had worked her way to San Francisco and had tried to survive by haunting the waterfront and catching the ships as they came into port.

She barely managed that first year, but when gold was discovered most of the crews were more interested in jumping ship and heading for the gold fields than in paying to jump into bed with her.

Times became very hard, and Miss Molly had found her penniless and hungry down on the docks. She had brought her back to the Land of Gold and given her some food. After hearing her story, she had offered her a job working for her. Not knowing how else to support herself, Pearl had accepted the offer.

The working conditions had been better than anything she had ever known. Miss Molly had been extra careful to see they all were checked by a doc regularly. She had even shown them how to keep from getting a babe in their belly if they didn't want one. After three years, Pearl did not regret her decision one bit.

But instead of this making her have more patience with those who were talking of leaving, it made Pearl even madder at them. They didn't know, or care, how good they had things working at the Land of Gold. They could all just as easily have been working for Belle Cora or even, she shuddered, Ah Toy.

Conditions at either of them houses were plushy for the customers all right but hell for the girls.

Pearl looked over at Julie fondly. She had always been a friend to her, to all of the girls. Even though she knew what they were, she had never looked down her nose at them or acted as though she were better than they were.

She realized how hard things were for Julie, what with Miss Molly laid up hurt. Pearl decided she would see to it that none of the girls left, but she would do it her way. Miss Julie was far too nice a lady to understand that patience would only get you so much, while a good kick in the right place could get far better results.

What Miss Julie didn't know couldn't hurt her and, in this case, might even help her, Pearl thought to herself, as she and Mae started to leave the office and return to the other girls.

"Oh, Mae," Julie called after them.

Turning at the doorway, Mae looked back and replied, "Yes, Miss Julie?"

"Which room is the Gold Room?" Julie could not prevent the blush that crept across her cheekbones as she spoke.

Mae and Pearl both noticed it, but they refrained from embarrassing Julie by saying anything. Mae only smiled as she replied, "The second on the right, at the top of the stairs."

As they moved down the hallway toward the waiting girls, Mae turned to Pearl and said, "I think we had better do what we can to keep the special customers happy until Miss Molly is well. I think Miss Julie has her hands full already with that new husband of hers."

Pearl grinned. "I think you may be right."

Back in the office, Julie sat, unaware of how she was to be guarded by the caring girls. She would have been relieved had she known and had her mind not been so preoccupied with her plan to steal away from the casino unnoticed.

Having gathered as much information as she could from her careful perusal of her father's papers, she was at that moment contemplating whether it would be better to leave before or after midnight.

She tapped at her upper lip with a carefully manicured fingernail as she decided after midnight would be best. Then, she would be able to slip away through the throngs that usually gathered to enjoy the nocturnal life of the Plaza.

Luckily, she had been able to glean a few interesting tidbits that Matt had conveniently forgotten to mention to her when they had jointly gone over her father's papers.

It seemed her father had had a meeting with one of

the controlling families of the Six Companies in Chinatown shortly before he had been killed.

According to what she had been able to discover, he had met with them to discuss the Barracoon. She intended to visit them herself . . . that night.

Slipping the papers back into the desk, she gathered the few notes she'd made and left the office.

As she made her way back downstairs, she could not help but smile to herself. No wonder Lee Tang knew where Matt and Carlo could be reached. It was his family her father had visited two days before his death.

She wondered why Tang had never mentioned anything about that meeting to her? He had been visiting his family at the time. Surely he must have seen her father? It puzzled her. But she knew now was not the time to bring the subject up. He would immediately be suspicious. A watchful Tang was problem enough, but a suspicious Tang was an unshakable shadow.

She already had good reason to know where his true allegiance lay. Hadn't he delayed Molly long enough for Matt to place her in a compromising position?

"Tut-tut," her small voice warned her. "You are forgetting you had as much to do with compromising Matt as he did with compromising you."

"He did keep Molly away!" she hissed quietly but aloud as she began to argue with herself.

She had no doubt that Tang would side with Matt against her. He had been too pleased to see their marriage take place. He had even gone so far as to wish Matt felicitations and the blessings of many sons and no daughters!

If she hoped to make her escape unobserved, she

would have to be very careful. She could not do anything that was out of the ordinary. The slightest deviation could alert Tang. Once alerted, he would stick to her side and make it impossible for her to leave.

The next hours, until dark, were some of the hardest Julie had ever spent. She forced herself to carry on with her work as though she hadn't another thing on her mind.

It was nearing eleven and Matt and Carlo had yet to return. Julie had finished her last circuit of the tables before going upstairs when Mae came over to her and whispered in her ear. "There's a special customer who has asked for you, Miss Julie."

"What!" Julie nearly shouted. Not now, she was screaming inside!

Looking around the crowded room, she tried to guess who the special customer might be as she asked, "There's no mistake? You're certain he is one of Molly's . . . special ones?"

"Very sure, Miss Julie," Mae replied.

"Where is he?"

Mae saw the way Julie was scanning the crowd and, smiling to herself, she said, "He's already upstairs waiting in the Gold Room. I told him you would be right up."

Julie knew she would have to go upstairs and explain to whoever was waiting for her that she was terribly sorry, but that she had not taken over *all* of Molly's duties. As she ascended the staircase on fear-laden feet, she didn't even care if her announcement cost them a good customer. There was no way she was going to go to bed with a perfect stranger!

Unfortunately, at that moment her eye was caught by

the sight of a drunken and filthy miner. He was leering at her from the top of the stairs. Her heart began beating heavily against her ribs. Not only was he filthier than any man she had ever seen—she could smell him from where she stood, frozen, on the stairs—he was also ugly. He had a scar that started at the top of his head above one eyebrow and ran down the length of his face diagonally to disappear into the dirt-encrusted collar of his shirt. His leering grin showed to full advantage the blackened stumps of his rotten teeth. Julie wondered vaguely if she were going to be sick right then and there.

She was opening her mouth to tell him there was no way he was anyone's special customer when a figure brushed past her on the stairs and ran into his arms with a cry of, "Polecat! I've missed you!"

It was, of all people, the sturdy Pearl! Julie tried not to show the mixture of relief and astonishment she felt. Nor, did she fail to note the aptness of the name Pearl had called out with such apparent joy. A polecat was certainly what he smelled like.

Julie watched in stupefaction as Pearl threaded her arm through his and began to lead him back downstairs, passing her. She was batting her eyes and smiling at him as though he were the handsomest man in the place! Without a doubt, Pearl had to be the best actress Julie had ever seen, on or off the stage!

Reaching the landing, Julie glided across toward the once-forbidden corridor, her dress a whisper of silk on the polished floor.

Reaching the second door on the right at the top of the stairs, as Mae had instructed, Julie hesitated before taking the ornate doorknob in her hand. It was getting closer to midnight and she did not want to waste time fighting off an overamorous customer who thought she was a whore!

This was not to her liking at all! The sooner she entered the room and explained the misunderstanding to the man waiting inside, the sooner she could sneak off to her room and change. No matter what, she planned on leaving at twelve.

Opening the door, she entered the room. It was a shock to her senses! There were mirrors everywhere! The walls were covered with them, as was the ceiling above the oversize brass bed! But, there wasn't anyone else in sight! She was alone in the room!

Releasing a giant sigh and thinking whoever it was must have gotten tired of waiting and left, Julie turned to leave.

As she turned, she heard the ominous sounds of the door being closed and locked behind her. She gasped aloud as she saw Matt smiling at her. He carefully placed the key to the door in his pocket and started walking toward her.

Chapter Fourteen

"YOU!" JULIE EXCLAIMED AS SHE TOOK A STEP BACKWARD, an astonished look on her face. "What are you doing here?" she demanded as she felt a knot forming in the pit of her stomach. "You'll have to leave! I am supposed to be meeting someone and . . . and . . ." She couldn't tell him why she was meeting someone! The knot in her stomach grew tighter.

"Yes?" Matt smiled, waiting for her to go on with her explanation.

"Why did you lock the door?" Julie asked nervously.

Had he somehow found out about her plans to sneak away? Or had he discovered she had overheard his conversation with Carlo? Julie mustered all her arguments in favor of the former and against the latter. She would need them to defend herself, should he confront her with the knowledge of either.

She was not ready for him to shake his head slightly, look at her with a wounded expression, and say, as he advanced slowly toward her, "Is that how you talk to all your special customers?"

"Special customers! How did—Don't be ridiculous!" Julie snapped back in surprise. "You speak as though I do this on a regular basis! They aren't *my* special customers, they're Molly's!" She glared at him as she moved back to the door. "Now unlock this door, and let me out of here!" she demanded.

Matt stopped barely a foot away to lift his hand and trace the curve of her cheekbone as he spoke softly. "But I was told that you had assumed *all* of Molly's duties." He paused for a moment and stared down at her, a teasing light dancing in his golden eyes, before adding, "You have assumed them, haven't you?"

"I may have taken over some of Molly's duties, but not all of them!" she protested.

"I know that." Matt smiled as he lowered his head and claimed her lips with his. "I wanted to hear you say it," he murmured, his lips lightly pressed to hers.

Drawing away from her slightly, he whispered, "Don't even think of taking over this end of Molly's work. You would be making a big mistake to try to handle it. You're lucky it was me waiting up here and not someone else. Special customers expect special treatment, not explanations."

She pushed him away from her exclaiming, "You knew! You say I'm lucky you were the one waiting up here! I don't like what you are inferring, Matthew

Thorn! How dare you! In spite of what you may think of me, I am not, I repeat not, one of Molly's girls!"

"This wasn't what I had in mind, when I started." Matt frowned at her. "I only wanted to explain to you the hazards of allowing the world to think you've taken Molly's place. I couldn't very well come up to you and warn you when you were working downstairs. Trying to explain something like that in a room full of people is not my way of doing things. Besides, that's not the only reason I went to all the trouble of getting you alone." His frown deepened. "I thought I should try to make up for our missed wedding night."

He stared into her eyes as he sighed, adding, "And, you push me away. Is that any way for a new bride to treat her husband?"

"Started? Missed wedding night? What do you mean, all the trouble you went to? What are you talking about?" Julie questioned him as she moved a few paces away, trying to break the growing hold his eyes had on her. She had to fight the fascination she felt when she watched his eyes change from a dark color to bright gold as he spoke.

Matt's sudden and unexpected appearance wasn't making it any easier for her to sneak away. Turning she faced him with her hands on her hips and declared, "I may be a new bride, and you, my husband, but I'll be damned if I am going to act as though I'm grateful for your veiled insults! One minute you all but call me a whore, and the next you expect me to fall into your arms grateful that you have found the time for me!"

Matt loved the way she held herself so erect when she was indignant. She looked magnificent. Her cheeks were flushed with temper and her eyes shot sparks as she glared at him. He knew he shouldn't say it, but he did anyway, just to see her reaction. "Did you miss me?"

"Miss you! I was glad you were gone, and out of my way!" Julie exclaimed heatedly. "I was finally able to attend to some of my work without your interference! As far as you're concerned, only your time is important. Mine matters little to you. You have consistently taken it for granted since the day we met that I can blithely"—she waved her hand in the air as she spoke— "rearrange my schedule and responsibilities to suit you. This is a perfect example!"

"It is?" Now Matt was enjoying himself.

What she said was perfectly true. It wasn't fair of him to expect her to drop everything anytime he wanted something. But he was not about to tell her she was right. That might make the discussion broader than he wanted it to be, at least for tonight.

"You say you want to make it up to me for missing our wedding night. Heaven alone knows why you feel you have to make it up to me! But you have forgotten, I still have a business to run!" Julie threw both her hands into the air with exasperation.

Matt's words had started a chain reaction of feelings she could not ignore. Once she had started telling him what she thought of him and his actions she could not stop.

When she had first seen him walking toward her, all she could think of was that somehow he had found out about her plan to leave and investigate on her own. The possibility had frightened her. But hearing what he said and seeing his attitude had changed her fright into outrage. Now, she was so mad at him she didn't know what to think! He hadn't said a word about knowing anything about her plan. He had only tossed warnings and insults at her while he tried to make love to her! She didn't believe a word of his explanation and trusted his motives even less. What was he up to?

Matt viewed her outburst with zestful appreciation. She had let him have it with both barrels and still was primed for more. She was quite a woman!

Unfortunately, if he hoped to carry out his intentions of making passionate love to her for the remainder of the night, he would have to try to calm her down. If he did not, the only passion expended would be in argument.

"Have you any idea how hard it was to convince Pearl and Mae to tell you that it was expected you would take over all of Molly's duties." He shook his head. "Then I had to wait for the right time to have Mae tell you there was a special customer waiting upstairs." He tried to enlist her sympathy for all the effort he had gone to on her behalf.

His voice drew a picture of pained effort, all for naught, as he said, "Believe me, it hasn't been easy getting you alone like this!" He tilted his head slightly to the side and looked at her with narrowed eyes. "And, now that I have, I am beginning to wonder if it was worth the trouble. If, I'd known you'd be this upset about my absence last night—"

"That's not why I'm upset!" she sputtered. "Wait!" she commanded as his words sank in. "All this was your idea! But, why?"

"Molly thought it was a sure way to get you alone," Matt responded with a grin.

"Molly! You discussed this with her!" Julie spun

205

around in a circle, her hands in the air beseeching the heavens to save her. He'd done it to her again! She was the last to know! Stopping to face him, she glared at him, saying, "I can't believe you deliberately had the girls trick me into believing I was expected to . . . to—"

Her words were cut off as Matt reached over and pulled her into his arms and began to kiss her, saying, "Has anyone ever told you that you talk too much?"

Julie pulled her lips free and said, "And you listen only when it suits you!" Pushing against his chest with her hands, she struggled to break free of his grip. "Did it ever occur to you to ask me if we could be alone? All this elaborate trouble you complain about might have been avoided that way. Besides which, I find it hard to believe you engineered all this merely to have some time alone with me. Now, what is going on here!"

"If I had asked, would you have said yes?" Matt questioned her softly.

"That would have depended on when you asked," Julie replied reasonably, still trying to break free of his embrace.

"I thought so," Matt said as he nuzzled her neck. "My way is better. You never have time for anything, but work."

"Your way! Since when is your way the only way?" she demanded. "In case you've forgotten, we are in business together. I haven't forgotten! And I've been trying the best I can to keep it from falling apart!" Julie protested through clenched teeth as Matt's tantalizing teasing of her neck awoke the first fingers of desire in her.

She tried to ignore the soft ache that began to tiptoe

across her nerve endings. It was a battle of determined effort on her part. She was not going to give in! He hadn't listened to a word she'd said about her time and responsibilities, yet he still expected her to fall into his arms. He was impossible!

As she fought her own growing response, she tried to think of some way to make her escape. Matt's touch made thinking difficult—the teasing way his lips brushed hers, his hand caressing the soft swell of her breast through her dress. She could not deny the love she felt for him, but there was too much danger involved if she allowed herself to succumb to it now.

There was no way she was going to allow him to get away with his cavalier attitude toward her. She refused to subordinate herself to him merely because they were married! She could not live that way. There had to be more to a relationship than that for her to be happy. Much more was at stake here than her only wanting to investigate on her own.

At the sound of Matt locking the door, her plans to leave at midnight had suffered an unexpected blow. His words had delivered a blow of a different kind. He had lit the fuse of her temper and now he was reaping the results.

She could tell by the way he was behaving that he had plans for them that did not coincide with her plans for the night. She would have to think of a way to stall him before the night was spent in trying to keep him from bedding her. If she allowed him to make love to her now, she would lose more than her chance to leave!

Matt wished things had not taken the turn they had. He had wanted the time alone with Julie, had wanted to speak with her and tell her how he really felt about her.

He wanted them to have hours undisturbed, in which to make love and begin their marriage as they should.

He felt Julie stiffen in his arms and leaned back to look down at her questioningly. "You're really upset with me aren't you?"

"I think I have more than enough reason to be," Julie answered him. "You will be wasting your time, if you think kissing me is the way to make me less angry," she warned him.

"We'll see about that." Matt grinned as though she had issued him a challenge instead of a warning.

Before she could move away, he reached out and, pulling her closely against him, began to kiss her. His strong hands molded her hips against him and she could feel the heat of his desire. She steeled herself for the onslaught of his lips, but was unprepared for the gentleness of his touch.

She had expected him to take what he wanted roughly and as quickly as he could. Instead, he was acting as though he had all the time in the world, as though nothing mattered more than his slow arousal of her desire.

When his lips moved to her ear and he began to nip at it, as he blew tiny puffs of air at its sensitive shell, Julie opened her eyes and fought the increasing tingle of pleasure that was flowing through her veins. She could not allow her body to rule her mind!

No, she insisted to herself! She was stronger than this. She would not allow the pleasure his lips and hands promised to sway her into giving herself to him.

She looked behind Matt and saw the immense brass bed with the mirrored ceiling above. Into her mind flashed images of the two of them entwined in each others arms, making love, and the twin scene that would be reflected from above. Blinking quickly to force the sensuous images from her mind, she pulled her eyes from the beckoning expanse of the bed. Her eyes narrowed slightly as she saw the table next to it, upon it an ornate china vase and flowers. She could feel her control beginning to weaken and she knew she would have to act soon if she were to be able to live with herself.

It took great effort for her to do what she did next. This was not the way she wanted things to be. But if she intended to go through with her plan, she had no other choice. She allowed herself to become pliant in his arms and to lean against him.

He held her a moment before whispering in her ear, "I prefer this to fighting. Don't you?"

She couldn't trust her voice and her knees were beginning to feel weak. She didn't say a word as he slowly led her to the side of the bed. It wasn't fair that he should affect her like this, while he seemed perfectly in control, she thought wildly.

Glancing out of the corner of her eye, she saw the bedside table behind her, and as Matt leaned across her to pull back the covers on the immense bed, she acted swiftly. Reaching for the china vase, she lifted it and brought it crashing down on his head. He slumped soundlessly onto the bed, wet flowers scattered around him.

Setting the still-intact vase back on the table, she was filled with remorse. She hadn't wanted any of this to happen. Leaning over him, she reached into his pocket and withdrew the key to the door. Palming the key in a tight grasp, she looked down at his unconscious form.

Laying her free hand against his chest, she felt the steady beat of his heart and saw the slow rise and fall of his breathing. He was still alive, but he would be madder than hell when he regained consciousness and realized what she had done. Without thinking, she moved one of the pillows under his head as though to cushion his anger.

Julie knew she was committed now. She hurried to the door and unlocked it. Carefully stepping out into the hallway, she glanced to the right and left to make sure her exit was unobserved. The muted chiming of a clock in one of the rooms signaled midnight, and lent haste to her feet as she moved quickly toward her room.

Once inside, she closed the door heaving a sigh of relief. She had made it so far. Now to change clothes and implement her plan of escape.

It took her little time to change; she had left a dark skirt and a shirtwaist of plain design close at hand. Grabbing her brush, she quickly removed the pins from her elegant hairstyle. Brushing her hair into a long curtain down her back, she swiftly parted it and began to plait it into two thick braids which she coiled at the nape of her neck and pinned securely. One last look around the room to see if she had forgotten anything and she was ready.

Cracking her door open, she peeked out to see if anyone was nearby. The hallway appeared deserted. Knowing its empty state could change at any moment, Julie slipped through the door and moved quickly toward the back stairs that led down to the kitchen below.

Descending the staircase, she paused near the bottom to listen and see if the way was clear for her to make a break for the back door. She could hear the sounds of the crowded main room spilling into the kitchen, but the kitchen itself was quiet. She laid her ear against the wall on her left. She could not hear anything from the storeroom that was on the other side. Taking a deep breath, she moved down the remaining steps to the kitchen floor.

She was about to reach for the handle on the back door when she heard the sound of boots scraping against the wooden floor leading from the main room to the kitchen. Startled, she jumped back onto the bottom step of the back stairs and crouched down hoping to go unnoticed by whomever was coming.

The footsteps sounded thunderous in her ears. Or was that the frightened pounding of her own heart she heard?

Her attention was riveted on the kitchen. She recognized the thick arm of Lukes as he reached out and opened the storeroom door. She sat frozen in fright, praying that he wouldn't find her and begin asking unanswerable questions as to why she was crouched on the service stairs. One look at the way she was dressed and he would know something wasn't right. A soft sigh escaped her as he moved into the storeroom, unaware of her presence.

She could hear the clinking of bottles and the grunt of effort as Lukes moved cases of liquor closer to the storeroom door.

Business must be brisk tonight; she had to stifle a nervous laugh at the incongruous thought.

It was clear to Julie that now was her best chance to sneak out the back door. Lukes would not be there much longer and, she had been lucky to arrive on the scene during one of the infrequent lulls in the normally busy kitchen.

She moved silently toward the door. Without hesitating, she opened it and slipped out onto the darkened porch. Her action had been taken none too soon. Lukes chose the next instant to move from the storeroom, carrying three cases of what looked like empty bottles. He turned toward the back stairway and lowering the cases to the floor stacked them near the wall at the bottom of the stairs.

Julie flattened herself against the side of the building and watched as Lukes moved back to the storeroom and made two more trips to stack cases by the stairs.

A fine sheen of perspiration coated her body as Julie realized she hadn't moved a moment too soon. One second longer in her hiding place and she would have been caught!

She shivered in the damp mist that shrouded the night air and lay its clammy fingers on her skin. It was cold and uncomfortable, but she knew it was her ally. It would help to hide her as she made her way toward Chinatown. She shivered again as she realized it would also hide anyone who tried to follow her.

She knew the weather-roughened porch was not a silent pathway to freedom. Its warped planking had a song of its own to sing if stepped on incorrectly. Because of the misty darkness around her, Julie couldn't see clearly enough beyond the splashed halo of light from the kitchen to cross the porch and go down the steps into the alleyway without a sound. Not wanting to test her luck any further, she waited, immobile, until Lukes had finished and left the kitchen area.

Seeing him leave, she quickly scampered across the porch, her light footsteps leaving a trail of groans and squeaks. Reaching the dirt of the alleyway, she hurried off to her right, to be quickly swallowed by the mist and the deep shadows of the night.

She tried to leave a convoluted trail to confuse anyone who might be following her. She didn't think she was being followed but could not be certain. Lee Tang was not an easy man to fool.

Confidently, she made her way through the maze of alleyways and back streets of the Plaza, glad that they held no hidden terrors for her. She had played and raced through these same lanes as a child. She used her familiarity with them to her advantage, doubling and, once, tripling back upon her route to see if she was being followed. She maintained this circuitous path until she neared the edges of Chinatown.

Chinatown held no fear of the unknown for Julie. She knew its ins and outs, its laws, even its history. Sacramento Street or Tong Yan Gai, as it was called by its Oriental residents, was the birthplace of the first cluster of eight hundred Chinese to settle in San Francisco.

With time and effort, they settled and spread to Grand and Kearney, and soon Chinatown was born. Since its birth and under the direction of the ruling families of the Six Companies, Chinatown had grown to thirty-five retail stores, five popular and bustling restaurants and seventeen pharmacies. All established to serve the Chinese population of San Francisco, but also catering to the needs of its neighbors. Wah Lee's laundry at the corner of Washington and Grant, with its sea of washtubs, worked day and night keeping the clothes of San Francisco clean.

Julie felt a kind of peace begin to settle over her as she moved through the noisy and bustling panorama of the Chinese quarter. It was always alive with the noise of many dialects and the bustle of commerce. Some said Chinatown never slept. The colorful decorations with their fluttering ribbons, distinctive calligraphy and brightly hued ornamentation drew the eye from exotic shop to exotic shop. Many a San Franciscan spent time lost in wonder as he moved through this self-contained civilization with its ties to the Manchu government in China.

It was not unusual for the Chinese people to maintain their obedience to such a faraway power. Many of them still had families in China. And it was not unusual for business ties to stretch the great distance across the Pacific Ocean to the homeland. Their sense of duty, honor and country would shame many a casual citizen of San Francisco.

Turning onto Dupont Street Julie heard the sound of Chinese music, which hurt most Western ears, and she glanced over her shoulder to see if she were being followed. To her, all this was only a journey to see old friends. None of the well-known danger of Chinatown at night affected her. She was as safe as if she were at home in her own room. She and her father were under the protection of the Kong Chow family, one of the most powerful among the Six Companies. Lee Tang was Kong Chow's grandson and heir apparent, and it was to this family's seat she was heading.

The sound of fighting behind her made her turn

around. She saw two Orientals beating a swarthy man dressed in seaman's garb. She quickened her pace, not wanting to see whether this was a private matter between the three men or whether the Orientals were appointed shadows of her safety, intercepting someone on her trail.

She saw her destination ahead and moved toward it with renewed confidence. Soon she would be able to ask some of the same questions her father may have asked and more of her own. She hoped the answers would be the ones she sought.

Reaching the gateway of the whitewashed house, she knocked. A small panel in the solid gate opened and the gatekeeper asked her to state her business.

It took much effort on her part, but she was able to answer him in what she hoped was understandable Chinese. In her urgency to get there, she had forgotten that few of the household spoke or understood any English. The panel closed and the sound of locks being drawn reassured her.

The gate swung open on well-oiled hinges and a wizened hand beckoned for her to enter the courtyard. She did so, leaving the cacophony of the business district behind her as she stepped into a pool of serene silence.

The sounds of crickets chirping and of water trickling from a small fountain in a corner of the garden were all she heard as the gate closed behind her.

Following the old gatekeeper, she entered the foyer of the large house and sat down where he pointed. As she waited in tense anticipation, she looked around the stark room. It was almost barren of decoration. Its white walls held only two hand-painted scenes of the

Chinese countryside on delicate-looking scrolls. Against the wall facing her was an intricately simple flower arrangement that rested only a few feet from the floor on a highly lacquered black table. Surprisingly, she found the sparsity of decorations restful to the eye and calming to the mind.

She did not have long to wait. Massive double doors at the end of the long anteroom opened and a tall, muscular figure emerged.

The blood draining from her face, Julie rose from her seat and exclaimed, "Lee Tang!"

Chapter Fifteen

LEE TANG CAME OVER TO HER AND LOOKED DOWN AT her knowingly as she sank to her seat.

"Miss Julie," he said in his deep melodious voice, "did you truly think you could elude my guard?"

"Yes," Julie found herself answering meekly.

A wide grin split his normally stoic face and Julie was astonished to hear laughter come booming from him. It resounded in the austerely furnished anteroom, making her ears ache.

Placing his hands on his hips, he grinned down at her, mirth lingering in his dark eyes as he said, "We of the Kong Chow family have been guardians of far wilier than you for generations. There was no hope of your eluding my watchful eye."

"Oh!" Julie said to him in surprised disappointment. "You knew all the time?"

"Yes. I also knew of your destination. Where else could you go in San Francisco to obtain the information you so ardently wish to have?" Lee Tang returned.

"But how did you know?" Julie questioned. "I was so careful not to make you suspect anything."

"Exactly." Lee Tang nodded. "You should have acted as you normally do, Miss Julie."

"But I did!" she protested.

"That is not so." He shook his head. "Not once did you complain of being a caged pet. Not once did you tell me you were more than capable of watching out for yourself. This is not normal for you," Tang explained. "I became suspicious. It did not take this one long to determine the reason for such odd behavior."

"It didn't?" Julie gasped.

She had never heard him say so much at one time in all the years she'd known him. His every word radiated confidence and a sense of power. She had never dreamed what lay hidden beneath his cool mask of inscrutability.

"The lion does not growl when he is not hungry. The caged bird does not flex his wings with joy if he is to remain caged. I knew the reason for your odd behavior. You were planning on exchanging words for action." Tang showered her with the wisdom of his logic.

Julie suddenly felt humbled and ashamed. She had never realized how transparent she must be to him.

She had been so busy rebelling against what she considered to be a threat to her independence, that she had not given a thought to how he must feel. Nor had she thought about him at all, except how to avoid him whenever possible. She had not made life easy for him.

His voice told her he was more than a mere nurse-maid to a troublesome woman. Lee Tang and his family were the guardians of emperors and dynasties!

"I am truly sorry, Lee Tang." Her eyes asked for his forgiveness. "I have been stubborn and selfish, not thinking of how you must feel. Please believe me when I say I never meant to be a burden to you or to anyone."

Lee Tang nodded briefly, his usually serious mien replacing the stranger who grinned and laughed. "It does us both honor, Miss Julie, that you have the courage to see the error of your ways and ask my pardon. I freely give it, in respect." The indulgent smile returned. "But, you have not been so great a burden, little one. Is a feather a burden to a great mountaintop? You cannot always help the way you feel and act. You are, after all, a woman."

Julie knew better than to take offense at his reference to her gender. Lee Tang and his people had a far different attitude regarding women. They had an ambivalence toward them. They accorded them respect for their power to give life but felt their very womanhood controlled their actions, not their minds, which were known to be illogical. It was felt few could make their way through life without a strong man to channel their lives and protect them from themselves.

Tang lifted her lowered chin with a finger, and said admonishingly, "You should have come and talked to me about your plans. I would have advised you. Has not my Family advised yours in the past?" He made the word family sound all powerful.

Julie saw the logic of what Tang said. If she had gone to him, he would have advised her. But she had unfairly placed him in the same category as Matt and Carlo. She had taken it for granted that he would side with them against her.

"What am I to do now? Return home?" she asked him.

Another surprising smile lit up his face as though he relished his response. "No. I have consulted with the Head of my Family. It has been decided that, though you are but a woman, you are not as foolish as most. Your father taught you well. And as is known to happen with some women, you do have flashes of insight."

"I do?" Julie's eyes widened at the news.

He paused a moment to watch the play of emotions that crossed her face before saying, "Now is the time to exchange actions for words. I have been given the information you came here to find."

"What!" Julie had not expected things to turn out like this. "Are you allowed to tell me?" she asked him, fearful that she was to be left in ignorance.

"I am entrusted with the safety of your life and the location of what you seek," Tang replied.

"Do you know who killed my father?" Julie rose to her feet in anxious dread.

"Of that matter, I cannot say for certain," Tang told her. "I can only take you to the place your father asked about on his last visit with my Family. Maybe there you will find the answers to your remaining questions."

"The Barracoon?" Julie asked hopefully.

"Yes. I have been given the secret location of the

Barracoon." Tang's face hardened. "It has been decided by the Six Companies that this place brings danger to us all and should be exposed. Its existence here in Chinatown condemns us in the eyes of San Francisco. It should be expelled from our midst before it brings trouble upon our heads."

Julie's eyes widened in disbelief. "Am I expected to be the one to expose it?"

"You are only one of the instruments of its exposure. Those who follow you will see that its days are numbered," Tang explained to her cryptically.

"Follow me? I'm afraid, I don't understand." Julie frowned.

Tang smiled at her as if he knew something she did not and replied, "You will in time."

Julie knew it was useless to pursue this question any further. He had told her all he was going to for now.

"Where is the Barracoon?" she asked him.

"I will take you there only if you give me your solemn promise to listen and obey me when I tell you to do something," Tang warned her. "The danger there is great, and without your word, I cannot be responsible for your safety."

"But, I have to go!" Julie protested. "If I am to find out what I can about my father's murder, I must see this place and find out, if I can, who the people are who run it. One of them may have ordered my father killed."

"This has been discussed by my Family. It is known to them that you seek to avenge your father. My Family feels, though this is the duty of a son, you, as a true daughter of your father, have the obligation upon your head."

"True daughter? Why am I called that? I have an older sister," Julie said.

Tang looked at her as though she hadn't spoken, ignoring her question as he asked, "Do I have your solemn word?"

"Yes," Julie quickly replied. This might be her last chance to find out anything and she was not going to miss it.

"The place you seek is in a basement room under a joss house in St. Louis Alley," Tang informed her. "We will go there tonight. Our informants tell us there is to be a sale."

"But . . ." Julie quieted as Tang looked at her. The time for talk was over.

She followed him as he led the way from the anteroom out into the courtyard. She waited as he opened the window panel on the heavy gate and scanned the street outside.

Closing the panel, he turned to her and said in a low voice, "Stay close to me and remember your promise to obey what I say."

She had every intention of staying as close to him as possible. For the first time in her life, Chinatown frightened her.

Tang moved through the gate and she followed. Their route took them through dark paths and alleyways she never knew existed. They paused at every corner as Tang's eyes watched for danger.

She was hard pressed not to trip on the garbage strewn in her path or over the opium-stupored bodies of those tossed from the smoky dens.

Time became meaningless and Julie concentrated all her attention on placing one foot in front of the other as she tried to keep up with Tang's swift pace through the everpresent mist.

As they neared St. Louis Alley, Tang kept to the deeper shadows and motioned for her to do the same. From here on, they would be in the most danger of discovery.

Julie had heard tales of others who had tried to find the Barracoon and never lived to talk about it. Their bodies had been found with the eyes gouged out and the tongues severed, as if their killers would deprive them of repeating what they may have seen even in death. Her father had explained that such mutilation was a warning to any who might be foolish enough to follow in their footsteps.

They halted between two houses and Tang motioned with his hand for her to wait where she was. She crouched against the side of the whitewashed wall and shivered as the weeping eaves of the ramshackle house dripped cold beads of moisture onto her neck and shoulders.

Tang disappeared into the mist and Julie felt isolated. She strained her ears trying to follow the path of his silent feet but she could hear nothing except the persistent dripping of the mist-induced rain off the surrounding roofs. She fought the urge to follow Tang. He was her only way in or out of this area. She didn't think she could find her way back through the many paths and alleys now; but he had told her to wait, and she had given her word to obey.

The deserted street in front of her was a frightening contrast to the Chinatown she had always known. The mist and darkness made everything take on a ghostly aura.

She had been waiting for what seemed like ages when a large hand appeared from behind her and covered her mouth to prevent her from screaming.

She struggled as an arm wound around her middle and she was lifted bodily from the ground. The hand across her mouth smothered her cries. She tried to bite it, but she could not get a good grip with her teeth. She kicked back with her feet, hoping to throw her captor off balance. One foot connected with what felt like a kneecap and she heard a loud grunt of pain. But the arm about her did not loosen its hold.

She was being carried across the narrow street when Tang suddenly reappeared from out of nowhere. He launched himself at her captor, knocking him to the wet ground.

The man's hold on her tightened and she went down with him, hitting the ground with a jolt, the pins from her hair raining about her. Her plaits uncoiled and fell about her face onto the dirt beneath her. The air was knocked from her lungs, and she could not breathe as she felt Tang drag her captor off her.

The sound of a fist hitting flesh filled the night air. Tang quickly followed the first blow with another. His opponent was returning his blows, adding vicious kicks wherever he could.

Julie rolled free of the fighting men and drew her knees protectively to her chest as she tried to pull the air back into her tortured lungs.

Slowly her lungs were restored and she could breathe again, though painfully. She watched in horror as the two men rolled and fought on the ground a short way from where she lay. She prayed that Tang would be the victor. She did not want to think of what her fate might be if he were beaten.

Feeling dangerously exposed should her would-be kidnapper have friends, she crawled toward what she hoped was the relative safety of the alley.

Taking up a position near its corner house, she leaned against the rough foundation for support and returned her gaze to the silent battle being waged on the deserted street.

The mist had lifted slightly, so she had a clear view of the two men as they wrestled and strained to best one another. Tang was the larger of the two, but what his opponent lacked in height, he more than made up for in strength and endurance.

It was eerie the way neither of them uttered a sound even as painful blows were landed. Tang pinned his foe to the ground with the strength of his legs. The pinned man flip-flopped like a fish out of water, trying to break Tang's grip.

Tang was relentless. He tightened his scissor grip and Julie could hear a crack as though a bone had snapped. She then realized with fright they were fighting to the death. Tang would have to kill this man or be killed himself!

Fear clutched at her throat. She had to do something! She couldn't lie there and watch Tang fight for his life alone. But what could she do? She looked around her in search of something she could use as a weapon. There were only rocks of various sizes and shapes left over from the building of the foundation of the house.

Reaching over she picked up one of them and tried it for weight. It fit nicely in her hand and was not too heavy to throw with accuracy. She looked back over at the combatants, eyeing her chances of hitting the right man. In the dim light and mist, she would have to wait for an opening or risk hitting Tang instead.

She rose on her knees to a crouch, biding her time. She had little doubt she could hit her target, given the opportunity. She had spent many an hour throwing rocks at makeshift targets and skimming stones across the water as a child.

As she watched and waited, she saw the shorter man reach down and pull a knife from his side. He raised his arm in the air to bring the knife down into Tang's back.

Julie cried out a warning to Tang as she let fly with the rock she held.

The rock smashed into the villain's wrist and the knife went spinning from his hand to land harmlessly out of reach.

Tang had heard Julie's cry and reacted instinctively, bringing the flat of his hand upward into the man's face. A horrible gurgling sound cut through the night as the blow killed him instantly.

The sound of feet running in their direction gave them no time to recover and regain their strength. Julie's cry had alerted the dead man's companions.

"Run!" Tang ordered her. "I will hold them off."

Julie did not need to be told twice. She knew she was no match for a grown man and lacked Tang's skills at defense.

She spun away from the sound of advancing death and ran as fast as her legs would carry her. She had no idea where she was going, twisting and turning down alleyways blindly. All she knew was she had to put as much distance as she could between herself and her pursuers. Her chest began to burn with the effort it was costing her to breathe. She would have to stop and rest soon . . . or collapse.

Rounding the corner of one of the alleyways, she grabbed the side of one of the buildings for support. Her lungs were laboring and fire was burning in her chest. She looked about her trying to find her bearings as she gasped for breath.

Tears of frustration sprang to her eyes as she realized she had been running in circles! She was almost back at where she had left Tang!

Stumbling to the next corner, she looked out onto the street. She could clearly see Lee Tang struggling with two men, while a third came up from behind him and hit him on the back of the head. As Lee Tang slumped to the ground, so did Julie's hope of escape.

She prayed he wasn't dead, but he remained motionless on the wet ground. The three he'd struggled with stood talking amongst themselves. Julie wondered if it was about her they spoke. One of them turned and stared in her direction as though he could feel her presence. She withdrew as much as she could, attempting to avoid his peering gaze while still keeping an eye on the fallen Tang.

After a short time, the three finished their discussion. Two of them bent down and grabbed the still-unconscious Tang by the arms and began to drag him with them as they followed the third. They headed off in the opposite direction from where Julie lay hidden.

She had to keep them in sight! Crouching down as low to the ground as she could, Julie followed the trio and their defenseless cargo. She was careful not to creep up too close and risk the chance of being spotted.

She trailed them for a number of minutes, through the twisting and turning avenues of this part of Chinatown, until they came to a halt near a nondescript-looking building.

As she watched, she saw what appeared to be an argument of some kind break out between two of the men. There was wild gesticulating and their angry voices drifted back to where she had hidden herself.

As far as she could decipher from their pointing fingers, the argument centered around Lee Tang and whether to take him inside the building or not.

Their problem was solved for them when the door to the building opened and another man stepped out. He must have been someone in authority over the three, for he moved with the air of one in charge. Seeing him, all three hit the ground on their knees and lowered their heads to the dirt.

Ignoring this display, the newcomer looked at their prisoner. Having seen all he cared to see, he turned and asked one of the men a question, which was quickly answered with much bowing and scraping. Whoever this newcomer was, he was important, Julie thought as she watched.

It was but a few seconds later when two of the men rose from their knees and grabbed Lee Tang by the arms. All four disappeared with their unconscious burden into the building, leaving the street as quiet and deserted as before.

She couldn't lose track of Lee Tang! She had to know where they were taking him. She had to know if he were still alive! He hadn't moved since he had been hit from behind.

Cautiously, she crept from her hiding place and

scurried across the narrow street. Flattening herself against the far side of the building, away from the door, she waited to see if anyone came out.

As she waited, she caught the faint sound of music and an eerie singsong chanting. It was coming from inside the rear of the building. Turning, she looked in the direction of the sound, trying to pinpoint its origin. Dropping to the ground, she crawled on all fours to a narrow window at the far end of the wall.

There was a narrow chink of light coming from the small gap in the heavy curtains which covered the ground-level window. Lying almost flat to the ground, Julie peered through it into the room beyond. What she saw made her skin crawl. She had found the Barracoon.

It was a basement room filled with smoke and people. There were chairs scattered haphazardly in small groups around a center platform. Toward the back of the platform stood four naked and obviously terrified young women, their hands bound together in front of them. At the front, there was a lone girl who seemed to be fourteen or fifteen years old. Her bound hands were being held high over her head by a large mean-looking woman who pointed and pinched at the young girl's breasts as she said something that made the crowd laugh.

A man Julie recognized as one of the nastier brothel owners rose to his feet from the audience and said something to the large woman. The woman nodded and motioned for him to come closer to the platform.

He came right up to the very edge and looked up at the young girl. Without a word, he reached out and grabbed her by the leg. She tried to struggle and was hit in the face by the big woman who held her.

The man ignored the struggle as he forced the girl's legs apart and stuck his hand between them. He moved it around for a second or two as the young girl writhed with pain and embarrassment.

Julie felt bile rise into her throat as nausea overcame her. What she was seeing was far worse than she had ever imagined it would be. Her teeth began to chatter from her nervous reaction. She leaned away from the window as her insides churned and she retched onto the dirt. Everything the man had done had been so unemotional and cruel. It was obvious to Julie that he did not even consider the young girl a human being, only a piece of merchandise to be inspected before purchase.

Returning her gaze to the window, she watched the brothel owner with loathing in her eyes. Apparently satisfied that the young girl was still a virgin, he pulled his hand free and returned to his seat.

Once he was seated, the big woman nodded to a small Chinese man who stood slightly behind her. He moved to the front of the platform and began the singsong chanting that had attracted Julie's attention earlier.

Next to the platform was a table set up with a cashbox and scales. A flinty-eyed man was measuring out the weight of a pouch of gold dust on the scales while a tall slender woman watched. It was Ah Toy.

Julie recognized her by her beauty and the proud way she stood. If she had had any doubt the tall Oriental woman was the infamous Ah Toy, one look at her feet would have identified her. They were not unusually small for her height. The majority of Chinese women of her rank and power all had tiny feet, their growth stunted by the tight bindings that they had worn since childhood. In spite of her rich clothing, which stood out against the dirty atmosphere of the basement like a splash of sunlight on a gray day, Julie could feel the danger of the woman. She was well known for her vicious temper and unyielding perseverance in protecting what was hers. Even at this distance, she frightened Julie.

The small gap she peered through limited her view of the room and she could not see everyone inside. She scanned the room, averting her eyes from the platform and the grisly tableau it held, searching to see if she recognized anyone else. She noted three or four of the owners of dives her father had been intent on closing, but none of them was important enough to be anything more than a customer.

Julie's attention was drawn to the far side of the room by the movement of three people toward a curtained alcove in a corner of the room. Two of them were moderately well-dressed men and the third was George Baldwin.

Julie was not surprised to see him. She had always suspected he was heavily involved in the dealings that went on here. Because of his and Ah Toy's presence, Julie wondered if anyone else of major importance might be there.

The singsong chant halted and Julie's eyes were drawn back to the platform. She saw the young girl, tears streaming down her face, being dragged from the platform by a fat woman. She recognized the woman as a procurer for the Countess.

The Countess ran one of the richest brothels in San Francisco and was not cruel to her girls. Many of the Countess's ladies, as she preferred to call them, had been known to marry into the higher strata of San Francisco society.

Julie knew it would be small consolation to the young girl if she knew, but her final destination could have been far worse had someone else bought her.

The noise level grew as the large woman in charge dragged forward twin girls. In their late teens, they both had long black hair that cascaded down their backs to their hips. Their skin was translucent and glowed even in the poor light of the basement.

They were not as frightened as the first girl. They smiled and posed for the audience of buyers. Obviously, this was not new to them. From the way they postured and encouraged the buyers, Julie guessed they were trying to drive up the bidding.

When one overeager buyer reached across the platform floor and tried to grab at one of them, he received a kick in the face for his efforts. Julie cringed as she waited to see the large woman in charge discipline the girl who had kicked him. She was surprised instead to see her laugh at the buyer.

As the singsong chanting of the auctioneer began again, Julie rose from her prone position on the cold wet ground and sat with her knees to her chin as she thought over what she had seen. Her skin crawled with a clammy feeling of fear. She was normally not easily frightened, but this was a situation she had never encountered before in her life. She could feel her heartbeat racing as though she had been running, the palms of her hands were sweaty and her teeth still clicked together.

When she had first discovered the narrow window, she had hoped to learn where Lee Tang had been taken. Instead she had found the Barracoon, and she was sickened at what she had seen. None of the rumors or tales that surrounded this hellhole had even come close to the reality.

Having seen the Barracoon firsthand, she realized the immensity of what she had so foolishly thought she could deal with alone.

She had seen Baldwin and Ah Toy in what appeared to be positions of authority. They and whoever else was behind this operation were far more powerful and dangerous than she had imagined. They controlled the lives of all who came near them. They held the power of life and death in their hands.

She grimaced as she thought to herself, what a fool I am! She had naively thought finding the Barracoon was the answer to all her problems, that finding it would tell her who had killed her father.

She'd never stopped to think about what would happen after she'd found it. All her energies had been directed toward sneaking away from the casino and searching for this hidden location as though it were the missing piece to a giant puzzle. Some detective she'd turned out to be! Lee Tang was now a prisoner. She was reduced to peeking through windows like a voyeur. What good had it done her?

She hit her knee with her fist in lonely frustration. Without Lee Tang to guide her, Julie knew she might not be able to find her way back to safety.

But, that did not mean she could not try her best to evade capture while she hunted for a safe place in the area to hide. Come dawn, she would find her way back to the Land of Gold.

But what then? She couldn't go to the authorities.

They'd turned a blind eye on the Barracoon from its beginning. They would be no help.

Julie was so involved in self-recrimination and her plans of escape that she failed to hear the approaching footsteps. Terror washed through her and a scream broke from her lips as she was grabbed and dragged roughly to her feet. She saw only a fist as it lashed out to connect with her jaw before blackness descended.

Chapter Sixteen

Slowly regaining consciousness, Matt stirred and moaned as alarm bells went off in his head. Opening his eyes, he realized that he was lying at an angle across the bed, with, of all things, a pillow under his head! Why? What had happened? Had they been attacked? Where was Julie? The questions only increased the pounding in his head.

Rising to an upright position evoked another moan, and he rested his aching head in his hands as he remembered. He had been bent over the bed, pulling back the covers, when something had crashed into the back of his head. Julie had hit him on the head with something! Why? And with what had she hit him? Lifting his head from his hands, he saw the wilted flowers strewn about the bed and the empty vase resting on the bedside table. At least she hadn't broken the vase, he thought. But he wasn't too sure about his head as another groan slipped from his lips.

But why, he wondered? She had not been faking the desire he'd seen in her eyes or felt in the way her body had responded to his touch. He knew she had been mad, but he didn't think she had been mad enough to hit him. There had to be another explanation for all of this.

Where was Julie now? He looked around the room seeing nothing but his reflection thrown back at him from all angles. What he saw did nothing to make him feel any better. He was a sorry sight, his clothes all wrinkled and damp and a night's growth of beard on his face.

Rising slowly to his feet, he stumbled over to the door. Opening it, he looked out onto the corridor. It was empty, and from the lack of sound filtering up from downstairs, he knew the casino was closed.

Using the wall for support, he made his way toward Julie's room. He had more than a few words to say to her.

Reaching her room, he opened the door and went inside. Viewing the room, the words he started to say died in his throat. Her evening clothes were strewn across the bed, and her wardrobe door was hanging open. Julie was nowhere in sight, and her bed had not been slept in.

"Damn!" he exploded sending shock waves through his throbbing skull. She was gone! He knew instinctively that she had gone off on her own to look for her father's killers.

236

Leaving her room, he made his way back to his, intending to change and try to follow her. Anger at her stubborn foolhardiness cleared his head of any lasting effects from the blow he'd received.

"The little idiot!" he muttered. When he caught up with her, she would be sorry she had ever met him. He had warned her not interfere, that it was too dangerous for a woman alone.

Reaching the office, he walked straight through to his room, unbuttoning his damp shirt as he went. Moving into his bedroom, he threw his discarded shirt onto the bed and reached toward his dresser for a fresh one.

Sitting atop the dresser, was an envelope addressed to him. Ripping it open, his eyes went quickly to the signature at the bottom of the page. It was from Lee Tang. Why would Tang be leaving him a note, he frowned as his eyes moved to the top of the page to read its contents.

Tang explained in concise words that he had suspected Julie might try to go off on her own and that he had a fair idea of her destination. He would be intercepting her there.

He then left instructions for Matt to bring Carlo and follow him.

The grim lines on Matt's face did not ease at reading this news. Even though he knew the competent Tang was with Julie, he was still angry.

Angry with himself for not anticipating Julie's actions, as had Tang. But he could not in all fairness stay angry at Julie. He realized that one of the reasons he loved her as much as he did was because of her independent nature. He should have known she would be unable to sit back and watch while others found out who had killed her father. He cursed himself for not seeing this sooner.

If she and Tang had gone to Chinatown, Matt had a good idea of their destination there. This knowledge made the adrenaline level rise in his blood. If his guess was right, they would be dealing with more danger than even Tang could handle alone.

Glancing over to the window, he noticed for the first time that it was bright daylight outside, and his frown deepened. It was far later than he'd thought. Surely they should have returned by now?

Tossing the note back on the dresser, Matt quickly changed clothes and left to search for Carlo. As he moved from room to room in the bordello, hunting for Carlo, he went over Tang's instructions in his mind.

Matt was to go to the Kong Chow family in Chinatown. They would be able to tell him where Lee Tang and Julie had gone.

Once he found Carlo, together they would go to the Kong Chow and see if Lee Tang and Julie were there. He hoped they would find them. If not, they were in trouble.

Matt found Carlo in Mae's room. Waking him, he told him what had happened. Carlo rose at once and quickly dressed, muttering under his breath the entire time in a mixture of English, Spanish and Italian, about the insanity of allowing women to become too independent.

The two men left the casino and headed in the direction of Chinatown. They were silent as they made their way through the noonday streets. The way they carried themselves and the grim looks on their faces discouraged even the more daring street scum from bothering them. The pair looked too dangerous and deadly to attack for the possible gain of a few coins.

Reaching the Kong Chow enclave, they were quickly ushered into the presence of the Head of the Family, Kong Woo, Tang's grandfather.

From the activity going on in the household it was obvious that something was amiss.

"Honorable Sir." Matt bowed slightly as he greeted the vigorous old man in perfect Chinese.

"It has been too long since you have honored this house with your presence, Matthew Thorn," the old gentleman responded, as he slipped into the plain shirt being held for him by a servant. "It is a bad time that draws us together again."

Lee Tang's grandfather was an older and more mature version of Tang. He had the same tall build and steely frame. His dark eyes were penetrating and reflected the power of the man. He moved with the ease and muscular grace of men half his age. Time had left its mark only in the silver stripes threading through his long pigtail.

"Tang and my wife are not here," Matt stated flatly as he took in all the activity about them.

It took but a few words with the older man to discover Lee Tang and Julie had left hours earlier to go to the Barracoon . . . and that they had not been seen since.

It was assumed by Tang's grandfather that they had been either waylaid or taken prisoner. He informed Matt of the measures he had taken once his suspicions had been confirmed by his informants.

Kong Woo had spent the morning hours in trying to arrange the return of his grandson and the daughter of his old friend through the customary method of ransom. But all his efforts had been crudely rebuffed. Rather than discouraging him as the rebuff was meant to do, it served only to fuel his anger.

He explained what he had done and the response he'd received to Matt and Carlo as the bustle of activity increased around them.

"Those in charge are barbarians without honor." He spat on the floor. "They care not for the honorable ways of negotiation and compromise. They understand only force."

Hearing the discussion between Matt and Kong Woo, Carlo understood only part of it. But, the part about force was very clear to him.

He turned to leave at once, but was stopped by Matt's hand on his arm. "Wait," Matt said. "We're not going alone. Kong Woo says it's too dangerous. We are to be accompanied by him and the men of the Kong Chow."

Julie opened her eyes and bit back the scream that started to bubble to her lips. She couldn't see a thing! Everything was black!

She blinked her eyes trying to clear them, but still she couldn't see. Lifting her head from the damp floor and turning it in all directions, she strained her eyes to focus on something, anything! All she saw was unending blackness.

She tried to sit up and lift her hands to her face, but couldn't move. Her arms were bound securely behind her back.

The way her jaw and head hurt from the blow that

had knocked her cold, she wondered if she had been struck blind!

Unable to move her hands or see with her eyes, she strained her ears to catch any sound that would tell her where she was . . . and if she were alone.

Silence slammed at her like a physical blow. The panic she felt grew and spread throughout her body, making her limbs tremble uncontrollably. This couldn't be happening! Her childhood nightmare had come true!

For months after her mother had died, Julie had suffered from the same recurring dream. She was lost in a land of total darkness, unable to find her way out and with no one to help her. She would call out for her parents, but they didn't come. She would call out for Sara, and cruel laughter would echo through the cloying blackness.

In her nightmare, the blackness became almost alive as it wrapped about her like a cocoon and tried to smother her. She would wake up screaming, bathed in cold sweat and tearing at her bedcovers to escape.

In childhood, Molly or her father would come into her room and hold her in their arms comfortingly, soothing her until the terror had gone and she had drifted back to sleep.

Now neither would come to comfort her. She was alone!

A horrible weakness hit her and she laid her face back on the floor, ignoring its damp grittiness as she fought the waves of terror that washed over her, threatening her very sanity.

"No!" she screamed in defiance of the demons that

hid in the darkness surrounding her. She knew they were there. They had always been there, waiting. Waiting for her to give in to her terror. They fed on it and grew stronger. When they were strong enough, she knew they would come for her and she would never be free of them again.

Forcing herself to breathe slowly and deeply, Julie tried to stave the demons off. Think of something else, she ordered herself!

"Pretend its a game of blind man's bluff," she whispered aloud, trying to push back the utter silence that surrounded her.

She hadn't played the game since childhood, but she had been one of the best players among the children of the Plaza.

She forced herself to remember how she'd planned out each move before acting, instead of groping fruitlessly about her as her friends had.

First, she had inspected her immediate position; then she had moved so many steps to the right and then to the left, always returning to her original position so as not to lose her bearings and become confused.

As she remembered, the terror threatening to engulf her began to fade slowly into the background. It did not go away, but lurked on the fringes ready to rush back in should she loosen her rigid control.

Finding it comforting, to whisper aloud to herself as she began to slowly inspect her prison, she questioned, "Where am I now? What am I lying on?"

Her senses answered her. The floor under her was hard and smooth like stone. It had a fine gritty covering —sand?—and it felt damp and chill against her skin and through the fabric of her skirt.

"Where have I felt something like this before?"

She kept her breathing steady and with incredible effort built a wall within herself against the lurking terror.

A small feeling of triumph helped her reinforce that wall as she said aloud, "The basement at the Land of Gold. The floor there feels like this."

This was a basement room somewhere. Was she still at the Barracoon? Or had enough time elapsed while she was unconscious for them to take her somewhere else?

"No!" she insisted aloud. She refused to become lost in questions she had no possible way of answering. She would concentrate solely on answering the most basic questions.

The time passed with agonizing slowness as Julie spent the next few hours exploring her surroundings. She had to move an inch at a time and feel her way with her feet as she crawled. When she wanted to explore anything further, she had to twist around so as to be able to use her bound hands. It was painfully awkward, but the more she learned about where she was, the less terror she felt.

When exhaustion riveted her aching body, making it too great an effort to explore any further, she lay her head down and slept. Waking later, she assembled all the information she had so painstakingly gathered.

She knew now that her prison was small, without any discernible windows, and it had a thick solid door at its entrance. The ceiling, she had painfully discovered, was low. Leaning against one of the walls, she had tried to inch herself erect. When only half erect, she had crashed quite unexpectedly into this low barrier.

There was no way for light to enter the room. The walls were all made of stone, as was the floor, and the door was tightly fitted to its frame.

Knowing this helped to expel the lurking demons in her mind; it explained the total darkness that surrounded her. She knew she was not blind, as she had originally feared.

Over in one corner, she had discovered stored goods. She had tried searching through them, but in the darkness, with her hands tied, it had proven impossible. She consoled herself with the thought that it was very doubtful that her hands, were they free, could help her to escape, for the people who held her prisoner were far too smart to lock her in a room containing anything that she could use against them.

She would have to be patient and try to work free of her bonds anyway. With her hands free, she would not feel quite so helpless. And with her hands free, she might be able to find a way of escaping.

Holding that thought uppermost in her mind, Julie grit her teeth and began the tedious and painful process of trying to loosen her bonds.

His earlier overtures ignored, Kong Woo had issued the call to the men of the Kong Chow to gather. It had taken most of the afternoon to assemble the men and plan their strategy.

Those hours had grated on Matt and Carlo's impatient nerves. Carlo had wanted to storm the Barracoon at once and rescue Julie and Lee Tang. He had listened with growing irritation as Matt and Kong Woo had sat and carefully planned out their attack.

"We are only wasting time sitting here like old

women and discussing what to do!" he had exclaimed. "I say hit them now!"

"They are expecting us to do just that." Matt tried to reason with the hot-blooded Carlo. "If we do as you say, we will more than likely get Julie and Lee Tang killed."

Matt understood how Carlo felt. The urge for action was also hot in his veins. But he knew it would be suicide to go in unprepared. He tried to make Carlo understand this by adding, "We are planning to make sure nothing like that does happen. We want Lee Tang and Julie back alive."

Carlo held his tongue after that. But he could not restrain a giant sigh of relief, when the signal was given to depart. This was more his style. He was not as patient and careful as Matt and Kong Woo. He was a man of action, not words.

Matt did not feel as patient as he seemed to Carlo. The hours spent in planning had been necessary, but they had also been a living hell for him. His first impulse had been the same as Carlo's, to storm the Barracoon and free Julie and Lee Tang. But his innate sense of danger had warned him against it.

The hours that he and Kong Woo had spent organizing and planning had been filled with the agonizing fear that they would not be in time. When the word had gone out that they were ready, a deadly calm had come over him. He was prepared to do whatever was necessary to free the woman he loved.

The lengthening shadows of early evening served as an umbrella of concealment when Matt and Carlo followed closely behind Kong Woo as they left the family enclave.

Kong Woo led the men of the Kong Chow, forty in number, through the narrow, twisting paths of the Chinese Quarter toward the Barracoon.

Those who saw them moved from their path and returned to the safety of their homes and stores, their eyes fear-widened. They were grateful that they were not the ones who'd wakened the sleeping dragon. The wrath of the Kong Chow was legendary in Chinatown.

The small army of the Kong Chow moved with the precision and silence of one man. Well-trained and deadly, they slipped between the buildings and through the area.

All communication was done by hand signals as Kong Woo deployed his men to their prearranged positions. Once set, they began the vigil which would last until nightfall.

It had been decided to wait until then so they might use darkness as a cover for their further advance. Kong Woo and Matt had agreed that it was unwise to boldly storm the Barracoon and risk the possibility of a full-scale battle that could spread throughout Chinatown, endangering the innocent.

Kong Woo had no thought of ending the Barracoon. He knew it would take more power even than that held by the Six Companies to close its doors forever. He was more concerned with the safe return of Lee Tang and of the wife of his friend, Matthew Thorn.

Julie's wrists were raw and the cords that bound her were soaked with sweat and sticky with blood.

It had taken the most intense concentration and patience to work her wrists slowly back and forth against her bonds hoping to stretch them.

She had ignored the lancing pain of the cramps that had attacked the muscles of her forearms, causing them to knot up painfully and come close to crippling her efforts. Sweat coated her body and rolled in irritating rivulets into her eyes and between her breasts.

The continued effort was taking its toll on her strength. But she thought she could feel the cords loosen slightly. She prayed she would have enough strength left to loosen them completely.

She rested a moment to give the burning pain a chance to subside. A choking thirst ate at her throat, and her empty stomach reminded her that she had not eaten since leaving the Land of Gold.

In all the hours since she had regained consciousness, she had not seen or heard another living soul. For a time, she had held onto the hope that by now she would have been missed at the casino and that Matt was searching for her. But as the hours dragged on, she began to doubt that he, or anyone, would ever find her.

A thought more horrible than she cared to imagine had begun to take root in her fear-driven mind. Maybe she had been left here to slowly die of thirst and starvation.

Gathering what strength she had left, she once again began the painful process of flexing and twisting her wrists. She had to bite her lip to keep back a cry of pain as the cords once again cut into her raw flesh.

Not long after, she fainted from loss of blood and exhaustion.

When she came to, she was astonished to see the door open and light streaming in like a beacon. A sob of relief came from her parched throat, to be quickly followed by one of intense pain as her wrists were grabbed in a cruel grip and she was roughly hauled to her feet.

Through the mist of pain she heard a voice saying, in heavily accented English, "The bitch has injured herself. The master will not be pleased when he learns of this."

She could barely stand she felt so weak. She came close to fainting again as a knife cut through the cords that had bound her, and they were yanked free.

The man who had cut her bonds thrust her arms forward into the light and the large woman she had seen earlier and dubbed the Frog grabbed them and inspected them.

A hand lashed out and slapped Julie across the face. "You fool! You have only made things worse for yourself by doing this."

She grabbed Julie by the chin and lifted her head as she spoke. "Listen to me, girl. Your fate is now in my hands. You will do as you're told or suffer the consequences. There is no escape."

The hand that hit her moved to the neckline of her shirt and with one quick yank ripped it open, the buttons snapping off and flying in all directions. Her chemise was the next to be torn, and then her skirt, until she stood totally exposed to the woman's gaze.

"Yes, yes." The Frog almost drooled the words. "You will bring a high price." Her large hand reached out and painfully squeezed one of Julie's breasts.

Julie could not suppress the shudder of revulsion that went through her at the woman's touch.

The Frog saw her reaction and squeezed harder as she laughed.

What happened next made Julie scream. The man grabbed her from behind and held her immobile as the woman stuck her hand between Julie's legs and violated her painfully with her fingers.

"It is too bad you are not a virgin. But, we might be able to overlook that, depending on the customer," the Frog said as she removed her hand and straightened to her full height.

"Take her away! Clean her up and feed her before she becomes sick and is worthless to us," the Frog ordered the man with her. "Bring her to me when you're done. The master wishes to inspect her."

The woman's words made Julie gather the last bit of pride and strength she had left. She glared steadily at the Frog, hatred pouring from her eyes.

The woman laughed as though Julie's defiance amused her. "That's right, girl. Hate. It may keep you alive."

Julie promised herself that if she ever escaped, she would return to wipe the evil grin from the woman's face.

An hour later, after she had been thoroughly bathed, fed and her wrists attended to, Julie was once again ushered into the Frog's presence.

Her hands had been bound in front of her, and she had not been given any clothing with which to cover her nakedness. But her inner reserves of pride shielded her as though she were fully dressed. Drawing on these hidden reserves and on her determination not to allow herself to be broken, Julie faced the woman coolly.

A small glimmer of respect glowed briefly in the Frog's eyes as she recognized the strength of character

Julie possessed. But it was quickly hidden, and she harshly repeated her earlier warning that Julie's behavior would decide what her treatment would be.

Julie stared wordlessly into the woman's eyes. The fear that had earlier tortured her had been replaced by an implacable anger.

Frowning slightly as though she had never been confronted by such defiance, the woman turned and led the way down a narrow corridor. Reaching a door, she paused and knocked twice. A muffled summons to enter could be heard through the thick wood.

Entering the room, Julie was thrust forward as the Frog and her companion guarded the door behind her.

Sitting at a rough table, with papers neatly stacked in small piles in front of him, was George Baldwin. Turning in his seat, he looked at Julie with cold appraising eyes.

Julie felt as though his hands, not his eyes, traveled over her, making her feel dirty while his eyes lingered on her naked breasts.

"You have caused me a lot of trouble, Miss Leighton. I do not like people who cause me trouble," Baldwin told her. "I have my own ways of dealing with those who do."

"You must be a busy man, Mr. Baldwin," Julie said sarcastically.

"You were warned, Miss Leighton. You should have accepted our generous offer to buy the Land of Gold while you had the chance."

"Go to hell," Julie said flatly.

"I probably shall, Miss Leighton," he responded, with a smile that disappeared as he added, "but, I will see you there first."

"Not if I can help it," she told him in an icy voice.

"Ah, but you can't, Miss Leighton," Baldwin responded. "You won't have the time. At this moment, one of my preferred customers is on his way here to see you. I think when he does, he will be more than happy to pay what I am asking."

Julie stared at him unflinchingly as she said, "It doesn't take long to squash an insect."

Baldwin rose from his seat and lashed out with his hand, catching her across the cheek and leaving a livid mark. "You had better keep a civil tongue in your head, or your life will be far worse than you can ever imagine."

Julie threw her head back, causing her hair to ripple in waves along her spine as she laughed in Baldwin's face. "Little man, you don't frighten me."

Baldwin's face turned a mottled red at her insult. But, he raised his hand to stop the Frog from hitting Julie again, saying, "No. She mustn't be too badly marked. It will affect her price."

"That's right. Mustn't mar the merchandise," Julie snapped. "It might affect your sales figures."

"Shut up!" the Frog ordered her roughly.

Ignoring her warning, Julie eyed Baldwin and asked, "Tell me, what do you plan on doing when my husband comes for you?"

Baldwin's eyes narrowed at her words. "Your bravado will get you nowhere, Miss Leighton. And as for your imagined rescue by your husband, don't raise your hopes. By the time he realizes you have disappeared, you will be long gone from here, and I shall be innocently attending to my business in a public place."

Turning to the woman behind her, he ordered,

"Time is wasting, we have a customer waiting. Gag her. I don't want her causing a scene."

A dirty cloth was bound over her mouth, effectively preventing her from speaking as she was led from the room and back down the corridor.

The atmosphere grew smokier as they traversed the narrow passage toward the main basement room. Julie could hear the auctioneer chanting his singsong account of the bidding.

She knew that what was to come next would be the greatest test of courage she had ever faced. She silently prayed for the strength to face what lay in the room beyond.

When they entered, Julie was assaulted by the stink of fear that permeated the air. She avoided looking at the platform off to her left as they skirted the back of the room, but she could not close her ears to the sounds of terrified weeping that accompanied the small Chinese orchestra in the far corner. The discordant music seemed to thread through the heartbreaking sound and form a background of spine chilling horror.

As she was led to the curtained alcove where she had seen Baldwin on the previous night, Julie kept her eyes on the back of the ugly woman in front of her.

She was led to the rear of the curtained area and ordered to be still as the Frog took up a position next to her. Baldwin left them and moved to the front of the alcove. Julie guessed he was joining the preferred customer he had mentioned earlier.

As she waited she could hear voices through the velvet curtain. One of them was Baldwin's. The other sounded oddly familiar to her. She listened as she heard Baldwin extolling her beauty and spirit and adding a warning that she might not prove as docile as past purchases.

The blood in her veins ran cold as she heard the second voice respond, "The last two you sold me only lasted a week. I hope this one lasts longer."

The noise in the room and the thickness of the curtain in front of her distorted the voice of the buyer, so she could not be absolutely certain where she had heard it before.

The curtain in front of her parted and she was pushed forward. Shock such as she had never felt before washed over her. Sitting next to Baldwin with a look of keen anticipation on his face was her brother-in-law, Adam!

Chapter Seventeen

JULIE'S EYES WIDENED, AND THE BLOOD DRAINED FROM her face. What was Adam doing here? Where was the "preferred customer," she had heard speaking to Baldwin?

She looked about the small viewing area to see if anyone else was seated in the few seats that lined the space in front of the platform on which they had made her stand. Her heart went to her throat as she realized that the smirking Baldwin and the stunned Adam were the lone occupants of the viewing area.

It was Adam she had heard! The shock this sent through her made her knees weak. Did Sara know he was here? Did Sara know about his "preferred customer" status?

These questions remained unanswered as she watched her brother-in-law turn to Baldwin and heard him say, "Is this your idea of a joke? I find no humor in it, if it is! I came here expecting to find a prime buy and you show me my sister-in-law!"

Baldwin had planned this from the moment he'd known Julie had been caught. He knew of Raleigh's sadistic tendencies and could think of no better way to even the score with Julie for all the problems she and her father had given him through the years.

He found he liked the idea of her suffering and being debased at the hands of her own brother-in-law. And her death, which was a foregone conclusion where the rapacious Adam Raleigh was concerned, could not be laid at his door. Baldwin found it an ideal way to deal with one of his more vexatious problems and to make a more than tidy profit at the same time.

He feigned surprise at Adam's outrage as he replied, "But you specifically requested that you be notified the moment we received a real beauty. You made no disclaimer regarding any possible relationship to yourself!"

He leaned closer to the shaken Adam and, leering up at Julie, commented lasciviously, "Come now. Having married one sister, you must have been curious about what it would be like to bed the other?"

Adam kept his eyes averted from Julie's face as he thought over Baldwin's words, for he had indeed wondered what it would be like to bed her.

He had grown bored with bedding Sara soon after their marriage. She had been equally disenchanted with him and suggested that he find an outlet elsewhere for his animal lust. He had brought a young whore home and taken her, in their bed, to see how Sara would react.

She had not objected to his bedding a whore, only to his doing it in their bed. She told him he could have all the whores he wanted if that meant he would no longer bother her. She would prefer that he not use their bed, but other than that, she did not care what he did or with whom he did it. She did not want to take the chance of becoming pregnant. She had no intention of ruining her figure to bring some squalling brat into the world.

It was soon after this that one of his friends had introduced him to the Barracoon. He had discovered that there they had exactly what he wanted, and at a price he was willing to pay. It was not long before he had become a regular customer.

Baldwin had struck a responsive chord by saying what he had. Adam could already think of things he would like to do to his snooty sister-in-law if he was given the chance.

"Come man. Look at her," Baldwin insisted as he saw the look in Adam's eyes. "Forget the bandages on her wrists," he told him. "She foolishly tried to escape from her bonds. And, the reason for the gag should need no explanation. You know better than most what a vicious tongue she has."

Baldwin gloated as he watched the glow in Adam's eyes brighten. He decided to tease Adam further. "Are her sister's breasts as perfectly formed? Look at them. See how they seem to reach out to you of their own accord. Can't you just see yourself buried inside her as she struggles beneath you?"

Adam's breathing became shallow as he listened to

Baldwin's prurient words. He found he could not take his eyes off Julie's nude form. She made Sara look insipid by comparison.

Yes. He could see all that Baldwin described. The images that flashed through his mind caused a fine film of perspiration to form on his forehead and upper lip. He wiped it away with the back of his hand. Tearing his eyes from Julie, he asked, "How much?"

Julie uttered a garbled cry of outrage and disgust that was swallowed behind her gag. Adam wanted to buy her!

When she had first seen him, the shock had been so great that she had not stopped to think of anything except that he had somehow found out she was being held prisoner and had come to rescue her.

But from the conversation between him and Baldwin, she knew Adam was as surprised to see her as she had been to see him. And now, after she had felt his eyes upon her, she feared him as she had never feared a man before. His glazed stare and the way he kept wiping at his face told her more clearly than any words that he had no intention of releasing her should he agree to Baldwin's price.

She held her breath waiting to hear Baldwin's reply.

"Twenty-five thousand dollars."

Adam gasped at hearing the enormous sum. "No woman is worth that!"

"This one is," Baldwin assured him confidently.

Adam stole another glance at Julie. She was without a doubt the most beautiful woman he had ever seen. And, it would be worth it at twice the price to know she was his. But, his normally greedy nature refused to let Baldwin win so easily.

"I still say you are overcharging," he told the flesh peddler. "She isn't even a virgin!"

Baldwin used Adam's outburst as an excuse to add to the bait that would seal the deal. "But, that's where you are mistaken," he told him.

"What!" Adam frowned. "Are you telling me that Matthew Thorn has not bedded her!"

"Have I ever lied to you?" Baldwin asked him, as he set the hook. "Haven't I always given you good service in the past? Believe me, when I say, their marriage was but a business arrangement."

Adam's pulse quickened. Baldwin was offering him the opportunity to even the score with the hated Matt Thorn by deflowering his wife! And maybe getting her with child! That would be something to relish for the rest of his life.

But, he asked himself, was Baldwin telling the truth? He found it hard to believe that any man, especially one as virile as Thorn, could resist bedding such a woman.

Baldwin saw the lingering doubt on Adam's face and said, "If you don't believe me, check her for yourself."

Julie's insides tightened in dread of Adam's taking Baldwin up on his offer. She steeled her muscles, ready to jump from the small platform and make a break for freedom. She refused to stand still and allow Adam to touch her.

Baldwin saw the tensing of Julie's leg muscles and nodded to the woman behind her. The Frog moved forward and grabbed her by the arm in a punishing grip.

Rather than take Julie's reaction as revulsion, Adam

took it as the sign of a virgin not wanting to be touched. It more than anything convinced him that what Baldwin said was true.

"Of course, you'll waive the usual rules for such a large sum of money," Adam stated as he accepted the price Baldwin had set.

Pleased with himself, Baldwin decided to add to his enjoyment by dangling the prize a bit further from Adam's reach before he began to reel him in.

"You know we can't make any exceptions to the rules. Cash only. If, you don't have it . . ." He shrugged and held out his hands as though to say the matter was out of his control.

Adam lifted his wallet from his pocket and counted the bills it contained. "I haven't that much cash on me!" he said in dismay. "You know I'm good for the money! Can't you wait until I can get to the bank in the morning?"

"The rules are cash at the time of purchase," Baldwin repeated. Then he paused for effect before adding, "How much do you have?"

"Seven thousand," Adam replied, adding quickly, "but, I can get the rest as soon as the bank opens."

Baldwin pretended to give deep thought to Adam's words as he enjoyed watching him squirm. "Leave the seven thousand here as a down payment. And bring me the remainder first thing tomorrow," he said, in a tone meant to convey that he was doing Adam an enormous favor by bending the rules.

Adam fumbled the money from his wallet and shoved it into Baldwin's hands saying, "I'll have it here first thing!"

Having thrust the money at Baldwin, Adam rose from his seat and reached to grab at Julie and pull her from the exhibition platform.

Baldwin's hand on his arm stopped him. "Delivery when you have paid in full," he said in a voice of steel.

Adam was crushed. He had planned on taking Julie that night. To have to wait until after the bank opened and he had paid Baldwin was an excruciating blow.

"But! You know I'll come through with the cash!" He tried blustering.

"After you've paid in full," Baldwin repeated. "She will remain here until then."

Darkness surrounded the hidden force. They had waited and watched as the district had settled in for the night. They had seen the carriages and coaches pull up and surreptitiously disgorge their passengers before speeding away.

The door to the joss house had opened and closed countless times, swallowing those who sought entry. Matt and Carlo moved closer to the entry, so as to have a clear view of those who came to deal in human flesh. They saw many faces that they recognized. Some they were not surprised to see, others made them look at each other in disbelief.

The clientele was not restricted to only one class of people. They saw crib masters from some of the sleazier dives on the waterfront and some men with the most respected names in the community.

Seeing all this firsthand helped to explain how the Barracoon had survived as long as it had. The operators obviously had friends in much higher places than anyone had ever guessed.

Kong Woo motioned to one of his lieutenants to give the signal. The signal given, the small army crept forward on silent feet.

They infiltrated the joss house through unguarded vents and storeroom windows as quietly as the fog that had begun to drift in from the bay.

The sparsity of outlying sentries showed how invulnerable the operators of the Barracoon felt themselves to be. They knew they had little to fear from the authorities. Instead, the heaviest concentration of guards were positioned, facing inward, around the perimeter of the main room.

It was obvious to the advancing raiders that the guards were intended to protect the customers from each other and to prevent any of the sale items from escaping, should they be foolish enough to try.

Kong Woo gave another signal and the outer guards were slowly and systematically eliminated, to be replaced by his men. It was only a matter of a few minutes before the room was surrounded by the men of the Kong Chow.

Waiting at the end of one of the corridors, Matt had an open view of the room. He searched the main platform to see if Julie was among the poor unfortunates waiting their turn upon the block. Not seeing her, he turned his gaze toward the corner across from him. What he saw made a feral growl rumble in his chest.

Someone was leaving the curtained alcove. And as he did so, he flipped the curtain open, briefly revealing Julie's nude form to Matt's eyes.

Carlo grabbed him as he started to bolt from the corridor. "What is it?" he demanded.

"Julie!" Matt grated as he nodded toward the curtained alcove. "Raleigh!" Matt hissed as he recognized the departing figure and struggled to break free of Carlo's restraining hold. "I'll kill the bastard!"

"Wait," Carlo cautioned him under his breath as he watched Adam Raleigh leave the room. "We will both kill him . . . later," he promised.

Carlo maintained his manaclelike grip on Matt, waiting for him to regain control. "Now is not the time to rush in there like a mad bull. You will only get yourself hurt. And, what good would you be to Julie then?" he said to him.

Matt nodded his head as he took a deep breath. He did not trust his voice to speak. The fury that boiled in his blood was only barely under control.

Carlo reluctantly released his hold on Matt's arm. He waited, ready to grab him again should he try to bolt across the room.

When he saw Kong Woo signal for them to take the alcove while he and the rest of his men handled the main room, Carlo said in a deadly voice, "It is time."

"Baldwin's mine," Matt told him as they moved from their hiding place.

The noise of the music and the milling customers, hid them as they stealthily made their way toward the far side of the room. Reaching the side nearest the alcove, Matt motioned for Carlo to take one end of the curtain, while he took the other.

Once Carlo was in position, Matt held up three fingers, signaling that they would both go on the count of three.

Julie watched her brother-in-law depart and her insides turned over with disgust. He had practically fainted when Baldwin had hinted that he might not sell her to him.

Suddenly the curtains at either end of the alcove were thrust open, and all manner of hell broke loose within the room. Julie had little time to react as she saw Matt and Carlo enter the secluded viewing area.

"Matt!" she cried out behind her gag as she was hustled from the small platform and away from the basement room.

She had been dragged a short distance into the adjacent corridor when the Frog halted. Looking behind them with fear-widened eyes, she quickly grabbed the bolt locking the door on their right and opened it. Pulling the door open, she forcibly shoved Julie inside the dank room and slammed the door behind her. Turning, she began to run, more concerned with making good her own escape than with Julie.

Julie could not stop herself from falling, and she was stunned when she unexpectedly crashed into someone already in the room. A scream began to build in her chest, but it was quickly cut off as she heard Lee Tang's deep voice say, "Quiet girl!"

"Tang!" she mumbled with joy, wishing he could understand her. If only she could be rid of the gag, she raged as she reached her bound hands up and tugged at it wildly.

Pulling it free, she repeated her joyous greeting, "Tang!"

"Miss Julie?" His response was unbelieving. The feel of naked flesh in his arms had told him it was one of the girls they planned to sell. But the possibility of it being Julie had never entered his mind. He thought she was safely away from the Barracoon.

"What is going on?" he added as he stripped off his shirt and used it to cover her before he tried to untie her hands.

"I haven't time to explain now," she croaked harshly, her mouth and throat dry. "Matt and Carlo are here."

Lee Tang paused in his efforts to free her hands as he heard her news. "Kong Woo!" he exclaimed.

"No. Matt and Carlo," Julie repeated wondering what had made Tang mention his grandfather's name at a time like this.

Tang quickly undid her bonds, and as she donned the shirt he had draped over her, he said, "Kong Woo and the men of the Kong Chow are with them. I left word with Matthew to take Carlo and go to my grandfather."

"Oh!" Julie exclaimed in surprise. "Why weren't you tied up?" she asked, surprised that the muscular Tang had been left free.

"I was unconscious when they dumped me in here, and they saw no need to bind me," Tang explained. "You are the first person I've seen since I've been here. I think they had decided to lock me up here and forget me."

Julie shuddered as she listened to Tang's matter-of-fact recital of the events since his capture. She had been afraid that she had been left to suffer the fate they had planned for Tang.

Further conversation was halted by the sounds of gunshots and screaming. Moving to the closed door, Tang tried the handle and grunted in satisfaction as the door moved toward him slowly.

In her haste to escape, the Frog had neglected to lock the door.

264

Tang led the way as he and Julie moved out into the narrow corridor. Off to their left in the main room, the sounds of a major fight could be heard.

There was the crashing of furniture, mens' voices yelled in anger and terrified women screamed piercingly as they were caught up in the raging battle that surrounded them.

Warning Julie to stay in the corridor, Tang moved toward the fighting. The doorway was blocked by two men struggling to escape the chaos.

Julie could hear their cries of fear as Tang loomed unexpectedly out of the dark. She crept as close as she dared and saw Tang grab them by their collars and, with one quick movement of his wrists, knock their heads together. She watched as he released their unconscious bodies and stepped over them as they crashed to the floor in a heap.

Feeling cut off and alone in the depths of the corridor, Julie crept toward the end, hoping to find Matt.

Flattening herself as much as she could against the wall, she peered into the basement. What she saw was enough to frighten anyone.

Some of the customers had managed to conceal guns from the searching hands of the guards posted at the entrance when they had first arrived. The room echoed with the sound of their shots. And the air was acrid with the smell of gunpowder.

The room was awash with men engaged in life or death struggles. The captives lined up on the platform had seized their chance and banded together to attack the few who had remained to guard them. The shrill cries of their efforts added to the din.

Julie strained her eyes in the confusion trying to find a face she knew. She could not tell the men of the Kong Chow from the guards of the Barracoon, and as the fighting grew fiercer, she knew it wasn't safe to remain where she was much longer.

Looking down at the unconscious men in front of her, she saw that one of them held a pistol in his hand. Bending down she pried it from his grasp. Checking to be sure it was loaded, she moved from the corridor and along the edge of the wall toward the main door.

It was the small passageway, just prior to the main door, that interested her. She would find Matt or Carlo later. Now, she had a few scores of her own to settle.

As she edged her way closer to the passage, a figure leaped out at her from the side. As hands settled themselves around her waist and tried to drag her to the floor, she brought the barrel of the gun down as hard as she could on the head of her attacker. It was one of the women Julie had noticed when she had been taken to be bathed and fed. Julie kicked her away as the woman slumped to the floor.

Almost immediately someone else came at her. This time it was the Frog's man. Julie smashed her knee into him as he tried to grab her. His wail of agony was a high-pitched keening as he crumpled retching to the floor. Julie did not spare him a second glance as she continued on her course toward the passageway and Baldwin's office.

She pushed and shoved her way through struggling bodies until she reached the passage entry. Taking a quick look about her, she ducked into the dim passage and moved toward the door of Baldwin's office.

The sound of fighting dulled to a muted rumble

behind her as she made her way around the stacked crates that lined the sides of the passage.

She had to avoid the scrambling of frightened rats that shot out from their hiding places amid the crates and scurried across the dirty floor. Her grip on the gun she held tightened as she neared Baldwin's hidden office.

Hearing the sounds of a struggle up ahead, she quickened her pace afraid that Baldwin had already made good his escape. She frowned as she saw the door to his office gaping open.

Reaching the open doorway, she gasped. The inside of the office was a shambles. The table Baldwin had used as a desk was now a pile of kindling on the floor, and the papers that had earlier been so neatly stacked upon it lay in scattered disarray around the tiny room.

Standing amidst the rubble were Matt and Baldwin with their hands at each other's throat. Each was trying his best to choke the life from the other.

Julie stared in horrified fascination as the two men fell to their knees, neither releasing his grip on the other. The sound of their labored breathing rasped through the air like a buzz saw that needed oiling.

She lifted the gun and tried to take aim, but couldn't maintain a clear field of fire as Baldwin's leg came up and he tried to knee Matt in the groin.

Matt had anticipated this move and twisted his body out of the way. Baldwin's knee failed to connect with its target, and the effort left him off balance. Taking advantage of this, Matt crashed down to the floor on his shoulder and rolled free of Baldwin's punishing grip on his throat.

The two men eyed one another carefully. Aware only

of each other and nothing else, they waited for an opening that would spell their opponent's doom.

Julie watched spellbound and unable to move. Her limbs were paralyzed with fear for Matt's life. Baldwin might be a smaller man than Matt, but he was as vicious as a cornered rat in defending himself.

If either of the men had an advantage, it was Baldwin. The cramped room in which they fought made it easier for him to maneuver than it was for the larger Matt.

Julie was so intent on watching the men, she did not see the hand that came from out of nowhere and smashed into her forearm causing her to drop her gun.

The pain that lanced up into her shoulder broke the spell she was in. She reacted instinctively by ducking and turning, while at the same time she struck out with the fist of her good hand.

Keeping tucked low in her stance, her fists protecting her face and head, she faced her assailant. It was the Frog.

Julie ducked to avoid the fist that was aimed at her face, and she parried with a blow to the midsection of the bigger woman.

She knew she was outweighed and could be hurt pretty badly should the Frog's hamlike fists connect a second time. The pain that still radiated from her forearm into her shoulder told her she must avoid such an occurrence at all costs.

It took all the childhood training she had received from Carlo to maintain her protective stance. She resisted the urge to go straight at the Frog. She parried the blows that came at her like buckshot and landed a few of her own to let the Frog know she wasn't dealing with a defenseless woman, but an opponent capable of beating her should she lower her guard for an instant.

Julie watched and waited for the perfect opening. When it came she flashed out with her fist and caught the Frog on the cheek. The force of her blow split the skin and blood began to drip down the woman's face.

Julie knew she would only have one or two such chances and tried to follow her advantage by sending another blow to the Frog's jaw.

The larger woman stumbled slightly and bellowed with rage as she lashed out with her own fist catching Julie a glancing blow to the shoulder.

It was enough to send Julie reeling away from the office door and down the passageway. She caught herself on a stack of crates before she crashed to the floor.

"Oh shit!" Julie could not help exclaiming as she saw the Frog reach into her waistband and pull out a wicked-looking knife.

Looking frantically about her for something with which to defend herself, Julie saw a broken crate lying on its side near her feet.

Keeping a wary eye on the Frog, Julie reached down and, grabbing one of the wooden slats, held it in front of her like a club.

The Frog laughed at the puniness of Julie's weapon in comparison to the six-inch razor-keen blade she held. Her arms held wide, the Frog began to advance toward Julie, saying in her heavily accented voice, "When I'm through with you, you'll be fish bait. You have caused Magda problems for the last time, you troublesome bitch."

Julie could not stop the laugh that bubbled from her

throat at hearing the woman's real name. "I like the name Frog better," she called back as she watched the woman advance.

"Frog? You call Magda a frog!"

Julie drew in her breath and released it slowly as she balanced all her weight on the balls of her feet as Carlo had taught her. Seeing the expression of virulent hatred on Magda's face, she wondered if she had made a mistake in telling her what she had named her.

Magda had come within three feet of her before stopping. She stared at Julie with her froglike eyes and began tossing her knife from hand to hand, trying to confuse Julie.

She was doing a good job of it. Julie wasn't certain which side she should be ready to defend.

The eyes! Watch the eyes! Julie's inner voice screamed at her.

"That's right!" Julie whispered to herself. "Carlo always said to watch the eyes. They will tell you when to move."

She concentrated on watching Magda's eyes ignoring the flick of the knife as it changed hands. It helped erase the confusion she had felt a moment earlier. Now she had something definite to watch and prepare to defend herself against.

She saw Magda's eyes flicker briefly to the left, and she swiftly countered the lunge of the knife with the board in her hand.

Retreating a step, she waited alertly for Magda's next move. It was fast in coming. The knife whisked through the air by her face and the end of the blade thudded against the board as Julie held it up in defense.

The wood splintered slightly from the wrenching pull

of the blade as it was forced free by the increasingly furious Magda.

Julie knew she could not spend the rest of the day warding off Magda's repeated attacks. Sooner or later, the blade would slip by her guard and she would be hurt. She decided to try something she hadn't done since she used to practice knife fighting with Carlo behind the Land of Gold.

She knew she would only have one chance, and crouching, she balanced all her weight evenly between the balls of both feet. Bringing the board down in front of her, she grasped it firmly with both her hands.

Taking a deep breath, she screamed at the top of her lungs as she brought the board up from the floor with all the strength she possessed. It crashed into the hand that held Magda's knife sending it flying straight up into the air.

In the split second all this took place, Magda immediately charged at Julie reaching for her throat with both her hands outstretched. Her fingers had closed around Julie's windpipe and begun to tighten their grip, when a look of astonishment came over her face and she released her hold. She backed away from Julie, her hands grabbing frantically behind her.

"Noooo!" The wailing cry issued from her lips as she crashed to her face on the floor in front of Julie.

Julie stood and stared in horror at the hilt of the knife as it quivered from the middle of Magda's back.

The big woman had moved straight into the path of the falling knife when she went for Julie's throat. It had proved to be one of the last moves she would ever make.

The sound of a shot rang out from the direction of

Baldwin's office. Stepping over Magda's body, Julie cried out Matt's name as she hurried back down the passage. Reaching the office door, her hand went to her mouth and a cry of anguish sprang to her lips.

Lying motionless on the floor was Matt with Baldwin's unmoving body on top of him and Carlo standing over them both, a smoking gun in his hand.

Hearing Julie's cry, Carlo turned in time to catch her as she fainted into his arms.

Chapter Eighteen

WHEN SHE CAME TO, JULIE FOUND HERSELF LYING ON a strange bed in a strange room. She sat up straight, gasping.

"Matt!"

Two hands reached for her shoulders and held her; then Matt sat on the edge of the bed, saying, "I'm here. It's all right now."

Unwilling to believe her eyes and ears, Julie moved her hands to his face and traced its contours as she stared at him in disbelief. It couldn't be him! She had seen him lying dead on the floor of Baldwin's office!

Her fingers caressed the skin of his cheek and moved to his eyelids in wonder. This couldn't be so! She was dreaming! Those weren't Matt's golden tiger eyes looking at her so warmly. She was only imagining he was there.

Tears started to roll from her eyes and coursed silently down her cheeks as she whispered, "You're not real."

"Maybe this will convince you," Matt said as he claimed her lips with his and seared her soul with a kiss that sent flames of sweet longing flicking through her.

There was no way she could imagine such a feeling. It wasn't a dream. Matt was there, holding her tight and making her feel as though molten lava ran in her veins! She laced her arms about him and clasped him against her, afraid of ever losing him again.

The remembered pain of losing him once already made her exclaim in a rush of words, "Are you all right? When I saw you lying on the floor in Baldwin's office, I thought he'd killed you!"

Silencing her spate of words, he kissed her again taking her breath away. Holding her close to him, he said, "That should tell you, I'm fine. You're the one we've been worried about. You've been unconscious since late last night."

Julie leaned against him reveling in the sound of his voice and the beat of his heart in her ear. It wasn't a dream! It was Matt holding her in his arms and speaking to her. The feel of his lips on hers had sent an electrifying surge of pure joy through her. She had been certain he was dead. It was seeing him lying unmoving like that on the floor of that filthy office that had made her realize she might have lost forever the chance to tell him how much she loved him.

But, what had happened since then? She pushed slightly away from him and said, "I guess I'm a bit confused. What happened? All I remember is seeing you, and you were dead!"

Matt tightened his embrace and replied, "Baldwin had tried to bash my brains in with the leg from a broken table. Carlo saved my life by shooting the bastard. I was exhausted and had closed my eyes in relief when you appeared on the scene." He leaned down and kissed her on the temple. "You scared the hell out of us collapsing like that!"

"I scared you!" Julie exclaimed. "How do you think I felt when I saw you lying on the floor like that! Don't you ever frighten me like that again!"

"I won't if you promise not to go around hitting me over the head and getting yourself involved in dangerous situations," he told her. The hollow ache that had been inside him ever since he had seen her unconscious in Carlo's arms still gnawed at Matt. He had come far too close to losing her forever.

"Oh!" Julie murmured guiltily. "I'm sorry, I hit you like that. I won't do it again if you promise to tell me what's going on. It was awful worrying about what you were doing or planning! I was afraid you and Carlo might get yourselves hurt or, even worse, killed because of me!"

"What are you talking about?" Matt asked her in surprise.

Julie haltingly told him about the conversation she had overheard between him and Carlo on the night they had gone after Molly's attacker.

Matt listened to her and said, "You only heard half of what we had been discussing and filled in the other half with that wild imagination of yours! Maybe this will teach you not to listen at keyholes."

The echo of her cry was still in his ears. It was a sound he would never forget. When she had slumped unconscious into Carlo's arms, Matt had thought the worst. He worried about what might have happened to her, and the realization of what she must have gone through tore him apart. Needing to know she was all right, he gazed into her eyes looking for any sign of concussion. What he saw looking back at him made him enfold her even closer to his heart as he kissed her once again.

Her response filled him with love for her, and he swore he would never let her go. She was the woman he loved.

"How did I end up here?" she asked him as they broke apart trying to catch their breath. "I don't remember a thing after seeing you."

He cuddled her closely and went on to explain what had happened since she had fainted. "We couldn't find anything wrong with you. We brought you back here and had Kong Woo's physician take a look at you. He said, you were suffering from a shock to your system and that you would regain consciousness when your body felt it could once again handle the stress."

Unable to keep her love a secret any longer, she placed a finger on his lips silencing him. Looking into his eyes she shook her head slightly and whispered, "He was only partly right. When I saw you, and thought you were dead, a part of me died. I love you, Matthew Thorn. I couldn't bear life without you."

Her words released a tide of feeling within him that Matt never knew existed. She loved him!

He started to tell her how he felt, but she wouldn't

let him speak as she continued, "I know you think of me as a brazen whore. I can't force you to believe me, when I say I'm not. But you had better believe me when I say you are the only man I have ever loved."

"What!" Matt exclaimed at her believing he thought she was a whore. "You're wrong," he tried to tell her.

Hearing the shock in his voice Julie cringed inside, but she refused to take back a word she had said. "I'm not lying! You should know I was a virgin the first time you made love to me."

Matt's hand came over her mouth forcing her to be quiet. He glared down at her, his eyes radiating sparks. "Don't!" he commanded her harshly. "Don't you ever call yourself a whore! You are my wife and the woman I love. I won't allow you or anyone to say such things about yourself."

Julie's eyes widened in shock and surprise as she listened to him. He'd said he loved her! Those were the only words that mattered. He loved her!

She reached up and pulled his hand from her mouth, whispering, "Say it again!"

"I will not have—" Matt started.

"No!" Julie stopped him. "The part before that."

Matt read the emotion in her eyes and said, "You are my wife and the woman I love."

Julie gazed at him wordlessly allowing all her love for him to shine forth. She melted into his arms as he gathered her to him and kissed her.

It was well that Kong Woo had given orders that no one was to disturb them. For Matt and Julie spent the remainder of the day and most of the night rediscovering each other and exploring their newfound love.

Their loving carried them on a continuous and ever increasing wave of tenderness and sharing that lifted them to unknown heights. They were no longer two but one, each indistinguishable from the other in their mutual fulfillment.

Their love made them a part of each other. They shared the secret of life between them. They bared their souls to the touch of the other. They kept no secrets but the ones they shared. Time and the world no longer mattered now that they loved.

The terror and fears of the past days healed and forgotten, they slept contentedly enfolded in each other's embrace.

It was pitch black inside the room when they awoke and gloried once more in their love.

Resting with her head on Matt's chest, Julie giggled as she felt the rumbling complaint of hunger. She was starving and she needed a bath. She tickled Matt awake and asked him, "Are you going to feed me? Or are we going to stay here forever?"

Matt listened to her with a smile on his face and replied, "I would prefer staying here forever, but I guess we do have to eat sometime."

"And bathe . . .", Julie sniffed as she raised her head from his chest. "We both reek!"

Matt pulled her back to him and kissed her soundly saying, "You smell good to me."

Laughing, Julie pushed free saying, "I don't to me. Now, get up. You'll have to go find us something to eat and see if you can't have bathwater sent up."

"Why can't you do it?" he asked as he tried to snuggle into his pillow.

Julie poked him in the ribs. "I don't think Lee Tang's shirt would be considered appropriate dress. But if you are too lazy to do it, I guess I'll have to chance offending our host, and do it myself."

She started to climb from the bed, only to be hauled back by Matt's hand as he rose saying, "No, you don't! I'm a selfish husband and don't like sharing my wife's charms. I'll go."

"Yes, dear." Julie's eyes twinkled up at him impishly as she snuggled beneath the covers. "Try not to take too long. This bed is really comfortable."

Pulling on his clothes, Matt tossed Lee Tang's shirt at her, saying, "And, you call me lazy! Be careful, woman. Or, I might change my mind and join you. Then you can stay hungry."

It was only a matter of a few minutes before Julie heard a discreet knock on the door. It opened and two servants came in bearing a tub and pails of hot water. Another servant followed behind, bringing fresh clothing, towels and soap. Bowing to Julie as she buried herself under the covers, they filled the tub and laid out the fresh clothes. Placing the towels near the steaming tub, they bowed once again and departed as quietly as they had entered.

Julie was starting to leave the bed when she heard the sound of approaching footsteps. Jumping back beneath the covers, she waited to see who else had decided to call.

She did not wait long. Three more servants entered the room. One was carrying a table and the other two were laden down with trays overloaded with food.

The low table was set up and the food distributed on

it as she watched in silent amazement from the bed. Completing their task, these servants bowed, as had the others, and departed.

The combination of steam rising from the heated tub and the mouth-watering aroma of the food made Julie throw caution to the wind. She hurried from the bed and into the tub; grabbing the soap, she began to scrub herself vigorously. Her stomach told her this was not the time for a leisurely soak.

She was drying off and preparing to slip into the soft silk of the gown that had been brought for her when the door opened again. She froze, having been taken by surprise. There hadn't been any knock and she was caught in the act of dressing. Matt entered the room, closing the door behind him.

His hair was damp and combed back to dry, and he had shaved. It was obvious by the Chinese silk housecoat he wore that he had bathed before returning.

"What not ready yet!" He quirked an eyebrow at her teasingly. Moving toward the food, he said, "You had better hurry or there won't be anything left for you to eat."

"That's what you think!" Julie exclaimed as she hurriedly dressed and scampered to the table. Taking a seat on one of the large pillows set out for this purpose, she picked up the chopsticks that rested by her plate and began to eat from the bowl of rice placed in front of her. The use of chopsticks was not foreign to her. She had learned to use them so long ago, she had forgotten when. To her, they were as interchangeable as knife, fork or spoon.

Taking a seat next to her on the floor, Matt helped himself to the abundant feast, saying, "Carlo asked if he could join us. I told him to wait twenty minutes or so, before he did. Otherwise, our mouths would be too full to talk."

Julie laughed, choking on some of the rice she was eating as it went down the wrong way. Matt clapped her heartily on the back, saying, "Careful! I don't want Carlo to show up and find you have choked to death on a bowl of rice. He would never forgive me!"

Sipping at the hot fragrant tea held in a small handleless cup, Julie replied, "It wasn't the rice that made me choke."

"It wasn't? Then, what was it?" Matt asked her as he ladled some of the bird's nest soup into a bowl and set it by her plate.

"Why do you always tell everyone I am about to die from hunger?" she demanded. "You make me sound like a bottomless pit!"

"I think you have a beautiful bottom!" Matt leaned over and looked at where she was sitting. "And, I do not tell everyone that you are starving to death . . . only those capable of doing something about it before you do."

"Ohh!" Julie exhaled in exasperation.

Matt smiled over at her as he heaped food on her plate. "Come on now, we mustn't let any of this go to waste."

She couldn't help but laugh at the teasing expression on his face. She looked over at his plate and said, "Are you sure you have enough?"

The plate was piled with enough food to feed two normal people. But smiling up at her husband, she knew he was not an ordinary man. She never wanted to try to change him. She laughed softly. Matt would probably go on telling people she was starving for the rest of their lives.

A knock on the door interrupted any further conversation. Matt called for whoever it was to enter. And Carlo came in bearing a single flower in his hand.

He also was dressed in the Chinese fashion. He bowed most formally and handed the flower to Julie saying, "Please accept this poor token of my affection."

The meekness of his voice made Julie's eyebrows go up as she looked at Matt for an explanation. Matt smiled as he watched Carlo seat himself on the extra pillow he had brought with him, saying, "Carlo has decided to pursue the wisdom of the East. One of Lee Tang's cousins, Lee Mei, has opened his eyes to the beauty of this ancient culture."

Understanding came to Julie at once, and she asked Carlo, "Is she beautiful, my friend?"

Carlo lifted his hands in what was a purely Latin gesture of praise. "Words fail me, *cara*. Lee Mei is a lotus blossom in a world full of weeds."

Matt restrained his laughter as he asked, "Have you eaten?"

"Yes," Carlo replied as he took one of the extra plates and began to heap food on it.

Even though he had already dined, Carlo could not pass up the chance to eat again. His poverty-stricken background had taught him that you eat when you can because you never know when you will have another chance.

Julie watched him with affectionate amusement while he settled back and began to stuff himself as though it were his last meal.

"Speaking of Lee Tang, is he all right? The last I saw

of him, he had knocked two men out and was heading into the thick of the fight," she said to the men.

"He's fine," Matt reassured her. "He sends his regards and bade me to tell you that he has returned to the Land of Gold to watch over things until our return."

Looking at Carlo, she asked, "What happened after I passed out?"

"I aged thirty years," Carlo replied as he helped himself to seconds.

"Carlo!" Julie reprimanded him. "I'm serious. I want to know what happened."

"I am being serious, *cara,*" he replied. "When you cried out like that and collapsed, I did age at least thirty years. I thought you were dead."

"No, I was the one who was dead." Matt corrected him from the sideline.

Julie reached over and slapped his leg, saying, "Stop it! I want to hear what Carlo has to say, not listen to your idea of humor."

"After I caught you"—he nodded to his friend—"Matt came off the floor like a bolt of lightning and grabbed you from me."

"He did?" Julie asked. She glanced lovingly at Matt.

Carlo nodded, while Matt busied himself refilling his plate. "Together, we worked our way out of the basement and back onto the street. Matt insisted on carrying you the entire way back here," he told her. "The rest you already know."

"No, I don't!" Julie exclaimed. "What about Ah Toy and the others at the Barracoon? What happened there?"

Matt took over the explanation allowing Carlo to

finish his meal. "Ah Toy wasn't there. She was at the opera with one of her rich customers. As for the others," he went on, "they were either taken to appear before the tribunal of the Six Companies or, as in the case of the other girls being held for sale, taken to where they could be cared for and looked after, until their families could be found and notified of their whereabouts. Now tell us what happened to you?"

Julie related all that had happened from the time she had left the casino until she'd fainted. She could not bring herself to say anything about Adam or what had gone on in the alcove. Thankfully, neither Matt nor Carlo seemed to notice this omission. For neither of them questioned her about it.

When she related the fight between herself and Magda the Frog, she thanked Carlo for all his patience when they were young and he had taught her how to defend herself. When she came to the part where Magda died with a knife in her back, she fell silent for a moment.

She had never wanted to kill anyone in her life. But now she had. Self-defense or not, it still made her feel guilty. Shaking her head to clear away this gloomy thought she went on with her tale which ended with her finding Matt and thinking he was dead.

"I think we both have had a rough time," Matt told her as he gazed lovingly into her eyes. "Hopefully, we can put all this behind us now and get on with living."

"But what about the Barracoon itself?" Julie asked him.

"That will continue," Matt replied grimly. "Maybe not at the same location. But it will continue. The Barracoon is not just a place. It's a service rendered to the disturbed and uncaring element of society, those of them willing to pay the price."

Matt looked over at Carlo as he continued, "I'm afraid it will take more than our small show of force to close its doors. It will take a major change in society itself. When the honest, decent citizens of San Francisco have reached the limit of their tolerance, then and only then will we see places like the Barracoon closed down forever."

"I'm not so sure, my friend," Carlo disagreed. "There will always be places like the Barracoon, as long as there are people like Baldwin. They may not be as visible or brazen, but they will be there just the same."

"I hope you're wrong, Carlo," Julie whispered. "I truly hope and pray you're wrong."

"So do I, *cara*," Carlo returned.

Julie sat silently as she thought of what Carlo had said. The odds were, he was right in his assumption of the future of the Barracoon and places like it. It sickened her. It also made her ill to think that after all that had happened she wasn't any closer to finding out who murdered her father than when she started.

She shivered. All she had found out, was that Adam was one of the people who kept such places open and in business. She couldn't believe Sara knew the kind of man she had married.

"What has you so serious?" Matt asked her.

"I was thinking," she replied.

"They must have been heavy thoughts to make you frown like that," Matt remarked.

"I was thinking about how I will probably never know who was responsible for my father's death," Julie told him.

"Julie, love. We will find out," Matt reassured her as he moved next to her and put his arm around her shoulder drawing her close to his side.

"We haven't given up, *cara,*" Carlo told her.

"Something else has you upset?" Matt said as he lifted her chin and looked into her face. "What is it?"

Julie closed her eyes and saw Adam's leering face looking up at her as Baldwin whispered in his ear.

"Julie?" Matt asked her again.

"I was thinking about Adam," she admitted to him. "Matt, he was there. I couldn't believe the way he acted, when he saw me." She shuddered as she remembered the look in his eyes and the way he had kept wiping his face. "He even tried to buy me from Baldwin for twenty-five thousand dollars!" Julie told him as she buried her face against Matt's chest.

Matt's face hardened and his lips became a grim line as he hissed, "Raleigh!"

Carlo looked at him and said so Julie could not hear, "Remember my promise, *amigo.* Later, will come. And, when it does, we shall take care of him together."

Matt nodded his head and held Julie tightly against him as she cried softly.

When Julie had stopped her weeping and looked as though she might fall asleep in Matt's arms, Carlo decided it was time for him to go. Rising quietly to his feet, he nodded farewell to Matt and departed.

Matt shifted Julie in his arms and, rising, carried her to their bed. Laying her down gently, he returned to his place by the table, poured himself another cup of tea and lit a cheroot.

He was surprised when he heard Julie's voice asking, "When can we return to the casino?"

Turning to the bed Matt told her firmly, "We will return when I think you are up to it and not before." Anticipating any objections she might have to his decision, he added, "Any work you think you have can wait. I want to be certain things here are settled before we leave."

"Shouldn't I go on ahead and you can come when you're finished here?" Julie asked him.

"No!" Matt stated flatly. "Your place is here with me."

Julie found she wasn't upset by his insistence that she stay with him. It warmed her more than anything else. She knew Matt felt as she did. If she could, she would much rather spend all her time with him.

It had been habit more than true desire that had made her push to return alone. She was realistic enough to know she would have to return to work sooner or later, but for now, she wanted to savor every minute they had together.

"Matt?" she called softly.

"Hmm?" Matt replied.

"Come to bed."

Chapter Nineteen

ONE OF THE FIRST THINGS JULIE DID UPON HER RETURN
to the Land of Gold was send word to Sara that she
wanted to speak to her. But her message was returned
with a note saying that Sara had left San Francisco to
return East on an extended visit to friends. The note
had gone on to say her husband had remained to take
care of business and would be available should she wish
to speak with him.

The last person in the world she wanted to speak with
was Adam! Julie hoped that Sara would never return
from the East and be forced to discover the truth about
the man she'd married.

Time moved on and she became immersed in the

Land of Gold and in her growing relationship with Matt. Adam and Sara faded from her mind.

Now Julie smiled as she made her way upstairs toward her office. Things were not at all as she had expected them to be upon her return from the Kong Chow's.

The chaos and confusion she had thought to find was nonexistent. Matt had laughed at her surprise when, upon their return three days earlier, she had been amazed to see how smoothly things were running.

Molly had received permission from the doctor to resume most of her duties as long as she allowed the faithful Bet to take over the heavier items.

All orders had been placed and paid for on time, wages had been disbursed and business was booming!

Matt had teased her, saying, "Looks like you've lost your excuse of having work to do."

"It does look that way, doesn't it?" she had answered.

Julie laughed to herself as she thought of what Matt had said to her that morning. He had asked her if there wasn't any work she needed to do. When she had asked him why, he had told her he hoped there was because he needed some rest!

She'd told him that she had delegated most of her work because he had made her promise she would.

Hearing this, he had groaned and swept her into his arms, nuzzling her neck and saying, "Undelegate some of it before you kill me!"

"I what! You're the one who keeps us awake all the time, not me!" Julie had told him.

"You're as much to blame as I am." Matt had

groaned. "I wasn't the one to wake you up this morning! Besides, it's your fault I can't keep my hands off you. You didn't have to be so beautiful"—he'd kissed her on the cheek—"so soft to hold"—he'd kissed her on the shoulder—"or so damn wonderful to make love to! Now, I think for both our sakes you had better see about undelegating some of that work you delegated. If we both keep busy, we might be tired enough to get some rest for a change."

She had frowned at him and asked, "Aren't all newlyweds like us?"

Matt had grabbed her and wrestled her to the bed, their laughter filling the room. "No, my love, all newlyweds are not like us. Some of them sleep once in a while."

"So do we!" she had protested.

"Obviously not as much as some," Matt had replied with a gleam in his eyes. "Lee Tang stopped me last night to give me a belated wedding gift."

"What?" Julie asked puzzled.

"It was a packet of powders the Chinese swear will enhance a man's stamina! And if the cook serves me any more raw oysters, I think I will start producing pearls!" Matt had replied.

"Oh no!" she had gasped at hearing what he said. "You too!"

"Me too, what?" Matt had asked.

Julie had begun to laugh and had a difficult time controlling herself as she replied, "Molly gave me a jar of cream she said the doctor had given her to give to me. It is supposed to prevent the soreness of something she called, 'Honeymoonitis'. Whatever that is?"

"Does it?" Matt lifted an eyebrow.

"I haven't had to use it," Julie admitted with a blush. "What about those powders Lee Tang gave you? Do they work?"

"I haven't heard any complaints from you," Matt had replied with a wide grin.

After that, their conversation had ended in the same way the majority of their conversations seemed to be ending these days.

Julie's cheeks still could feel the heat of her blush as she realized that everyone had noticed how often she and Matt seemed to want to be alone together.

When Molly had given her the jar of cream, she had noticed the dark circles under Julie's eyes and commented on the ones' she had seen under Matt's eyes, muttering, "Newlyweds!"

With things going so smoothly, running the casino was not as demanding as before, and Julie found she had time on her hands. She even tried to hunt for things to keep herself busy, but little remained for her to do now that Molly was back on her feet and in full control of the bordello operation.

This pleased Julie no end. The last thing she wanted was another chance to be a madam. She had discovered the hard way that she wasn't cut out for the position.

Going up to her office, Julie decided she had better start on the paperwork that surely had piled up waiting for her attention. Matt was off attending to some business he had at the wharf. So now was her perfect chance to attack the accounts without fear of interruption.

Entering the room, she was stunned to see Annie Isaacs sitting at her desk, neat piles of paper stacked around her as she busily wrote.

"Annie!" Julie called out her name in surprise. "What are you doing here?"

Annie looked up from her work and, seeing Julie, sprang from her seat and ran to hug her, saying, "It's so good to see you! That was a foolish thing you did, running away like that. Why your poor husband must have been frantic!"

Annie led Julie over to the sofa and sat down next to her, smiling with happiness at seeing her back safe and well.

Julie glanced back over at the desk and then at Annie, asking, "What are you doing?"

Annie shrugged unconcernedly as she replied, "Your Mrs. Fitzroy, Molly, she told me to call her. Wonderful lady, your Molly."

"Annie!" Julie pressed her to come to the point.

Annie placed her hands on top of Julie's, took a deep breath, saying, "Anyways, she says she needed help with all the paperwork that was driving her crazy. And my Sam, he hears her complaining, and he tells her I can handle figures better than anyone he has ever seen! Such a thing for him to say! I never knew he had even noticed! And"—she held her arms out wide—"here I am."

"You're doing the paperwork for the casino!" Julie gasped. "But, Annie, you don't know anything about running a casino!"

"So what's to know?" Annie asked her. "All it is is putting the right numbers in the right columns and adding them up. Two and two make four, no matter what business you're in."

"I guess you're right, Annie." Julie couldn't help laughing. "But I'm back now and can take over. So, you can get back to your Sam and his figures."

Annie looked at her as though she had suggested something obscene. "Annie Isaacs does not quit when a job's half done! I have only a few more entries to make and everything will be the way it should. After I've done that, you can take over. I won't have it said that Annie Isaacs is a quitter!"

Julie was astonished. She had never intended to upset Annie. "I never meant to imply you were!" she said.

Embarrassed at her outburst, Annie smiled shyly at Julie and patted her hand saying, "I know that. And I didn't mean to snap at you like that! Forgive me? My Sam keeps telling me my mouth will be the end of me yet."

"There's nothing to forgive. If anything, I should be asking you to forgive me, for barging in here and bothering you while you were working," Julie told her dear friend. "Why don't you finish what you were working on when I came in, while I go and get us some lemonade to drink?" she suggested with a smile.

"That sounds wonderful!" Annie said as she rose from the sofa and returned to the desk. "Working with figures can be a thirsty job," she added as she picked up her pen and began adding the columns on the page in front of her.

Matt laughed that night when Julie related to him what had happened as they were getting ready to go to bed. "Tell me, you didn't offer to take over her job? Don't you know Annie well enough by now to know she takes pride in the work she does? Your offer to relieve her must have sounded as though you weren't confident she could do the job right," he told her as they climbed into bed.

Julie cuddled into his waiting arms and resting her cheek on his muscled chest, said, "Annie and Sam are good people, and I'm proud to call them my friends. But I never guessed that Annie was vain about her ability to work with accounts. It caught me totally by surprise when she reacted like she did."

Matt placed a kiss on her temple and murmured, "I would suggest you don't forget it. We can't have you going around unintentionally alienating all our friends! We would soon run out of friends if you did!"

Julie reached over and tweaked the hair on his chest saying, "You're accusing me of losing all our friends. What about you and Lee Tang ganging up on Carlo like you did?"

"We didn't gang up on him!" Matt protested his innocence. "We merely sat down together with him and asked him, as friends of the Kong Chow, what his intentions were regarding Lee Mei. Now, how can you call that ganging up on him?"

Julie rose up on her knees and gazed down at him saying, "Very easily! You had the poor man convinced you were the official representatives of the entire Kong Chow, which we both know you weren't! Not only that, you and Lee Tang had him believing he was expected to offer marriage to Lee Mei or never see her again! How could you do that to Carlo!"

Matt's hands went around her waist and he pulled

her down on top of him, kissing her on the end of the nose as he said, "Carlo isn't that defenseless! He told us he had spoken to Kong Woo personally regarding just that!"

"He what!" Julie exclaimed. "What did Kong Woo have to say?"

"Carlo told us that Kong Woo was pleased that Carlo had enough respect for Lee Mei to come and speak with the head of her family and ask permission to see her," Matt replied, trailing a finger across her collarbone and down into the valley between her breasts.

Julie wiggled a little as Matt's finger tickled her and sent gooseflesh radiating across her skin. "What else did Kong Woo have to say?"

"He told Carlo that he wished Lee Tang and I were as respectful. He is worried that Lee Tang seems in no hurry to take a wife of his own and ensure the succession by having a son of his own. Kong Woo also said he had burned incense, asking added blessings upon our marriage, because he felt we would need them."

"Do you think we need them?" Julie asked him as she leaned back down and snuggled against him.

"They couldn't hurt," Matt murmured as he claimed her lips in a kiss.

That kiss led to another and another, and soon they had forgotten all about Annie Isaacs, Lee Tang, Carlo and Kong Woo.

Julie marveled anew that even now, when she and Matt made love they still were discovering new things about each other. She hoped it would remain that way forever.

They were awakened later by the sound of a loud

crash and the breaking of glass downstairs in the closed casino. It was not long before the smell of smoke began to filter upstairs and the crackle of flames could be heard from below.

"Firebomb!" Matt cried as he leaped from the bed and threw on his clothes. "Julie, go wake Molly and get out of here. I'll wake the girls and tell them."

Checking the handle on the door to see if it was hot before opening it, Matt leaned over and kissed Julie. On opening the door, the sound of flames grew louder and they could hear the screams of Molly's girls as they were awakened by the smell of smoke.

Julie stumbled, bent low to the floor and coughing, as she made her way to Molly's rooms. Pounding on Molly's door she screamed, "Fire! Molly the casino's on fire! Wake up!"

Her fist hit air as the door swung open when she hit it, and inside the room she could see Molly struggling with a man. He had a firebrand in his hand and Molly was trying to stop him from setting her room ablaze. Who was he? How did he get in there? And why? Julie thought all this as she saw Molly struggling to prevent him from setting the drapes on fire.

Julie rushed to Molly's aid. She screamed as she was grabbed from behind by a second man who had been hiding on the other side of the door.

"What have we here?" Adam's voice sounded in her ear as he twisted her arm painfully behind her back. "Well, well, if it isn't my sister-in-law, Julie," he said as he dragged her toward Molly's bed.

"Adam!" Julie choked as the smoke coming in through the open doorway thickened.

"You've caused me all the trouble you ever will," he told her as he began to bind her arms behind her.

"You started the fire!" Julie exclaimed as she realized that he and his companion must have come through the front after tossing the firebomb through one of the windows. "Why?"

Molly was dragged over next to her and tied; then Adam replied, "I'm correcting an error, a massive injustice. You weren't supposed to inherit the Land of Gold. Sara was," he told her. "She is the eldest, and everyone knows the eldest inherits everything at the death of the father. But your father flew in the face of accepted behavior, as he always did, and left this casino to you."

Julie couldn't believe what she was hearing. Adam had set the fire because she had inherited the Land of Gold and not Sara!

"You're insane! What can you possibly hope to gain by burning the place down?" she demanded.

"I will gain enough to keep my shipping line afloat and still be able to live in a style that I have become extremely accustomed to," he replied.

"What are you talking about?" Julie choked. She hoped to keep Adam talking long enough for Matt to notice that she and Molly were missing and to come looking for them.

"Your father thought he was so smart leaving this place to you. He figured that without the revenue it brings in I would soon have to face my creditors and be ruined. He knew what a fine line I was walking. I'd come to him about a loan to cover my debts and he laughed at me. In fact, he even bragged to me about how not one cent of his money would be spent by me." Adam didn't need much encouragement to vent his hatred of her father. "It was a boast that would cost him his life."

Shock like ice water hit Julie. Adam was the one responsible for her father's murder! She felt as though she had been hit between the eyes. She had never once suspected him. All her suspicions had centered on Baldwin and his group. What a fool she had been!

"You! You had him killed! Why?" she cried at him. "If you knew he wasn't going to give you any money, why kill him? It doesn't make any sense!"

"It made perfect sense at the time," Adam informed her. "You see, then I was not aware that he had already altered his will in your favor. I thought Sara would inherit everything. His boasting that I would never see a cent of his told me I had to act fast before he could change the will."

"But if that's true, why did he leave all the real estate to Sara?" Julie pointed out to him.

"Ha! That is so tied up with legalities and leases that there's no way I can use it to raise the amount of money I need. He knew that when he made out his will. He thought out every angle but one," Adam told her as he walked about the room setting the drapes ablaze.

Her eyes stinging and her throat raw from the billowing smoke, Julie coughed out, "What do you mean, but one? I don't understand."

Pausing near the door of the bedroom, Adam motioned for his accomplice to leave before answering Julie's question. "He forgot about the insurance policies he had on the Land of Gold. He purchased them when you and Sara were still children. I think he may even have forgotten he had them. But I didn't. I did some searching of my own and found out they were still in existence, all their premiums paid up to date. The wonderfully efficient Mr. Washburn had seen to that."

"So there are insurance policies. What do they have to do with you burning the Land of Gold?" Julie pushed.

"The main beneficiary is Sara. At the time the policies were made out, you were considered too young to be a major beneficiary," Adam told her as he threw the firebrand across the room and ran out the door.

Left alone in the burning room, Julie and Molly struggled to free themselves of their bonds. They knew it was useless to yell for help. The roar of the flames would drown out any sound they could have made.

Using the flames that threatened to engulf them to burn free of their bonds, the two women made haste to escape the room, which was fast becoming an inferno.

Their visibility was blanketed by a thick pall of smoke as they made their way across the landing toward the staircase. It took all the strength they had to breathe.

Ominous sounds from the roof above their heads told them they did not have long to flee, and showers of embers and flaming pieces of wood warned them that the roof would soon cave in.

Reaching the head of the staircase leading down into the casino, Julie grabbed Molly and stopped her from going down. The entire bottom half of the once majestic staircase was totally engulfed in flames.

Searching about her for another way out, Julie gasped and reached for the railing at the top of the landing.

"Matt!" she screamed her voice lost in the roar of the flames that greedily consumed the wooden structure.

The smoke had cleared long enough for her to see Matt and Adam fighting with one another on the casino floor, flames threatening to surround them both completely.

Julie froze in terror as she heard the loud creaking and horrible groaning of the ceiling above them. The ceiling over the casino floor where Matt and Adam were engaged in their own life and death struggle was about to collapse!

Molly knew there was nothing she or Julie could do to help either man and that they had little time left to make their own escape. Grabbing Julie from behind, Molly forcibly moved her away from the railing and down to the far end of the corridor.

Once there, she kicked open the door that had always been used by customers who did not want to be seen patronizing a bordello. A gush of air hit them and fed the fire behind them as they made their way down the narrow steps to the street.

Julie moved as though she were in a trance. The only thing on her mind was that glimpse of Matt and Adam struggling as the ceiling had given way and they were cut off from view by the burning rafters that had crashed to the casino floor.

Reaching the street and what they thought would be safety, the two women were appalled to see the night sky aglow with the one thing the people of San Francisco feared the most—fire. The Land of Gold was not the only thing aflame that night.

They were soon caught up in the chaos and panic

created by the people who were trying to escape the encroaching flames and were separated.

Julie found herself carried along by the panicked tide of fleeing residents to a hillside area away from the fire's path.

She was numb with shock and didn't feel the buffeting or hear the angry words of those who pushed past her. All she felt was a hollow aching emptiness that blocked out everything else. Matt was dead. She had lost him forever. Her mind kept playing and replaying the sight of him and Adam surrounded by burning rafters and flames.

She wandered aimlessly through the crowds and streets until dawn was turning the horizon a sickly orange brown as the sun's rays mingled with the smoke of one of the biggest fires in San Francisco history. Before it was over nearly three-quarters of the town would be in ashes and many lives would have been lost.

Needing to be with someone who shared her grief, Julie began searching through the survivors for any sign of Molly or anyone else from the Land of Gold. Soon she was searching for any familiar face.

When one of the city's twenty-three volunteer fire companies rushed past her to battle a fire in a nearby row of buildings, she was roughly pushed to the side of the rubble-strewn street to which her search had taken her.

Julie continued to make her way back toward the Plaza. There she prayed she would be able to find some of her friends and not feel so devastatingly alone.

She found herself crying as she viewed the once-beautiful Plaza. What was once the heart of the city was now a mass of charred hulks, smoldering skeletons and ruins.

She steeled herself to look over at where the Land of Gold once stood with its doors open to the world. She quickened her pace to a run as she saw a coach standing in front. Beside it, standing huddled in Sam's arms, was Annie Isaacs.

Julie cried out their names as she struggled through the destruction to reach them.

"Annie! Sam!" Julie cried as she stumbled.

Hearing her name, Annie turned and saw a ragged, soot-blackened figure running toward her.

"Julie?" Annie questioned as the figure drew near.

"Annie, it's me," Julie answered her, through her tears.

Annie's arms opened wide and engulfed Julie in an embrace as the two women wept with joy.

Her emotions spent, Julie looked at the faces of her friends and said, "Thank God neither of you were hurt! I love you both too much to lose you. I've lost everything else I love. I couldn't bear it if I'd lost you too."

"What happened?" Annie questioned her softly as she tried to wipe the tear-streaked soot from Julie's face with her handkerchief.

Julie told them what had happened from the time she and Matt were awakened by the sounds of breaking glass until she had found the two of them here in front of the burned-out casino. Her voice was flat and unemotional as she related what she had been told by Adam. And she choked up slightly when she told them that he was not only responsible for the fire which burned the casino but also for the murder of her father.

Annie pulled Julie back into her arms and held her until Julie could regain control over the shudders that passed through her body.

"Where's Molly now?" Sam asked when she told of how she and Molly had become separated.

"I don't know," Julie replied worriedly. "I only hope she is safe."

"I'm sure she is," Annie told her as she threw a stern look at her husband. "Molly is a survivor like the rest of us. You'll see. She'll be fine."

"I hope you're right, Annie," Julie replied as she gazed with hollow eyes at what was left of her inheritance and what was now the tomb of the man she loved.

As she stared at the burned-out remains with its blackened rafters looking like a giant's carelessly tossed toothpicks, her heart skipped a beat and she held her breath. She thought she saw the rafters move.

She blinked her eyes, telling herself it was a combination of fatigue and shock that was making her see things that weren't there.

But the rafters moved again, and as she stared in speechless wonder, two figures emerged from the pile of wreckage.

Covered from head to foot with the black greasy residue of the charred remains of the building, they were still two of the most beautiful sights Julie had ever seen in her life.

Even though he looked like an apparition from the dead, Julie knew it was Matt who came to her and wordlessly clasped her to his heart.

Julie felt as though she were reborn. The numbness that had surrounded her melted away. She held him as tightly as he held her, fearful of ever letting him go.

Leaning back and staring up into his face, she saw that he was crying.

Lifting a finger she caught one of his tears and brought it to her lips.

A small smile creased his begrimed features as he lifted a finger to the tears that streamed unnoticed down her face and did the same.

They had no need for spoken words. They knew, as deeply and surely as they both lived and breathed the love they felt for one another. But their joy was so great they had to share their feelings with the world.

"I love you!" they whispered simultaneously.

They flowed together in a kiss that brought tears to the eyes of those who looked on.

Annie looked up at her Sam and the love she felt for him shone from her eyes as he put his arm about her and drew her close to his side. They knew what Julie and Matt were feeling. They had lived through terror in the old country. They understood what it was like to find what you'd thought was gone forever.

"What about me?" a plaintive voice asked.

Matt and Julie broke from their kiss and looked at the equally blackened figure of Carlo as he said, "Isn't anyone glad to see me?"

Julie and Matt opened their arms and welcomed him into their embrace.

Without hesitation Carlo joined with what had become two of the most important people in his life. He loved both of them as deeply as he did his numerous sisters and brothers.

Having made Carlo a part of their reunion, Julie asked the men what had happened. She told Matt of her thoughts when she had last seen him struggling with Adam amidst the burning rafters.

Matt looked over at Carlo and pulled him closer in an embrace. "If it were not for you, my friend, I wouldn't be here to answer Julie's questions. I owe you my life."

Julie watched as the two men shared unspoken thoughts with their eyes. In her heart she felt a glowing pride that they could share the way they felt with one another. Only one other man she had ever known could be as open and honest with other men, and that man was her father.

Turning back to Julie and including Sam and Annie in what he had to say, Matt spoke, "After I left you, I went door to door in the bordello and warned everyone to get out. Carlo was with Mae and he said he would warn the others while I went downstairs to make sure there wasn't anyone trapped down there."

He took a breath and a hard look came over his face as he continued, "I found Adam and his accomplice raiding the bar for anything of value they could find as they set the rest of the room on fire. The room was pretty destroyed by the firebomb they had thrown through the window, but they were determined on setting the entire place ablaze.

"Adam had his back to me when the other man saw me and ran for the kitchen and out the back door. I tried to stop Adam, but he fought like a man possessed, screaming things about insurance and justice being done."

"He admitted hiring the men who killed your father," he told Julie, sadness in his eyes.

"I know," Julie replied. "He bragged about it to me

before he left Molly and me tied up in her burning bedroom."

"He what!" Carlo growled.

"He told me he'd done that," Matt said to Julie. "He said he had taken care of you as a problem once and for all and now it was my turn."

"How did you manage to escape after the ceiling caved in?" Julie asked him.

"After the ceiling caved in, I thought I was a dead man," Matt explained. "Adam had me pinned near one of the rafters and I knew it was only a matter of seconds before the smoke and fire got both of us. There was a crashing noise off behind us from the kitchen, but I was too busy trying to stay alive to pay much attention to it. When I thought it was all over and both Adam and I were dead men, Carlo appeared out of nowhere like some avenging angel. He grabbed Adam and pulled him off me. It was about then that the rafter I'd been pinned against gave way and I was buried beneath it." Matt grimaced.

"I think I'll let Carlo tell you what hapened after that," he said as he drew Julie closer to his side.

"When the rafter broke and buried Matt, I forgot about Adam and concentrated on getting Matt out of there. It wasn't until after I had dug Matt free that either of us thought about Raleigh," Carlo told them. "We looked and saw there was no way we could do anything for him. He had tried to make a break for it by running toward the bar. The remainder of the ceiling caved in on top of him," Carlo explained looking at Matt to finish the tale.

"After seeing there was nothing we could do for him, we pushed our way through the flames to the kitchen and out the back. I wanted to go back in and see if I could find you and Molly, but by that time the entire second floor was a solid sheet of flames and Carlo restrained me from returning," Matt continued. "We moved out toward the front hoping you had somehow escaped and we would find you there. But, you weren't anywhere in sight." The bleakness in his voice told Julie of the loss Matt had felt when he thought she was dead.

Carlo picked up the tale again. "We weren't out front very long before we were drafted into one of the fire companies, and we spent the remainder of the night trying to keep the rest of San Francisco from going up in flames. We ran into Sam and Annie near their shop, which luckily suffered only minor damage, and the four of us came back here." He looked at Matt with understanding in his face as he went on. "Matt insisted we search through the rubble for proof that you had not escaped."

"We were planning on searching some more after the embers had cooled," Matt added as he looked toward the smoking ruins.

Julie felt once again the joyous relief of having Matt beside her and she placed a kiss on his lips. Matt understood how she felt and kept his arm tightly about her.

Julie knew everything was close to being perfect, except she was still worried about Molly. She repeated what she had told Annie and Sam earlier about being separated from her and asked the men, "Did either of you see any sign of Molly?"

"No," they replied.

The sound of a fire wagon pulling up next to them

made them all turn to look. What they saw made them all laugh with relief and disbelief.

Lee Tang was holding the reins and sitting next to him, clad in a grimy nightgown with a soot-blackened parasol over her head, was Molly. She accepted his help down from the wagon and moved toward Julie who broke away from Matt to greet her.

Pulling her back to where Matt and the others stood, Julie kissed her on the cheek and whispered, "I was so worried about you."

"Worried about me!" Molly laughed as she moved around the group hugging everyone. "Julie, my dear, don't you know by now that it would take more than a fire to beat Molly Fitzroy!"

Julie exchanged smiles with Annie. "You were right. She is a survivor."

Molly broke from the group to survey the damage done by the fire. Shaking her head, she turned back and said to them, "I'm glad you're all here."

They listened in amazement as Molly turned to Annie and said, "How would you like to be a full-time accountant?"

Annie gasped in surprise and looked to Sam for his approval.

Sam smiled down at her and said, "I've always said you can work with figures better than anyone."

Receiving his approval, Annie gave her answer to Molly. "Yes," she said.

Nodding Molly turned to Sam and asked, "Do you think you and your fellow tailors could outfit new wardrobes for Matt, Carlo, Julie, myself and eight of my girls?"

Such a commission would keep him in business for a year and the offer took Sam by surprise. "Yes, ma'am. I think we could."

"Good!" Molly replied. Walking the length of the burned-out hulk, she turned and faced Julie and Matt, saying, "Well, partners, it looks like we have a job ahead of us. Think you're up to it? I suggest we use brick and stone this time. What do you think?"

"Brick and stone it is," Matt replied as he smiled at the strength and tenacity of the older woman.

Julie looked at Matt and whispered, "Can we do it?"

Matt smiled down at her, and replied, "Together we can do anything."

Tapestry
HISTORICAL ROMANCES

Breathtaking New Tales

of love and adventure set against history's most exciting time and places. Featuring two novels by the finest authors in the field of romantic fiction—<u>every month</u>.

Next Month From Tapestry Romances

DAUGHTER OF LIBERTY
by Johanna Hill
CHARITY'S PRIDE
by Patricia Pellicane

POCKET BOOKS.